A chill skidded down Rhianna's spine

She looked around at the nearly deserted balcony. The Frito muncher was dozing under his hat, and the twosome in the corner seemed to have vanished into thin air. There was no one else up here—and she felt somehow there should have been. The main floor was packed. Why hadn't some of that mob dispersed to the upper level?

She saw the werewolf usher stroll past her. In the flickering light radiating from the screen, his white fangs gleamed with a malevolence that unnerved her.

She hunched deeper into her seat. The feeling of being watched was strong in her—stronger than it had been before. Maybe that was due in part to the eerie movie, but she couldn't quite rid herself of the sense of pervading evil.

It was more than just the movie, she realized. There was someone up here—someone who knew she was alone....

ABOUT THE AUTHOR

As far back as she can remember, Jenna Ryan has been dreaming up stories, everything from fairy tales to romantic mysteries. She's read Harlequin Intrigues ever since the line was first introduced, and inspired by Anne Stuart's *Hand in Glove*, she set out to write one herself. A resident of Victoria, B.C., Jenna has been a model, an airline reservation agent, a tour escort and a lingerie salesperson. She currently writes part-time, but hopes to turn it into a full-time occupation.

Cast in Wax

Jenna Ryan

Harlequin Books

TORONTO • NEW YORK • LONDON
AMSTERDAM • PARIS • SYDNEY • HAMBURG
STOCKHOLM • ATHENS • TOKYO • MILAN

Harlequin Intrigue edition published April 1988

ISBN 0-373-22088-X

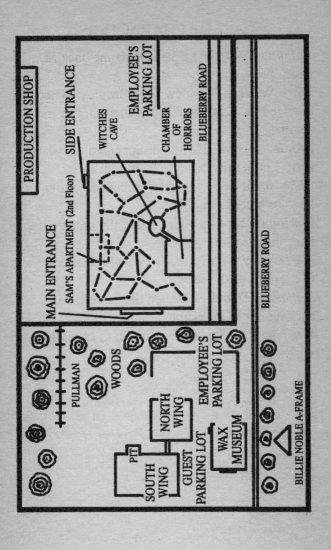

PRODUCTION SHOP

SIDE ENTRANCE

WITCHES CAVE

EMPLOYEE'S PARKING LOT

CHAMBER OF HORRORS

BLUEBERRY ROAD

MAIN ENTRANCE

SAM'S APARTMENT (2nd Floor)

PULLMAN

WOODS

NORTH WING

EMPLOYEE'S PARKING LOT

PIT

SOUTH WING

GUEST PARKING LOT

WAX MUSEUM

BLUEBERRY ROAD

BILLIE NOBLE A-FRAME

CAST OF CHARACTERS

Rhianna Curtis—The past had come back to haunt her.

Mark Reimer—He knew what Brodie had been involved in ... but wasn't prepared for the end result.

Brodie Morgan—He had disappeared ten years ago ... hopefully never to be found.

Billie Noble—She was out for revenge ... but how far would she go?

Marion Noble Betz—Had she really accepted her family's fate?

Joe Marinelli—A former west ender desperate to keep the past a secret.

Samantha French—She had the bracelet to connect her to the crime.

Dag Nichols—He had lied ... but to cover up what?

Prologue

"Rhianna, I have to see you. Tonight." Brodie Morgan's voice on the phone dropped to a raspy whisper. "It's about the east-end robberies. I know who's behind them—and why."

Drowsily, Rhiannan Curtis shook free of her mist-shrouded dreams. "See me where, Brodie?" she asked.

"Behind the production shop at Dad's wax museum—you know, where the expansion work is being done. Can you meet me here in fifteen minutes?" Her senior classmate sounded desperate.

Meet him all the way out on Blueberry Road, in the middle of the night, in the middle of a construction site? She hesitated for a second, then made the decision. "I'll be there, Brodie," she told him.

Fifteen minutes had stretched to fifty. Restlessly, Rhianna slid from the safety of her bulldozer perch to prowl the plowed ground behind the Bremerhaven Wax Museum. Two things were wrong. One: Brodie was nowhere in sight, and two: someone was doing God only knew what inside the recently expanded production shop.

She conjured up the exaggerated image of a mad bricklayer frantically walling in some poor, unsuspecting victim. Then she smiled to herself. She'd been reading too much Edgar Allan Poe.

2:24 a.m.

Instinct had her slipping silently into the shadows of a large oak. The scrape and grind noises from inside the production shop had ceased, to be replaced now by a different sound—surefooted steps on mossy earth. Possibly Brodie, but somehow, Rhianna didn't think so.

Holding her breath, she peered around the oak's massive trunk. There, on the threshold between darkness and moonlight, she spied the outline of a tall, slenderly built youth. A flash of blond hair caught her eye. Long, blond hair, similar to Brodie's in color and length.

Recognition was instantaneous, as was the feeling of apprehensive fascination welling up inside her. Transfixed, Rhianna stared at Mark Reimer's probing winter-blue eyes, at the lean line of his body and his remote features. She knew him, but not well. He was Brodie's cousin, a west ender with a reputation forbidding enough to make her hesitate.

Slowly, her eyes slid down the length of his rangy frame, over faded jeans and well-worn work boots, and she frowned a little at the splashes of red covering them. She knew he worked in the production shop of his uncle's wax museum, and that his job there involved the handling of various paints and dyes used to tint the wax figures. But even that knowledge couldn't prevent a sudden shiver of trepidation from rippling along her spine. Mark

Reimer was a total enigma to her, and she firmly strengthened her resolve not to reveal herself to him.

2:47 a.m.

Two minutes had felt like two hours to Rhianna. Her muscles were cramped and sore from the strain of not moving. But Mark's cool eyes were still surveying the wooded area, and she wasn't sure she trusted him enough to reveal herself.

Three seconds later, however, she forgot all about Mark's reputation, his steady gaze, the splashes of red on his clothes and every single one of her doubts about him. A small scream of revulsion rose in her throat, and she scrambled out from behind the oak, shaking her hand as if she'd just been bitten by a snake.

"Problem, Rhianna?" Mark seemed less than surprised to see her. A trace of a mocking smile touched the corners of his mouth.

"I . . . no. Yes!" She skidded to an abrupt halt on the uneven ground. "Is there a spider on me?"

"If there is you probably scared it to death with that shriek you let out." His lashes lowered to veil his eyes. "What are you doing here?"

"I'm . . . waiting for Brodie. Are you sure you don't see a spider?"

"There's no spider. Why are you waiting for Brodie?"

"He phoned and asked me to meet him here. He said he knew who was behind the east-end robberies." Too late, it occurred to her that Mark was the last person she should be telling about Brodie's call. "I've been here for almost an hour," she tacked on with one final sweep of her hair. "I'm worried about him."

"Don't be." Mark's tone was flat, and something else she couldn't fathom.

Intrigued in spite of herself, Rhianna tilted her head to one side. "You sound...different tonight, Mark."

He shrugged. "I have a cold. No big deal." Reaching out, he snared her wrist. "You should be home in bed, Rhianna, not standing around out here."

Her sentiments exactly. "But what about Brodie?" she persisted. "He sounded strange on the phone."

"Anyone who's obsessed with a wax figure of Dracula *is* strange," Mark countered wryly. "Besides, if he really does have information about the east-end robberies, he's going to need a lot more help than you can give him."

"Then you think he's in trouble, too, don't you?" Ineffectively, Rhianna struggled against the pull he was exerting.

"How the hell should I know?" Mark snarled. "His life's his own problem. Just drop it, Rhianna, and get out of here before you wind up in more trouble than Brodie."

More trouble than Brodie...

All the way home, Mark's words shot and echoed through Rhianna's head. Brodie *was* in trouble, she could feel it. In trouble, and possibly in danger.

THE NEXT DAY, her fears for Brodie's safety were confirmed. He was missing, and no one in town seemed to have any idea where he might be.

As a search team was organized, work in the wax museum's production shop continued. A brick wall, not quite complete Friday afternoon, was finished off Saturday morning. While the townspeople searched, the construction workers labored.

And still, there was no sign of the missing youth...

Chapter One

Damn, it was hot, every bit as hot and humid as the last time Rhianna had found herself out in the parking lot beside the wax museum's production shop. That had been ten years ago, and tonight, instead of staring at the nearly completed north wing, she was staring at a blackened shell, watching as firefighters extinguished the last of the flames that had all but consumed the wood-and-brick building.

It wasn't a pretty sight. Six people had been injured in the blaze, all of them employees at the museum. Fortunately, none of the injuries had been serious, smoke inhalation mostly, and a few fractured bones.

Rhianna winced as a sympathetic shaft of pain speared her own healing ribs. She'd been wounded in a scuffle two weeks ago with a woman fifty pounds heavier than her who had taken exception to the fact that her ex-husband had sent a private investigator down to New Orleans to find her.

The story was an old one, kidnapped children taken by the parent who had been denied custody. But while Rhianna had been prepared for the situation, she hadn't really expected to wind up tumbling down a flight of stairs. Still, she'd been successful in her quest. The children were now safely back in Boston with their father, and Rhianna was on a long overdue vacation, visiting an old friend from high school and recovering nicely from her wounds.

Out of the corner of her eye, she saw Samantha French coming toward her. Sam was a tiny woman, a former west ender, a punk rocker before the term had even been invented. Her burgundy-tinted hair was short and spiked, and Rhianna had to smile at the picture she made in her Lily Munster shroud and dramatic makeup. The crowd that had gathered this steamy August evening to watch the fire seemed a little taken aback to see Sam's ghoulish figure emerging from the wax museum's employee entrance, but Rhianna knew that the costume was all part and parcel of Sam's job there as a tour guide.

"How's your apartment?" she asked as the woman drew close enough to be heard above the confusion. "Any smoke damage?"

"Not really." Sam hopped up onto the hood of the fire chief's car, where Rhianna had been perched for the past hour. "What little air is moving out here must be moving away from the museum. The firefighters took a look around just to be sure, but they figured it would be okay for us to stay there tonight."

Rhianna glanced over at the neo-Gothic style wax museum and the living quarters above it. Sam had lived there for the past ten years, ever since the former occupant had moved out. She'd stayed on in Bremerhaven when Rhianna had gone off to college, turning a summer job into a full-time occupation, leaving her west-end tenement life well behind her.

"I heard someone say that Mark was on his way back up here from New York," Sam said, hiking her shroud up a little higher. "I wonder if he knows about the fire yet?"

Although she tried not to, Rhianna tensed at the mention of Mark Reimer's name. She'd been lucky in that during her eight-day stay at Sam's apartment, he had been out of town. Now, that luck appeared to have run out.

Upon his uncle's death in June, Mark had inherited the renowned wax museum, and for the past two months he'd been in town straightening out the estate. But then he'd been called back to New York City, where he apparently worked and lived, and Rhianna had been spared the necessity of dealing with the worst imaginable ghosts from her past.

Until now, that was. The moment he returned and she saw him, all the painful memories connected to that muggy June night when Brodie Morgan had phoned and asked her to meet him behind the production shop were going to come flooding back into her mind. Dammit, they were already, and she hadn't even seen Mark yet.

Well, maybe it was for the best, she reasoned, watching absently as the firefighters collected their hoses and reloaded them onto the trucks. She couldn't block out the past forever. Brodie was missing and presumed dead, and all the wishing in the world wasn't going to change that grisly fact. He'd known something about the east-end robberies, a strange series of thefts that had confounded the Bremerhaven police ever since they'd started up in October of Rhianna's senior year in high school. He'd known, and in all likelihood, he'd been killed for that knowledge.

Reminiscent stirrings of guilt started up on the outer fringes of her conscience. Maybe she hadn't been directly involved in Brodie's disappearance, but she couldn't help feeling that she was, in some small way, responsible for it.

She could have called the police after he'd phoned her. She hadn't. She could have pressed him for details about the robberies. She hadn't done that, either. Instead of thinking, she had acted on impulse, and now she could only wonder how different everything might have been had she thought her choices through before tearing off to meet him behind his father's wax museum.

Grateful that she was not the sort of person to thrash herself unfairly over unfortunate errors in judgment, Rhianna slid from the fire chief's car, careful not to jar her still-bruised ribs. If Brodie was dead—and she honestly believed he was—then the chances were good he'd been murdered by whoever had been behind the east-end robberies. And if that was the case, his murderer was the guilty party, not her. The real tragedy was that the murderer was probably still walking around free.

Somewhere in the back of her mind, she considered and dismissed Mark's name. West-end reputation notwithstanding, she couldn't quite bring herself to believe that he would have killed his own cousin. Why bother? He could have talked Brodie into just about anything. And yet, she couldn't really say she trusted Mark, either.

As the crowd started to disperse, Sam sauntered over to talk to a handsome, dark-haired firefighter, oblivious to the fact that she was still in full costume. The flames had been doused; the fire trucks were leaving; and Rhianna was on the verge of heading back to the apartment when she spied a charcoal gray Corvette pulling into the graveled parking lot.

She knew long before he extricated himself from the dusty vehicle that it was Mark Reimer. Except for the air of absolute detachment he radiated, Mark could almost have passed for his younger cousin.

He was older now, of course, thirty-five or so, but he was as tall as she remembered and as slenderly built as he had been ten years ago. His hair, still many shades of blond, was also still on the long side; his expression was still remote and unrevealing; and his eyes were still as clear and blue as a winter sky.

The resemblance between Mark and Brodie, however, started and ended on a physical level. Rhianna studied him covertly as he slammed the door of his car and looked over at the burned-out production shop. In every nonphysical sense, he and Brodie had always been polar opposites.

Mark had grown up in the west end of town, quietly tough and introspective. No fuss, no loud claims of strength. He'd been a leader over there, and if Rhianna's memory was accurate, he'd been one of only a few west-end youths who had not wielded a large knife.

Beyond that, however, she really knew very little about him. According to Sam, he'd been on his own since the age of fourteen or fifteen, somehow able to avoid the authorities who would have stuck him in a restrictive institution for homeless teens. He'd been more or less placed in his uncle's care, but he'd refused outright to live on the east side of town, and perhaps wisely, Reed Morgan had chosen not to force the issue.

Although it was doubtful he would have known she was in Bremerhaven, Mark didn't bat an eyelash when he caught sight of her in the employee's parking lot. To Rhianna's amazement, he halted his long stride not ten feet away from her.

"What happened here, Rhianna?" he demanded, shoving his keys into the pocket of his faded jeans. "Were you around when the fire started?"

So he had heard about it after all. She nodded. "I was reading out on Sam's rear balcony when one of the workers came out of the shop and told me that the north wing was burning. That was about five or so. I gather he was just finishing up his shift in the shop. He told me to call the fire department while he and Sam cleared the last tour group out of the museum."

Mark's expression was enigmatic as he surveyed the charred building. "Was anyone hurt?"

"Six people—two tour guides and four of the production-shop workers—but I don't think the injuries were all that serious. They were taken to the hospital a couple of hours ago."

The crowd had dwindled surprisingly fast in the aftermath of the blaze, leaving only the firefighter to whom Sam was talking, a walrus-mustached police lieutenant and a few other uniformed officers in the parking lot.

Rhianna saw Mark's steady gaze move past her shoulder to the woods beyond the graveled clearing. "Go home, Billie," he said, without raising his voice in the slightest. "The excitement's over for tonight."

Rhianna averted her head just in time to catch a glimpse of a scrawny, cowering form. At Mark's words, the woman's cringe deepened. She began to scurry for the shelter of the nearby underbrush, but not before lifting a gnarled finger and pointing it shakily in his direction.

Billie Noble looked like a cross between the Wicked Witch of the West and an aging Olive Oyl. A loose, black tunic hung from her skinny frame. Black stockings bunched around her bony ankles allowed a clear view of legs badly riddled with varicose veins. Her skin looked as dry as old parchment, and her brown eyes were sunk deep into their skeletal sockets.

Rhianna had seen her only once since coming back to Bremerhaven, but this second time shocked her no less than the first one had.

Ten years ago, Billie Noble had been the Bremerhaven High librarian. Today, she was a recluse, a pathetic little scarecrow, who lived alone in a tiny A-frame house across from the wax museum on this secluded stretch of Blueberry Road.

"I didn't notice her before," Rhianna murmured, her tone reflecting the disbelief she felt at seeing the woman. "What happened to her, Mark? She used to be so...different."

Mark shrugged. "She resented the bank for foreclosing on her family's diner, and my Uncle Reed for buying the land to expand the production shop."

"And that's what drove her crazy?"

"I guess so. She seemed all right for the first year or so, but after that, I gather she went all to hell. She stopped screaming vengeance and hid herself away in that house of hers. She babbles a lot, but I'm not sure if she really talks anymore." He shrugged again. "According to Marion, she's harmless enough."

Rhianna looked over at him, disconcerted to discover that he was standing less than two feet away from her. She masked the reaction and asked quickly, "I know they're sisters, Mark, but has Marion ever considered having Billie committed?"

Mark shook his head. "She doesn't have the heart. Besides, working at the wax museum gives her a chance to keep an eye on Billie's activities. She won't commit her until it's absolutely necessary."

As he spoke, Mark's eyes shifted back to the charred production shop. The dark-haired firefighter was coming in their direction, trailed by Sam, who had given up trying to navigate the rough terrain in her stiletto heels and was now treading barefoot on the gravel.

"How bad is it, Joe?" Mark questioned the man, whom Rhianna suddenly recognized as Joe Marinelli, a former west-end cohort of Mark's. Minus his leather jacket and shoulder-length hair, he looked totally different than he had a decade earlier. Different and nice.

"It could have been a lot worse," Joe replied, with a nod in Rhianna's direction. "The north cellar's gutted, but the top floor just might be salvable, and the south wing wasn't even singed. Far as I can tell, you lost a big storage area, and that's about it. No problems in the offices, the pit or the museum. And the people who were taken over to Bremerhaven General are all going to be fine. One of the guides, Renee, broke her ankle and your costumer has a concussion. The rest are suffering from smoke inhalation. They'll be released tomorrow morning."

The news apparently satisfied Mark; however, in her usual forthright fashion, Sam was quick to point out a possible problem.

"Mark, if Renee's hurt, that's going to leave us awfully short-staffed in the museum. Don't forget one of the guides is on holidays, and Marion fired that new woman a couple of days ago."

Mark frowned. "Why?"

"I have no idea." Sam swatted impatiently at a buzzing mosquito. "But I'm sure she had a damned good reason. Probably the little east-end bitch got on her high horse, and Marion, thank God, doesn't take any crap from people like that."

A grin tugged at the corners of Mark's mouth; but he said nothing in response to Sam's general snipe at the town's east-end residents. There was no point, really. Sam had never been especially tolerant of east-end affluence, scorning it every chance she got, the way she'd scorned it all her life.

Living in the east end as she had, Rhianna wasn't really sure what she'd done to warrant Sam's friendship, but she supposed it had something to do with the fact they'd been partners in biology. She'd passed the rat-dissecting test with flying colors, an admirable enough feat in Sam's eyes to offset her flagrant disdain of all things east end and allow for the rare exception.

The sun had long since set, its burning rays giving way to a hot, sultry twilight. Disinclined to follow Sam's lead and return to the apartment, Rhianna left Mark and Joe to their speculations about the cause of the blaze and strolled to the rear of the production shop.

This far out on Blueberry Road, the countryside was heavily wooded. Except for the wax museum and Billie Noble's distant A-frame, the only sign of human habitation was the overgrown ribbon of railway track on a slight rise some two hundred yards behind the workshop.

No longer in use by Amtrak, the rails were rusty and broken in several spots. But Rhianna knew they led to an old junction about a mile farther north, and she was curious to see if the ancient Pullman—Bremerhaven's hottest make-out spot ten years ago—was still there.

Encouraged by a waft of humid air in the form of a gasping breeze, she walked down the path and scrambled up a dirt and grass incline onto the ties.

It was like Smalltown, U.S.A., revisited. She grinned, balancing for a moment on one of the narrow rails. At the same time, though, it was different. Probably, she reflected, because Bremerhaven was different from most other small towns in the country.

Located some ten miles northwest of Salem, this particular town was a center for folklore and superstition, for witches and ghouls and spooky fireside tales. It was also a thriving New England community. The wax museum alone drew hoards of annual visitors to the region. And then there was the Haunting, a gray stone mansion turned restaurant, to consider, as well as the fabled Witch's Cottage, Sutter's Ghost House and even the Raven's Wing Tavern, all of which were interspersed along Blueberry Road and all of which were centuries old and loaded with eerie tradition.

Smiling to herself, Rhianna hopped from the rail and kicked off her sneakers. Behind her, she detected the odor of scorched timber and wax, and she breathed a sigh of relief that the fire had been extinguished before it could spread to either the museum or the surrounding woods. Then her breath suddenly caught in her throat as she heard a faint rustling sound somewhere off to her right.

Maybe a walk hadn't been such a good idea after all. Blueberry Road may have been sparsely inhabited but there was still Billie Noble to think of, not to mention the transients who frequently loitered by the out-of-service tracks at night. Her ribs were better, but she couldn't really say she relished the idea of injuring them again, not for the mere sake of a walk in the twilight.

For a minute, she stood still and listened. Frogs and crickets and even the odd crow joined forces to fill the dusky air with summer song, a familiar, reassuring cacophony that had absolutely nothing to do with danger.

Rhianna relaxed. She could even taunt herself for her foolish overreaction. Eight days of inactivity had wrought havoc with her imagination. At this rate, God only knew what kind of shape she was going to be in when she returned to Boston and her next case.

She was counting ties and still heading in the direction of the empty Pullman when her ears perked once again. This time, she knew she wasn't imagining things. And this time, she knew instinctively who was behind her on the rails.

"It's not a good idea to wander around out here alone, Rhianna," Mark drawled, amusement evident in his deep voice.

Damn him anyway, she swore, willing her fists not to clench around her sneakers. Did he always have to be so stealthy? Couldn't he just once, tramp around like a normal person?

Rhianna whirled on him angrily. "You could have given me a heart attack, Mark," she accused, for some unknown reason acutely aware of every long, slender line in his body.

She saw a slight grin curve his lips. "I don't think so," he returned easily. "You're not the weak-hearted type. You wouldn't be much of a private eye if you were."

She regarded him warily. "How do you know I'm a private investigator?"

Mark lifted an indolent shoulder. "Sam mentioned it." His eyes slid over her baggy shorts and T-shirt, then down the length of her tanned legs to her bare feet. "She also said you hurt yourself on your last case."

"I did."

He arched a wry brow. "You don't look wounded to me."

"I'm a fast healer," she retorted dryly. And she was also little more than a fledgling investigator, although she couldn't be sure whether or not Sam had mentioned that to him. She'd been doing this for only eighteen months or so now, ever since leaving law school. The kidnapping case had actually been her first solo venture.

Aware of Mark's cryptic gaze, Rhianna dropped her sneakers and slid her feet into them. The twilight was fading fast. In another half hour, the woods would be in total darkness. Wisdom dictated that she abandon her quest to reach the deserted Pullman and return instead to the apartment. Wisdom, plus the fact that if she continued to walk, Mark would undoubtedly see to it she didn't do so alone. And somehow, the prospect of exploring an abandoned rail car, one that used to be nirvana for passionate teens, was not a pleasant one, not when done in Mark Reimer's company.

No, strike that, she amended, stealing another unobtrusive glance at his lean body. The prospect was pleasant enough, even if she didn't want to dwell on the reasons. The situation would simply be uncomfortable since, in all likelihood, he'd spent countless memory-filled hours in the Pullman.

Or maybe he hadn't. With Mark, it was hard to be sure of anything. He had a reputation for being more detached than romantic. And one thing he'd never been was a braggart. His sexual conquests, numerous or not, had never been made public.

Rhianna could feel Mark watching her as she laced up her Reeboks. Ignoring the strange effect he was having on her pulse rate, she lifted her head to inquire casually, "You're not going to close down the wax museum are you, Mark?"

"No. Why do you ask?"

Her task complete, Rhianna rose to her full height of five feet nine inches. It was rather annoying to have to look up six inches when she was accustomed to staring straight across at so many men. "I heard Sam mention that you were short a few tour guides," she replied as offhandedly as possible. "I thought you might not have enough staff to keep the museum open."

"I don't really," Mark told her with an unconcerned shrug. "The night tours might have to be scrapped until the gaps are filled."

"But the night tours are the most popular ones," Rhianna objected.

"Then the morning tours will have to go."

"But—"

"No buts, Rhianna," Mark interrupted her a little impatiently. He took her firmly by the arm. "Come on. It's getting late, and you know as well as I do that this isn't the safest place to be at night."

Yes, she did know that. She also knew he wasn't the least bit worried about being jumped by a vagrant, any more than he'd been worried about his own safety that night ten years ago when Brodie had failed to meet her at the construction site. He certainly wasn't a knight in shining armor, but he had a decent streak in him.

Decency tinged with danger, she decided. And she had a foreboding feeling that the danger readily outweighed the decency.

MARK WATCHED HER from behind as she proceeded him along the path to the wax museum. She was a beautiful woman, he would give her that—dark-haired, green-eyed and long-limbed. He'd seen her in her clingy Vampira gown when she'd worked part-time as a museum guide, in her prom dress of white satin and lace and even in a stunning *Gone with the Wind* Halloween costume. He'd also seen her in jeans and loose shirts, riding horseback with friends and poking around the west end of town with Sam. And he couldn't deny, he'd always been a little fascinated by her.

Why, he couldn't really say. He'd never been a pushover for a pretty face, and as a rule, he preferred lush curves to coltish lines, blondes to brunettes and down-to-earth west enders to wealthy east-side dwellers. But then, Rhianna had never been a snob. She was Sam's friend and she'd seemed to understand Brodie's quirky sense of humor. Those two things alone had been reason enough not to lump her together with her rich classmates, to view her as a separate and rather intriguing entity. And the fact that she reminded him of a dark-haired angel hadn't hurt either. Put a halo and a set of wings on her and she would look like she'd just descended from heaven.

Deliberately dropping back a few paces, Mark regarded her tanned legs and long, wavy hair. But the cynic in him wouldn't let him enjoy the sight. He'd been knocked around by his father too much in the past to give in to a hot, physical urge. If he'd been a wistful romantic as a kid, that part of him had long since died. He felt jaded and hard, and even an old fascination couldn't change that.

The moon had risen in a purple-tinged sky. It was a half-moon, pale and opaque and about as untouchable as Mark felt these days. Reed's death had forced him to return to Bremerhaven; a staff of thirty plus was, for a moment, holding him here in a state of suspended animation. But he'd have to decide soon on his next move. He knew that as surely as he knew he couldn't stay.

It seemed almost inevitable. Hell, it was inevitable. He'd have to sell out, or at least come up with a good overseer for the place. Cursing Reed and Brodie and the world in general, he tossed around those options. He owned his own construction company in New York. It was the kind of work he could sink his teeth into; the hard labor involved gave him a much-needed outlet for all the frustration and anger of a tough upbringing. He didn't need Reed's money. He'd never needed or wanted it, even if his uncle hadn't understood that about him. The wax museum was a headache, nothing more. It had to go, and the sooner the better.

Irritably, Mark shook the hair away from his face. He'd given up two months of his time to settle his uncle's estate. Yet, tempted though he was to dump the wax museum, he hadn't been able to bring himself to do it. The place needed work, no question about it. Running on reputation would keep it healthy for a while longer, but Reed had slacked off over the past few years. Something had to be done to combat the apathy that seemed to be overtaking the workers.

So what the hell was he supposed to do about that? Mark wondered bitterly. Sell out to a large corporation? Turn the place into a co-op? Find a private buyer among the swarm of slick operators who'd been hounding him since Reed's death?

Any of those things would send the employees into a tailspin. They were just getting used to him. An outsider would kill the morale and the wax museum within a year.

He thought then about Brodie and whatever screwup had ended his cousin's life. Ass, he swore under his breath. Jealousy over Mark's relationship with Reed had prompted Brodie to get mixed up with the wrong crowd. For some unknown reason, his cousin had thought that Reed had favored Mark, and in his reckless bid for attention, the only thing he'd wound up with had been an uncertain epitaph. Essentially, Mark reflected, Brodie had been a confused kid with a misdirected sense of adventure and damn poor taste in friends . . . With a couple of exceptions.

Mark allowed himself another look and a small grin at the woman in front him. Brodie had been plenty gullible. If she'd responded to his come-ons, Rhianna might have been able to keep him out of trouble. Too bad she hadn't gone for the weak-willed type.

Twenty yards ahead, he saw her pause on the edge of the employee parking lot. She was staring at a young, sandy-haired man in jeans and a plaid shirt, and Mark had to squint to get a better view. The man was Dag Nichols, an ex-classmate of hers, as weak as Brodie in terms of character, but far more vocal and arrogant.

As Dag glanced in their direction, Rhianna took a backward step, and Mark chuckled a little over that one. He drew alongside her and sent her a mocking grin. "Something wrong?"

She shrugged. "You try fending off an oversexed octopus for a while, and see how you like it."

"Tell him to back off if you're not interested."

"I did."

"And?"

"And nothing. He didn't believe me."

Hardly surprising, Mark reflected, as the younger man sauntered bow-legged in their direction. The guy was nothing if not persistent. But then, if she'd really wanted to, Rhianna could have discouraged him fast enough.

"Hey, Mark. Hey, sweet thing. Looks like there was a little excitement out here tonight." Dag shoved his hands in his pockets, preening for Rhianna's benefit. Not unexpectedly, she refused to lower her eyes. It was a point in her favor.

For reasons he didn't especially want to analyze, Mark distracted Dag long enough for her to slip away into the deepening shadows. "Where were you this afternoon?" he questioned, arching a cool brow.

Dag blinked, clearly torn between his desire to pursue her and to answer the question from his current boss. "Down in the pit, where else?" he replied, staying put.

Like hell he'd been down in the pit. "Lie to me again, kid," Mark warned him softly, "and you're out the door. Now, where were you when the fire started?"

"I was—" a sigh, then "—oh, all right; so I took off a little early." Jauntily, Dag offered one of his cigarettes. "You know what Friday nights are like, Mark. Pretty young things drifting into town for the weekend and all. Man, this is a hot season, in more ways than one. You should check out the action at the Seven Oaks Inn sometime." He slanted a look toward the museum apartment. "Not that the scenery's been bad around here lately, mind you."

"You're pushing it, Dag," Mark told him levelly, keeping his meaning deliberately ambiguous. "Make sure you show up for work tomorrow by nine."

"You're not closing down?" Dag sounded incredulous.

"Nope."

"What about the north wing?"

"Storage space only." Mark extracted his keys from the pocket of his jeans. "Nine o'clock," he repeated, crushing out his cigarette. "Don't be late."

He heard Dag's disgruntled mutter as he strode across the lot to his Corvette but didn't bother to acknowledge it. He really couldn't care less that the kid had taken off early today; what he hated was a bad lie. Dag was going to find that out quickly, or find himself another job.

From the museum apartment, Mark heard Sam's stereo blasting out an old Stones classic, and he had to resist the urge to stop and listen. To listen was to think, and he didn't want to think—not about Rhianna, at any rate. Seeing her again had brought too many memories home for him tonight. Starting in on a batch of new ones was the last thing he needed at this point.

With one parting glance at the lighted windows, Mark slid behind the wheel of his car and flicked the engine to life. Then, in a spray of dust and gravel, he roared out of the parking lot. The Raven's Wing held the only promise he cared to contemplate tonight.

But it wasn't a promise and Mark knew that the moment he saw Joe's face. Joe, who was lighting matches and blowing them out, one after another.

"It was set, Mark," his old friend informed him in the privacy of a corner booth. "Someone deliberately torched the north wing." He glanced up sharply. "It looks like we've got an arsonist on our hands."

THE HOURS ROLLED slowly on. It was dark outside, the full embracing dark of a hot August night. The damage was done. The fire, so impulsively set, was out, and the time was almost right to do what now had to be done, what circumstances would force to be done. It would take only half an hour, perhaps less, then it would all be over. There would be nothing left to worry about, no more ghosts to exorcise. Tonight, the burden of an endless decade would be lifted. At last . . .

Chapter Two

"Dag's not really so bad, you know," Sam said. "He's kind of like old Doc Jekyll here, except his Mr. Hyde's not a murderous lech."

Rhianna grinned. "Just a lech, right?"

"Right."

It was close to midnight and still over ninety degrees outside. At Sam's suggestion, the two women had gone down into the wax museum to take a look at the various macabre exhibits.

Rhianna loved the haunting atmosphere of the building and every one of the lifelike figures housed there. She recalled her high-school years when she'd guided weekend tours through the maze of ghoulish displays dressed in a clingy, black Vampira gown, hair loose and wild, nails painted a vivid shade of red. She'd enjoyed the job thoroughly, and it amazed her that she could still recite block portions of her walking spiel.

Of course, with the lights up and the cleaning crew banging around in the background, the marble stares seemed less malevolent; nonetheless, Rhianna felt a pleasantly eerie sensation seeping into her bones as she encountered them.

She wandered past Nosfuratu with his pallid skin, curved fangs and razor-sharp nails, and Bela Lugosi in his most notorious role as the evil Count Dracula, then stopped in front of Jack the Ripper, who was leering at her from his foggy old London Town abode. For reasons she couldn't fathom, she found herself asking, "What does Mark do in New York, Sam?"

Her friend shrugged. "I hear he's a building contractor, and a successful one at that. I gather he has his own company."

"When did he leave town?"

"About ten years ago. He took off around the same time as you college-bound grads and didn't come back until Reed died."

"Is he married?" Rhianna hesitated a little before voicing that one, but Sam merely laughed, a dry, throaty laugh.

"So you're curious about the new boss, huh? Well, I guess that's understandable. He's awfully sexy—for a west ender, that is." Her smile held no malice. "To answer your question, no, he's not married. And he's not living with anyone. At least, I don't think he is."

Rhianna tried not to let that bit of information affect her, but it was hard to keep Mark's enigmatic image out of her head. She saw his skill stamped on so many of the wax figures. In the expertly crafted features of Merlin and Mim and the expressive faces of Lady MacBeth and Joan of Arc.

He was good with his hands, she conceded, an artist really when it came to bringing two-dimensional drawings to life. She could picture him in a Bohemian setting creating fascinating street-life portraits; she couldn't picture him, however, in a New York gallery showing his work. He was too private for that.

Glad for any distraction, she willingly let Sam urge her through the Land of Oz and the Legends of New England witch scene, the Munsters' cobwebbed home and Lizzie Borden's nineteenth-century world. They spent a long time reminiscing about the days when they had both worked at the museum and the fun they'd had revamping their original costumes. It was one o'clock by the time the maintenance people packed up their mops and pails and dimmed the overhead lights, and a little after that when Rhianna and Sam finally abandoned their impromptu tour and went back upstairs.

The apartment, Rhianna noted for the umpteenth time, was comfortably messy. A battered blue pawnshop trunk served as a central coffee table. An exercise bike stood in front of a nineteen-inch color television, which in turn sat atop a large wooden orange crate. The curtains were starched burlap, the rug an ancient rust shag. Toulouse-Lautrec lithographs adorned three of the walls, and the fourth was covered with movie posters, everything from *The Last Picture Show* to *Mad Max: Beyond Thunderdome*.

In the kitchen, an aging Westinghouse made strange clanking noises, interrupted on occasion by a faddy wall clock with a cigar-chomping magpie replacing the usual cuckoo. The guest room, where Rhianna was staying, consisted of two mattresses thrown on top of one another, a rattan rocker that didn't rock straight, a small vanity and another old trunk that doubled as drawer space.

After stripping off her clothes and donning a huge white nightshirt, Rhianna made a quick trip to the bathroom, then climbed under the sheets. She would sleep, she decided. Tired or not, she would sleep. And she wouldn't think about Mark or his life in New York or how he made his living there.

The last time she looked, it was one-fifteen; the next thing she knew, it was after two, and she was sitting bolt upright in bed, trying to figure out why she'd awakened with such a start.

For a long moment she sat there, listening to the grumbling refrigerator and the distant whoops of exuberant teenagers out on Blueberry Road. A Boeing 747, likely destined for landing at Logan International, roared through the night sky in a blast of jet fuel and sonic noise. But that wasn't it. Something else had intruded on her dreams.

Rhianna waited until she heard the sound again, a solid crash she knew immediately had come from somewhere close by.

Because an electrical short had disrupted the air-conditioning system, the apartment windows were all wide open. Although the sound that drifted in had a muted quality to it, it had definitely come from outside. Perhaps from the burned-out production shop.

Quickly, Rhianna reached for her discarded shorts and top. She grabbed her Reeboks and went into the living room. Silently, she crossed the carpet to the French doors leading to the rear balcony. Another muffled crash convinced her that she wasn't hearing things; it also pinpointed a direction for her to take.

But who in their right mind would be poking around a fire-gutted building in the middle of the night? Who? And why?

As she laced up her sneakers, Rhianna detected a rhythmic series of chunking sounds emanating from the north-wing cellar. No doubt about it, someone was in there.

She ran down the outer staircase to the parking lot, then fifty yards back to the roped-off workshop. The door swung open fairly easily when she tried the knob; it creaked back slowly, allowing a shaft of moonlight to beam down the stone stairs.

For a moment, she thought she saw a movement in the shadows, but whatever it was, it vanished a second later. Giving her eyes a few seconds to adjust, she descended into the scorched chamber.

The chunking noises had ceased, if they'd ever even been there. Upon surveying the toppled mass of wood and bricks, which had once been a narrow storeroom wall, Rhianna had a feeling the only thing she'd heard had been the sound of that wall collapsing. What a disappointment.

She grinned to herself as she climbed carefully over piles of rubble and still-wet debris. Part of her had been hoping to catch a vandal in the act, although what she would have done had she run into a burly six-and-a-half-foot looter was something she hadn't stopped to consider.

No matter. Now that she was here, she might as well take a look around.

She was skirting a mound of damp wood and Lord only knew what else when her foot landed squarely on a jagged hunk of plaster. It wobbled, then snapped beneath her weight, sending her sprawling across a scattering of broken bricks.

Dammit! She swore bitingly to herself. One of the rough edges had plunged into her sore rib cage; another had lodged in her shoulder. She probably deserved this fate for walking around in here, but hindsight wasn't going to help her scraped palms or bruised knees much. And it wasn't doing a thing to alleviate the ache in her ribs. If she didn't watch it, she was going to wind up in a cast, or worse, in traction.

Cautiously, Rhianna levered herself up on her elbows. She was halfway to her feet when her eyes fastened on a piece of dull metal directly beneath her. No, not a piece of metal—two pieces of metal. One was circular; the other was oblong.

Sitting back on her heels, she dusted the objects off and prised them free of the rubble. In the dim light, it was difficult to read the label on the small box she was holding, but she was finally able to make out the print. It was a box of Sucrets throat lozenges, and by the look of the rusted container, it had been there for a while.

She turned her attention to the second object, a rolled silver bracelet, badly tarnished, but for some reason, strikingly familiar to her. Where had she seen it before? she wondered, studying it intently.

Maybe it was some inner instinct; maybe it was a brick still teetering precariously from her fall; maybe it was a sudden glimpse of off-white or the shape of the objects over which she was poised. Whatever the case, her eyes strayed beyond the metal objects to the littered floor. And what she saw there had a scream of revulsion bursting from her throat, echoing off the blackened walls. She scrambled dizzily to her feet and was halfway across the room before she even realized she was standing.

Her breath was coming in short ragged gasps. Ignoring the huge chunks of fallen debris, she plunged up the stairs—and straight into Mark's chest.

"What are you doing here, Rhianna?" he demanded, his fingers curving around her upper arms as he steadied her.

What she was doing here wasn't a pertinent question. It didn't even rate an answer. All that mattered was the thing she'd inadvertently stumbled across in the cellar.

Twisting around, but not quite wresting free of his grasp, Rhianna blurted out a breathless, "There's a— Mark, there's a body down there!"

He frowned at her. "A what?"

"You heard me. A body!"

Clearly, he didn't believe her. "You're sleepwalking, Rhianna," he said, relaxing his grip slightly. "No one died in the fire."

"Maybe not, but there's still a body down there. I should know, I was practically lying on the bones."

"Bones? Body? What's going on here?" Joe Marinelli appeared behind Mark, his expression quizzical.

"Rhianna's having a nightmare," Mark informed the firefighter over his shoulder.

That did it. All traces of shock vanished. "Rhianna is not having a nightmare," she stated angrily. "There's a body down there, and if you're not interested, I'm sure the police will be."

Mark's eyes narrowed. Either the word police didn't sit well with him or he was convinced she was sleepwalking. In any event, he was making no move to check out her story.

Joe nudged Mark's arm. "Maybe we should take a look," he suggested.

"Yeah, maybe we should," Mark conceded slowly, skeptically. "You wait here," he instructed her, removing his hands from her arms.

In the back of her mind Rhianna registered an oblique sense of loss; however, now was not the time to examine the reasons behind it. Nodding, she moved aside so Mark and Joe could gain entry to the basement.

It wasn't until they had disappeared into the darkness that she realized she was still clutching the metallic objects she'd picked up moments earlier. Now, she looked at them again. And this time, she remembered.

The bracelet, which had struck her as so familiar, was Brodie's. He'd worn it all through his senior year—a solid band of silver on his left wrist.

"Oh, my God," she murmured, staring in numbed horror at the two things in her hand. What had she found down there? *Who* had she found?

The answer was not long in coming, although Rhianna did her utmost to keep from even thinking Brodie's name. It was too gruesome a notion to entertain. Fortunately, once Mark and Joe saw for themselves that her so-called nightmare was, in fact, a very real skeleton, she was given no further opportunity to think about anything.

Joe used the cellular phone in his car to call the police while Mark dug a Durabeam flashlight out of the south-wing pit. Once he had a flare in his hand, Rhianna had no qualms about trailing him into the workshop.

She saw him crouched down beside a half-buried collection of bones in the rear of the narrow storage bin. It had definitely been that wall that had fallen. Perhaps a coincidence; perhaps not.

With the throat lozenges and bracelet safely tucked in the pocket of her baggy shorts, she ventured down the stairs, halting as Mark raised his head to spear her with his eyes.

"Stay back, Rhianna," he said, his gaze steady on hers. "The cops will be here any minute."

Precisely why she wanted to get closer. Once the police arrived, they would seal off the entire building.

Swallowing the lump of revulsion in her throat, she asked. "Do you know who it is?"

Mark slanted her an inscrutable look. "You're the sleuth, Rhianna. You tell me."

Did she really have to? "It's Brodie, isn't it?" she managed, unable now to take another step forward.

"That'd be my guess."

God, he said it so dispassionately, almost as if he didn't care. Brodie had been in absolute awe of his older cousin. Surely Mark had to know that. Surely, he had to feel something. Nobody could be that devoid of emotion. Unless, of course...

No! She wouldn't even finish that thought. Mark was no murderer. He may have been many things, but a murderer wasn't among them.

Almost unconsciously, her fingers moved to the rusty box of lozenges in her pocket. From where she stood, she could see exactly where they'd been lying—right next to the body, in a spot that had only this night been exposed. They'd been there with Brodie's bracelet all this time, hidden behind a wall of bricks.

She tried to block the grisly recollection screaming in her brain to be acknowledged. Something Mark had said to her the night Brodie had disappeared. Something that crowded in with the image of his red-stained clothing and the strange scraping noises she'd heard not five minutes before he'd cornered her behind the oak tree.

He'd had a cold. He'd told her that straight out. And again, she felt the throat lozenges in her pocket.

"Rhianna."

Her lashes flew up, and she realized he was standing, watching her through guarded eyes. Somehow, she held her ground. "What?" She felt like he was staring right through her. Thank God for the sirens out on Blueberry Road.

His features were unfathomable. "I asked you if you saw anyone down here."

"I . . . no." She bit her lip. "I thought I saw a shadow, but it could have been the moonlight." Her confidence bolstered by the approaching squad cars, Rhianna lifted her chin a fraction. "What are you doing here, Mark? I thought you'd left for the night."

"Did you?" His tone was as impassive as his expression. "I guess you were wrong then, weren't you?"

"But I heard you leave."

"I came back to make sure the north wing was locked up."

"Did Joe come with you?" she questioned hopefully, but he squashed that possibility with a shake of his head.

"We had a couple of drinks over at the Raven's Wing, then split up. I had no idea he was planning to follow me over here."

Rhianna edged toward the stairs. She didn't like what she was thinking. And it wasn't fair, in any event. Throat lozenges were not grounds for conviction, she told herself firmly. For all she knew, they might not even be Mark's. And the body might not be Brodie's. The bracelet she'd found, however, seemed to refute that last theory.

Emitting a sigh of futility and pent-up frustration, Rhianna forced herself to accept the inevitable. Brodie had been missing for ten years, and she'd found a body in the cellar of his father's production shop. The two things had to be connected. Oh, hell, they had to be one and the same, didn't they? There just wasn't any other conclusion she could draw.

Squeezing her eyes closed, she spun away from the blackened rubble. Brodie was dead. He'd been dead all this time. She'd known that from the start, but somehow never really believed his body would be discovered. Now that it had though, Rhianna was certain of one thing: she wasn't going to leave Bremerhaven until she had a lot more answers than she did at this moment.

SATURDAY MORNING brought with it a host of local radio and TV news stories, bold *Chronicle* headlines and a steady flow of police officers and curious townspeople to the wax museum.

The coroner's report was delivered with more alacrity than Rhianna had anticipated, but while it identified the remains as those of Brodie Morgan, it stopped short of revealing the details she really wanted to hear. Rumor had it that Brodie had been strangled or stabbed or clubbed; however, there was no confirmation forthcoming on that vital point, and the best Rhianna could do for the moment was guess at the cause of death.

Because Mark had decided to close down the museum for the weekend, Sam spent the morning sprawled on the sun deck, her body slathered with sunscreen, her mood strangely quiet and withdrawn. Dag was in much the same state when Rhianna passed him around eleven en route to the production-shop offices. He offered her a weak half smile and continued walking toward the main building.

Zombies would have been more responsive than either of those two, she thought without rancor, wondering absently if she looked as rattled herself. Probably. It was one thing to think a friend was dead, another thing entirely to be confronted with the stark reality of his skeletal remains.

But she had a plan, a way to gain access to Reed's old files and whatever else the wax museum might have to offer. All she had to do was get herself hired as a temporary tour guide. Thus her trip to the production shop's main level.

Marion Noble was sitting in the outer office when Rhianna stepped inside. Smoke from a long Virginia Slims floated hazily in the air above her head. At fifty-six years of age, she was a commanding woman. Her dark hair hung in a mid-length forties-style wave around her angular face. She had what could only be described as Bette Davis eyes, large and brown and discerning—eyes that reflected her inner strength. Unlike her sister, Billie, she'd always been an outspoken woman, determined to overcome any and all obstacles in her life, including the heavy hand of a domineering mother. She was also a very shrewd individual. Rhianna had a feeling that Marion would figure out her reasons for wanting a job the minute the request was voiced.

As if to prove that point, one of Marion's plucked brows arched. Her smile was canny. "A social call on a Saturday morning, Rhianna?" she queried, through a veil of smoke. "Or did you perhaps have something else in mind?"

Rhianna grinned. "Would you believe a little of both?"

"I'm flattered, my dear, truly flattered." Marion chuckled and her laugh was as raw and husky as her speaking voice. "You always were my kind of people. I think we understand each other, you and I. You're a private investigator, and I'm the office manager here. Now, what do you suppose those two things could add up to?"

Rhianna took a seat in front of her, not quite ready to launch into her request just yet. "I assume you've heard about Brodie?'' she hedged, propping her elbows up on the desk.

Lazily, Marion flicked ash from the end of her cigarette. ''I've heard nothing else all morning. Dag's wandering around like a lost soul, and Mark—well, Mark keeps everything inside, but he's shaken, too.''

Was he? Rhianna wasn't so sure. He hadn't seemed shaken at all last night. ''You know him pretty well, don't you, Marion?'' she ventured, consideringly.

The older woman spread her fingers. ''As well as anyone, I expect. He was never as amiable as his cousin, but he had his good points. He just prefers to keep them hidden.'' Her dark eyes gleamed. She leaned back in her padded chair. ''Rather like me, wouldn't you say?''

Rhianna had to laugh. With Marion there was no pretense. She could feel comfortable and relaxed, not on edge the way she'd felt in Billie's presence.

It was funny, she thought now, but as strong as Billie had once appeared, she hadn't possessed Marion's ability to speak her mind and be done with it. When their family's diner had been demolished, Billie had ranted and raved and cursed everyone in sight. Marion, on the other hand, had merely told the bank board precisely what she thought of their decision, then put the unpleasant incident behind her and moved ahead with her life. She'd been working at the wax museum for as long as Rhianna could remember, and in spite of her dry, laconic exterior, she was well liked by the staff.

Glancing up, Rhianna caught the speculative glimmer in Marion's discerning eyes. ''Mark told me you saw Billie last night,'' she said, exhaling a long, slow stream of smoke. ''Were you shocked by the change in her?''

"Yes." The admission came easily, and with it, a renewed surge of curiosity. "What happened to her, Marion? The last time I saw her, she was fine."

"No, she wasn't, my dear. I'm afraid she wasn't fine at all. When Mother died eleven years ago, part of Billie died with her. They were extremely close—too close, for my money. Billie's never really let go of that bond." Her eyes lifted then to the glass doors. "Hello, Mark," she said. "Come and join us. Rhianna and I are having a lovely heart-to-heart here."

The door swished closed, announcing Mark's quiet arrival, and Rhianna's fists clenched in her lap. Damn him, she swore to herself. His timing couldn't have been worse if he'd planned it that way.

She averted her head as Mark strode through the outer office. He'd obviously showered and changed sometime after his cousin's body had been taken away. His blond hair looked clean and rumpled, and his white T-shirt had given way to a light gray one. His Adidas made no sound as he crossed the carpeted floor.

"The police chief's outside, Marion," he told her, his eyes skimming coolly over Rhianna. "He wants to talk to all the employees. You're next on the agenda."

Nodding, Marion sent Rhianna an inert smile. "Then I'd better go see what he wants," she drawled, picking up her cigarette box and purse. "We'll talk later, shall we, Rhianna?"

"That'll be fine, Marion," Rhianna assured her. "It can wait."

Mark said nothing until the older woman had left; then he lifted a questioning brow. "What can wait?"

Rhianna refused to be intimidated by the fact that he was towering over her. "It wasn't important," she said.

A small smile tugged at the corners of his mouth. "I take it you're planning to stay for a while?"

She stiffened her spine. "Is that a problem?"

He poured himself a cup of coffee, rounding the desk to straddle one of the hard chairs. "That all depends on your reasons," he replied, blowing on the steamy brew. "But my guess is you want to do a lot more than nurse a few sore ribs."

"And if I do?"

He shrugged. "That's up to you. Personally, I think you're wasting your time. Brodie's been dead for ten years."

Rhianna employed every ounce of poise she possessed and rose to her feet. "That doesn't mean his murderer has left town, Mark," she maintained dryly.

He swallowed a mouthful of coffee. "You're grasping at straws, you know."

Was she? She didn't think so. "I still want to stay," she said, aware of the throat lozenges in her pocket and far too aware of the clean, soapy scent of Mark's skin and hair.

"Okay." Still grinning ever so slightly, he set the mug down and rested his arms indolently on the top of the chair. "So you're determined to stay. Now what, Sherlock? Would you like to see the storeroom again?"

"Isn't it cordoned off?"

"Yep, but I'm sure that won't stop you."

Ignoring the teasing remark, she shot back. "What I'd really like, Mark, is to know why there was such a large hole behind the wall. It was just waste space, wasn't it?"

A glimmer of amusement flickered in his eyes. "Reed had it bricked up on purpose," he revealed calmly. "The original specs called for a fireplace in that alcove, but there was a problem venting it, so he had the wall evened off and block storerooms built instead."

Which meant what? "Had the brickwork been started before Brodie died?"

"I have no idea."

"Is there any way to find out?"

"You could talk to the bricklayer who was assigned to do the job."

It wasn't much, but it was a start. "Do you know his name?"

Mark rose to his feet, shaking his head. "Forget it, Rhianna," he said. "The guy's retired, and the other construction workers are probably scattered across the country by now. And even if you were to find out that the wall had been spirited into place, all it would prove is that the murderer knew a thing or two about mixing mortar."

Rhianna refrained from asking him what he himself knew about mortar. She had a feeling he knew plenty about a lot of things.

"Tell me why you wanted to talk to Marion," Mark prompted her again, his voice so quietly authoritative that she very nearly complied.

She caught herself in the nick of time. "It really wasn't important," she repeated.

There was a mocking edge to his expression, underlined by a trace of impatience. "I don't believe you," he drawled. Then he reached out to lift her chin with his forefinger. "You'd do well to remember that Marion's only the office manager here. In the end, she answers to me."

Rhianna could have handled his subtle threats; she might even have been able to parry them, if only he hadn't touched her. The ridiculous thing was, she'd never had a moment's trouble resisting any other man. What, then, made Mark so different? What made him so attractive, so sexy?

"Tell me, Rhianna," he said again.

She managed to squirm away from him. Squaring her shoulders, she summoned a semidefiant look. Lying wouldn't do her a shred of good. He'd plainly spelled out the chain of command, and if he wasn't one hundred percent sure of her intentions, he was close enough. "I was going to ask Marion if I could work at the wax museum for a while—until Renee gets her walking cast, or you can hire a permanent guide."

Mark grinned at her quite openly, and she had to admit he had a nice smile—when he chose to use it. "In other words, you want to moonlight."

"Yes, I want to moonlight."

"As Vampira?"

"Yes," she said evenly.

He was going to send her packing, she thought. At the very least, he was going to turn her down flat. She waited for the ax to fall, preparing herself for a heated argument in logic. But then he moved his shoulders, and she wasn't sure what to expect.

"All right," he murmured after a lengthy period of silence. "You can play Vampira. But you have to agree to stay until after the Labor Day weekend. Renee won't be back till then."

Four and a half weeks... Perfect. She could get an extension on her vacation with no problem. And with free access to the museum, she might just be able to catch herself a murderer.

Nodding, Rhianna made the required concession. "I'll stay until after Labor Day," she agreed.

FOUR AND A HALF WEEKS...

What the hell had he been thinking, anyway? Mark wondered for the hundredth time since Rhianna had headed off to the museum library for a quick refresher course. He must have been crazy to give her Renee's job. She was a private eye, for Christ's sake. And even if she hadn't been, she possessed more natural curiosity than anyone he knew.

But she also possessed the features of an angel, he reminded himself ironically. Maybe he wasn't a pushover for a pretty face, but then she wasn't just your run-of-the-mill pretty face, either. She was different somehow, more spirited, much more of a lure to his calloused senses.

Deep inside, Mark felt the reminiscent stirrings of emotions he hadn't experienced for years, and while he would have preferred to ignore them, he knew that wouldn't be possible. Something about Rhianna had the power to shake the foundations of the stony fortress he'd built for himself as a youth. Something in those stunning green eyes of hers, in her voice, in her actions. Something in her fierce determination to expose Brodie's murderer.

She wasn't someone who would settle for half-truths. And for that reason alone, he knew he'd have to watch his guard closely. It had slipped once already today, making him give in when common sense had warned him not to. And now Vampira was back on staff. Vampira in a detective's cap, hell-bent on causing an uproar over a crime that had been committed a full ten years before.

With a rueful grin, Mark let his gaze travel to the window overlooking the employee's parking lot. A dark bank of storm clouds was scudding in from the east, but even minus the sun's illuminating rays, he didn't miss the trail of Rhianna's dark wavy hair disappearing into the trees by the old railway tracks. Nor did he miss the other female figure hunched down in the bushes bordering the lot. It was the figure of Billie Noble. And her sunken black eyes were focused intently on Rhianna's receding form ...

Chapter Three

By late afternoon, the air was so heavy with heat and moisture that it was barely breathable. A mass of dark, angry-looking clouds had moved in from the east to block out the hot sun, but the temperature had remained in the mid-nineties and the humidity had risen to even greater heights. After spending several hours hunched over textbooks in the production-shop library to brush up on the museum's history, Rhianna had been ready for a break. And a break seemed to lend itself to a trip out to the old Pullman.

The woods were still and eerily silent as she followed the railway tracks to the deserted junction. Occasionally, a breath of air rustled through the leafy treetops, but beyond that, not a sound emanated from the tangle of underbrush around her. Nothing except the low, off-key whistle of an unseen vagrant and the far-distant strains of carnival music.

It was going to pour any minute, she thought, tilting her head back to survey the black clouds. A summer storm to wet the heat even further. And by tomorrow morning, the sun would be out again and the ninety-plus temperature would push every air conditioner in the area

to its limit. More heat and humidity and no relief in sight
for the next week, at least.

Forcing her mind away from her physical discomfort,
Rhianna turned her attention to her present situation.
What she really had to do here, she decided, was deter-
mine who had been behind the east-end robberies. That
had to be the key to Brodie's death. Certainly that was
what his frantic late-night phone call had implied. Expose the thief or thieves, and in all likelihood, she'd also
expose her friend's murderer.

Rhianna climbed over a fallen tree as she neared the
junction. The carnival music was louder now, floating
south along Blueberry Road from Kruger's Meadow. The
summer carnival was a large sprawling fair that she remembered well from her high-school years. It was like
something out of a Ray Bradbury novel, or maybe a
nineteen-fifties horror movie. There were the usual rides
and midway attractions, but there were also fortune-
telling booths and sideshows in large, dark tents—cause
enough for even the most ardent skeptic to fall into a su-
perstitious stupor.

Above her, an ominous peal of thunder rumbled
through the afternoon sky. A crow glided noiselessly over
the rusting Pullman. Not a ripple marred the murky blue
surface of the junction pond, and before her, the dilapidated coach stood like an ancient sentinel, guarding the
small clearing.

Rhianna relished the feeling of fright, of solitude and
spooky isolation. She let the carnival music filter through
her, waiting for the next roll of thunder and for the
forked lightning that might or might not accompany it.
It seemed almost ordained that, at the moment she set her
foot on the crooked step leading into the Pullman, a
hoarse whisper should issue from the woods. In the dead

silence, she heard the raspy cry and then the crackle of twigs under someone's feet.

A nervous glance over her shoulder, however, revealed nothing except dense underbrush and tall trees. But the whisper had been real, and Rhianna knew with a jolt that she wasn't alone out here.

"No more...no more..." The whispered voice croaked again. The pitch resembled a low moan, a dreadful plea issued out of desperation—or fear.

A knot of apprehension formed in the pit of Rhianna's stomach. She could feel the skin on the back of her neck beginning to prickle.

Endeavoring to control her jumping nerves, she peered deeper into the bushes. And in between the tangle of leaves and vines, she spied tendrils of wispy black hair and a lined face. Billie Noble's face, wild-eyed and pinched, scrunched into a mask of animal terror.

"Billie?" She called the woman's name hesitantly. "Is that you?"

"No more..." Eyes darting in every direction, the spindly ex-librarian dashed out from her hiding place. "He's come back," she hissed, halting at the edge of the tracks. "You have to warn them."

She certainly hadn't lost the power of speech, Rhianna noted distantly, forcing herself not to back away from the cringing woman. "Warn who, Billie?" she asked, half tempted to turn and run back to the museum, yet determined not to bolt in fear.

"All of them." Her voice raw and shaky, Billie Noble squatted by the rails. "He's come back to hurt us—to have his revenge."

Rhianna swallowed with difficulty. "Who's he?"

The woman's thin shoulders hunched. "He knows who we are. He was one of us—once. But then he went away. He said it was my fault, and he went away."

"Who went away?" Rhianna managed, albeit a trifle shakily. This was positively creepy.

Whether Billie was coherent or merely babbling, she couldn't tell. She wasn't sure she even wanted to.

The sunken eyes blinked rapidly, then clouded over. "I had to pay them back," Billie warbled. "For Mama. For what they did to her—to me... I had to do it. I had to... And it was all so perfect. But then, he went away and everything changed. Now, he'll try to hurt us all."

"Us?" Rhianna echoed, taking a few discreet steps away from the tracks.

Billie shook her head. "No more..." she rasped hazily. "Please—you have to tell them. Warn them. Before it's too late. Before he..." Her voice trailed off as her eyes locked on a point just behind the Pullman. "No!" she breathed, springing nimbly to her feet.

Rhianna looked quickly to her right. There on the tracks, staring at Billie with the most inscrutable of expressions on his face, stood Mark.

Although she had no idea where he'd come from, Rhianna knew he had to have overheard some part of the old woman's ramblings. He continued to regard her calmly. "Before he what, Billie?" he enquired, not making any move in her direction.

Billie's entire body began to tremble. "No!" she cried, this time shrilly. "No!" One gnarled hand clutched to her sagging breast, she spun around and bolted into the woods.

Rhianna stared after her in disbelief. Then she turned to stare at Mark. "What was that all about?" she demanded, forgetting for the moment her half-formed suspicions toward him, not allowing herself to consider what he might be doing out here. "Why is she so afraid of you?"

Mark shrugged. "Damned if I know. Maybe she thinks I'm responsible for her mother's death."

"That's ridiculous," Rhianna snapped. "Her mother died of a stroke."

"And Reed died of a heart attack and Brodie died from a blow to the skull. But then you already knew all of that, didn't you, Rhianna?"

Not the last one, she hadn't. Her mouth grew dry. "How do you know about Brodie? The papers said the cause of death was undetermined."

Mark glanced up at the threatening sky. The light gray of his T-shirt made his blue eyes seem icier than ever. "I saw the body, Rhianna," he told her without expression. "The information's been deliberately withheld."

She eyed him warily. "How do you know that, Mark?"

His features were impassive. "An old friend of mine is a cop on the Bremerhaven force. He told me."

Well, that was a nice, pat explanation, wasn't it? Mark continued to regard the storm clouds as the first drops of rain began to fall. Now what? Rhianna wondered, a little nervously. The sky was going to open up, and her only refuge was the Pullman. If there was any chance at all that Mark was the murderer, it would be far too easy for him to dispose of her in there. He could leave her, and let the police draw their own conclusions. In all likelihood, they'd assume she'd been killed by a vagrant. And that would be that.

No one but her seemed to think the murderer was still in Bremerhaven. She'd heard the police chief talking last night. It was his contention that the killer was long gone.

He wasn't about to launch an in-depth investigation into any of this.

The rain was really starting to come down. Rhianna was pondering her options when she suddenly felt Mark's fingers close around her wrist. He'd reached her so quickly that she'd had no chance to evade him, and now he had her in his grasp.

Before she could kick or scream or even raise a word of protest, he was hauling her toward the Pullman. And then she saw the lightning, a jagged bolt of white forking to earth, beyond the junction pond. Death by strangulation or death by electrocution. It wasn't much of a choice. She let Mark propel her into the dusty coach.

A small, wry grin tugged at his lips as he followed her inside. "You can relax Rhianna," he said, shaking the droplets of water from his hair. "You're safe enough in here. Billie's a witness, remember?"

He knew. Damn him, anyway, he knew exactly what she was thinking. But he was only guessing, she reminded herself. If she was extremely careful, he wouldn't have any reason to harm her. And maybe he didn't have a reason to harm her in any event. Maybe Billie Noble was the murderer. She had a good motive for wanting Brodie dead. She'd certainly leveled all manner of dire threats against Reed Morgan for purchasing the land on which her family's diner had once stood. And God knew, she was deluded.

Thunder bowled through the darkened heavens, a deep reverberating sound preceding a torrential pounding of rain. It slammed against the thin metal roof of the rail car and streamed over the dirty windows, turning the enclosed space into a sauna.

Rhianna sought out one of the faded velvet seats and sank down onto the worn upholstery. She could feel the smoldering heat radiating from Mark's body, combined with the enticing scent of his skin, even with ten feet of air separating them. She ran a surreptitious eye over his long limbs, so sleek and slender in near-silhouette. And she had to struggle not to submit to the dull ache in her chest.

Still smiling a little, he took a seat across from her, resting his forearms on his thighs, letting his hands dangle between his legs.

Curious about a past she didn't really understand, Rhianna couldn't prevent herself from asking, "Did you get along well with your uncle, Mark?"

He lifted one shoulder. "As well as possible. We weren't particularly close."

"But he left you the wax museum. He must have wanted you to have it."

"I was his only living relative. He didn't have a lot of other options."

"What about your mother?" Rhianna inquired cautiously. "Is she still alive?"

"Nope. She ran off when I was three, moved in with an ex-con from Detroit and wound up dead about five years later."

"I'm sorry," Rhianna murmured, wishing she'd held her tongue.

Mark's shrug was indifferent. "Don't be," he said flatly. "I'm sure as hell not."

It was a telling statement and far more than Rhianna really cared to hear. No wonder he was so cynical, so distant. He'd probably never been close to anyone in his life.

Seeking to change the subject, Rhianna reached into her bag and found her notepad. "I wrote down all the information I could on the museum displays," she told him, keeping her voice carefully conversational. "I'll have my spiel ready by Monday."

He nodded. "Fine. Just make sure you're concise. Some of the guides are too long-winded. The tours start up every fifteen minutes, and you've only got an hour to get through the museum. I'm going to put you in behind a couple of the slower guides. If they're lagging, push them forward. If they bitch about it, tell them to come to me, not Marion."

Rhianna studied him. "You don't like running the museum much, do you?"

"I don't mind it," Mark retorted easily. "Reed didn't do much with it in the last few years, though. And the place needs more time and attention than I can afford to give it. The guides are fine, but the production shop's a mess; the pit's only operating at a third its original capacity, and Dag's not really motivated to push for more."

In a way, his remark about his uncle made sense. Reed Morgan had been gung ho on improving the wax museum ten years ago; however, after Brodie had disappeared, he'd lost much of his initial enthusiasm. In the months preceding Rhianna's departure for college, he'd turned the running of the place over to Mark. According to Sam, when Mark left town, he'd taken up the reins again, albeit with far less enthusiasm than before. Production had slowed, creating a backlog of orders for the exquisitely crafted figures. And that was a shame, since the workmanship was beyond compare.

With a heartfelt sigh, she returned her notebook to her bag and looked over at Mark. Try as she might, she couldn't read the expression on his face. His eyes had strayed to the window and the sodden landscape beyond. There was a brooding aspect to his countenance, one she didn't dare quiz him about, and wouldn't have in any event. The last thing she needed to do was let herself become involved with Mark Reimer.

The interior of the car had become a steam bath. Rhianna's skin felt hot and damp, and in spite of herself, she couldn't help the covert glances she continued to cast in Mark's direction, similar to the ones he was casting in hers. She was attracted to him, she realized with a start. It was stupid and wrong, but there it was. And she knew that if she didn't put some distance between them quickly, she was going to lose her objectivity as well as any hope she might have of finding Brodie's murderer.

"The rain's letting up."

Mark's mild observation had Rhianna looking out the window at the lightening sky. Gray clouds were gradually replacing the black ones. Within minutes the downpour had turned to a drizzle, and soon after, even that ceased.

Breathing a silent sigh of relief, she rose to her feet. "I guess we can go now," she said.

"I guess so." Mark stood, too, handing her her slouch bag.

"Mark?" She halted at the crumbling doorway and regarded him over her shoulder. "Why did you come out here today?"

A faint grin worked its way across his mouth. "I saw you leave, and then I saw Billie following you. I didn't want to risk endangering my newest employee, so I decided to see what she was up to."

Rhianna ignored the impersonal rider. "You think Billie's dangerous?"

"No. But she has a tendency to be unpredictable. You'd be smart to stay away from her as much as possible." The carnival music seemed to catch his attention then, and a faintly reminiscent smile curved his lips.

"Brings back memories, doesn't it?" he murmured. "I can remember spending whole days up there when I was a kid, sneaking into the tents hoping to catch a glimpse of something wicked."

"Sneaking?" Rhianna grinned. "And here I thought you were such an upstanding west-end boy. Did you ever see anything?"

"Not much," he returned, his tone obscure. With his head, he motioned toward the distant meadow. "As long as we're out here, do you want to go up to the carny and have a look around?"

Did she? Yes. Should she? No. But then again, why not take the chance? she thought, nodding her hesitant affirmation. After all, if he'd wanted to be rid of her, the Pullman would have been a better place to commit a murder than a crowded carnival. Besides, she might be all wrong about him.

She clung to that tenuous thread of hope as they walked side by side along the tracks toward Kruger's Meadow.

THE NOISE AND COLOR and confusion of the summer fair hit Mark long before he and Rhianna reached the thronging midway. It took him way back in time, back before he'd had any kind of a reputation to worry about.

He remembered the days and nights he'd spent here, with Brodie tagging along behind him and his friends like a bright-eyed puppy begging for a scrap of attention. He remembered, too, how he'd once ridden the merry-go-round three times running just to shut the kid up. Naturally, that had brought a round of good-natured jeers from his west-end buddies, but in the end Mark couldn't say he'd really minded the ragging. Brodie's happy face had lit up the carny for the rest of the night.

A pang of regret worked its way through Mark's ribs. Brodie might have been a pest and he might have been sorely lacking in good judgment, but all in all, he hadn't really been a bad kid. Certainly he'd deserved something better than to be slammed on the head and dumped behind a brick wall.

In an effort to dispel the painful memories, Mark glanced over at Rhianna, beside him on the dirt track leading to the carnival gates. It helped, although he couldn't really say why. Maybe it was just that he didn't associate her with the past. He'd thought last night that he would, but it hadn't turned out that way. When he looked at her now, he saw only the present. And that was a great deal more than he'd expected.

IT WAS GROWING DARK by the time they reached the carnival gates, a premature dusk brought on by the pervading cloud cover. The smell of damp vegetation gave way to the smell of hot buttered popcorn, roasted peanuts, hamburgers and hot dogs. Overhead, a double Ferris wheel made a swooping descent, the shrieks of its riders momentarily rising above the festive strains of midway chaos.

Rhianna looked around her. Penny-arcade barkers were enticing passersby to play their games of chance. Others with megaphones were attempting to cajole those same people into their tents. There were lineups for ticket and concession stands alike, and even the open-walled German beer garden was jam-packed.

"Do you like the roller coaster?" Mark asked her above the swell of sound.

Rhianna hesitated. She didn't really like it at all, but it was doubtful he'd believe that or even understand the reasons. She wasn't sure herself. "Do you?" she returned with as much enthusiasm as she could muster.

"Yeah, but you don't have to come with me if you'd rather not."

"No, it's fine. I like the rides," she lied.

He sent her a disbelieving look. "You sure?"

"Of course I'm sure. Let's go before the lineup gets too long." Or before I lose my nerve, she added, sighing.

Before she knew it, the cars were rolling to a halt on the raised platform. Gritting her teeth, Rhianna climbed into the second car. It would have to be so close to the front, she thought peevishly. At least farther back, she might have been able to prepare herself for that first monster of a dip. Now, the best she could hope for was... Come to think of it, there wasn't a best thing she could hope for.

She squeezed her eyes shut as the attendant slammed the safety bar in place. For the sake of her pride, she wouldn't scream. But she was sure as hell going to hold on and pray for a speedy end to this ordeal.

Of course, no ordeal could ever be speedy. Life just wasn't that obliging. The second the cars began to grind upward along the narrow ribbon of track, her heart started to thump. And it didn't help that Mark was sitting right beside her looking relaxed and at ease and smiling that lazy, knowing smile of his.

"You love the rides, huh?" he drawled, and if she could have prised her fingers from the crossbar, Rhianna would have plunged her elbow right into the side of his rib cage.

As it was, the best she could do was turn her head and glare at him. "All right, so I lied. I thought it might not be so bad this time around... Oh, my God..."

They'd reached the peak now, that horrible sickening moment when the first few cars just seemed to hang there in midair. And that's exactly what they did—hang there, suspended high above the ground, waiting for momentum to plunge then straight down.

In that treacherous second, Rhianna felt Mark's arm slide around her shoulders. And although she knew he murmured something to her, she had absolutely no idea what it was. Her mind became a void, her body as stiff as a board.

And then they were plummeting to the earth below. Falling, falling—for what felt like an endless stretch of time. Falling and swerving and falling once more, until Rhianna felt sure she'd never again know what it was like to have her feet on solid ground.

Her mouth was completely dry when the cars at last rolled through the tunnel and screeched to a halt by the platform. It wasn't until the riders began to climb out of their seats that she realized she'd been clutching Mark's arm instead of the metal rail. She could see where her nails had dug into his skin.

"Oh, Mark, I'm sorry," she apologized. "I didn't mean to do that."

He vaulted easily from the car, holding out a hand to her. "Don't worry about it, Rhianna." He smiled. "I've had worse injuries in my life." He eyed her unsteady knees as she joined him on the platform. "I think maybe you could use a drink," he observed shrewdly. "The beer garden's right below us on the midway."

"Wonderful. Which way?"

His lips quirked. "Down, Rhianna. We have to go down."

She managed a weak grin. "Well, as long as we can do it slowly."

To her relief, Mark rested his arm on her shoulders as they made the final descent into the heart of the carnival. And by the time they'd reached the lively beer garden, she actually felt semihuman again.

Long rows of wooden benches and tables filled the open-sided area. A huge canopy offered protection from the elements and also confined the noise a bit. There were knockwurst and fat sausages, crusty kaiser buns and a variety of cheeses available for consumption, as well as draft and bottled beer, soft drinks and cider.

Rhianna dropped onto one of the rough benches while Mark went off to the bar. Never again, she vowed, glad to be sitting on something that showed no sign of streaking like a rocket through the night. She was never going near the rides again.

Since it looked as though Mark might be a while, she dug through her bag, removing the rusted box of Sucrets and Brodie's rolled silver bracelet.

She'd cleaned the narrow band up that afternoon. It gleamed now in the golden lamplight, and for the first time, she noticed the inner inscription. Six numbers rather than letters. Well, Brodie's name had six letters in it, didn't it? He must have been interested in numerology, she thought with a sigh.

A glance at the crowded bar revealed that Mark was placing his order. Hastily, she pried open the lid of the small box. It was nearly full of foil-wrapped lozenges. Nothing earth-shattering there, she decided, snapping the lid shut and returning both objects to her bag.

Mark came back a few minutes later with a Lowenbrau for her and a Michelob for himself.

"Feeling better?" he queried, taking a drink of his beer.

"A little." She hesitated, then asked, "Mark, do you have any idea what Billie was babbling about back at the Pullman?"

"Nope. Do you?"

"No. But I'm sure she was trying to tell me something."

"I don't think so, Rhianna," he said quietly. "She's just a crazy old lady who had nothing better to do than make up wild stories."

Maybe. But she'd been so insistent. "Does anyone ever spend any time with her, Mark? Anyone besides Marion, that is?"

He picked up a pretzel from one of the wooden bowls on the table. "Not as far as I know. Billie seems to prefer ghosts to people. She spends a lot of her time visiting Marcie's grave over at the cemetery."

"Marcie... Is that her mother?"

Mark nodded. "Marion claims her sister's most coherent when she's talking to the gravestone."

"She talks to her mother's gravestone?"

"She talks to everything. Gravestones, trees, even that beat-up old Comet of hers. I've seen her sitting in it myself, chatting away to the steering wheel."

Well, that pretty much said it all, didn't it? The woman was obviously bouncing off the walls.

An equitable silence reigned while she and Mark drank their beer. Rhianna was toying with the idea of having her fortune told when Mark suddenly reached over and touched her arm.

"I'll be right back," he said, his eyes focused on a small chipboard building across the crowded midway.

Rhianna nodded, yet a small, perverse part of her brain instantly went on alert. He could have been going to the washroom, but her instincts said no to that simple idea.

Feeling like a would-be voyeur, she trailed him discreetly to the sectioned building. To her chagrin, however, he did indeed go through the door marked "Men."

With a shrug for her missed guess, Rhianna braved the woman's side. The air was thick with cigarette and marijuana smoke and overpowering disinfectants, and she escaped it as quickly as she could, gulping lungfuls of muggy air the moment she was back outside.

There was a partition separating the two washrooms and for a minute she leaned against it, staring at the whirling salt-and-pepper shakers and the wild mouse cars as they careened around brutally sharp corners. A gypsy fortune-telling booth beckoned, but before she could take even a step away from the partition, low voices from the other side rooted her to the spot.

One of those voices belonged to Mark. The other was Joe's. And they weren't discussing the weather or the carnival or even yesterday's fire. She edged toward the front of the wall, pressing her ear up against it.

"What are you doing at the carny, Mark?" she heard Joe ask.

"It's a long story," Mark said. "As long as we're both here, though, you'd better know that you've got a major problem on your hands. There's no way she can be trusted."

"Tell me about it," Joe muttered. "Still, what can we do? If we try to get her out of the way, someone's bound to notice, and this whole thing could blow up in our faces. Man, we're talking about murder here."

"Have you talked to the others, yet?"

"This afternoon."

"And?"

"And they're sweating buckets. But they don't know what to do, either. Hell, they don't even trust one another."

"Do they trust you?"

"No more than you do." Joe chuckled. "Hey, come on, Mark. We've known each other too long here. No one trusts anyone. Not really. Why should we? I mean, this thing's been dormant for ten years. If the shop hadn't burned, who's to say how long it would have stayed hidden?"

"But it's out now, isn't it?" Mark prodded softly.

"Only the body part. The rest is still buried, and I don't see anything more coming of it. You said yourself the cops didn't find a single clue down there."

Mark's voice roughened. "No, they didn't. But I think Rhianna did."

"Aw, Jesus. Are you serious? What's she got?"

"How the hell should I know? She's hardly about to confide in me."

"No, I guess not." Joe thought a second. "Do you know how he was killed, Mark?"

"No. Do you?"

Joe chuckled again. "Trust, old friend. We're right back to it, aren't we?"

"Looks that way."

"You going to tell her about any of this?"

"What do you think?"

Joe sighed. "Man, I don't know what to think. You lost me when you hired her."

"I had my reasons," Mark said simply.

"That much, I figured." A set of car keys jangled. "Listen, I'm going to take off. I have the early shift tomorrow. And I gather you have a gorgeous, raven-haired P.I. out there waiting for you."

That was it—an end to her eavesdropping stint. With a firm shake of her head to offset a torrent of confused thoughts, Rhianna made her way hastily around the building.

The conversation had been an unsatisfactory revelation. It hadn't told her nearly enough. That Mark was mixed up in something with his old west-end friend was obvious. That they'd been speaking about Brodie's murder was also abundantly clear to her. But who were the others they'd mentioned? Were they the same others as Billie's obscure them? And who was the her who couldn't be trusted, who was bound to be noticed if she was missing?

Rhianna shivered despite the oppressive heat. She might very well be that indistinct her. And if she was, Mark was onto her. He thought she'd found something down in the basement. Her only reprieve—and it was a shaky one at best—was that he didn't know what that something was.

Blending with the swarming crowd, she crossed to the fortune-telling tent. Mark had lied, she realized, reconstructing the conversation once again in her mind. He'd said he didn't know how Brodie had died. And yet, he'd told her his cousin's skull had been smashed. Why then hadn't he told Joe the same thing? And for that matter, why had he hired her to work at the wax museum?

There was only one answer to that question and no way to avoid it. He knew she'd found something in the cellar, some clue to the identity of Brodie's murderer. He knew, and he wanted to get it back. One way or another.

Her skin grew cold and clammy. But even as it did, her resolve to get to the bottom of this strengthened. She wasn't ready to become anyone's next victim. Not Mark's, not Joe's, not even the unknown others'. She still had her piece of evidence, and no one was going to wrest it from her. She would simply have to be very, very careful and watch her back.

Stiffening her spine, she slung her bag firmly over one shoulder and waited uneasily for Mark to find her.

THE NIGHT CLOSED IN on a claustrophobic wave of heat and moisture. Darkness was a state of mind now, an endless swirl of uncertainty. And all because a woman, an outsider, had stumbled in and seen Brodie Morgan's body.

The fire had been a foolish mistake, but the end result could still have been a positive one. Certainly, the plan had been perfect: remove the body and dispose of it. And the wall had crumbled so very easily.

But then she'd stumbled in and ruined everything—just as Brodie Morgan would have ruined everything ten years ago had he not been stopped.

Now, she, too, must be stopped. Before she deciphered what she had found down in that basement. Before she finished what Brodie had started. Before the damage was irrevocable.

Chapter Four

"Hand me those needle-nose pliers, will you, sweet thing?" Dag pointed to Rhianna's right on an overflowing workbench in the pit—the production shop's huge central work chamber. "Can't leave a piece of wire sticking out of the werewolf's head," he grinned. "Mark'd have *my* head if I did that."

Without moving from her perch, Rhianna tossed him the black-handled tool. In the four days that she'd worked at the museum, she'd guided tours, lent a hand in the costume department and helped set up a booth over at the Bremerhaven Bazaar. Today she was down in the pit, helping Dag repair some of the older wax figures, watching in fascination as the newest ones were completed. While students weren't required to stray beyond their designated duties, evidently full-time workers were—at least until such time as the staff was restored to its original complement.

Although some problem at his New York building company had taken—and kept—Mark out of town for the better part of a week, he had nonetheless made the decision to increase outgoing production levels as quickly as possible. That meant overtime and double duty for everyone, Rhianna included. The disadvantage was that it had cut rather heavily into her investigating time. She was no further ahead now than she had been last Saturday when she'd overheard Mark and Joe out at the fairgrounds.

A glance through the slatted windows of the pit revealed brilliant sunshine with a slight haze starting to creep in from the east. Huge cauldrons bubbled thickly all around her; cooling vats hissed, and the clank of machinery kept time with a Bruce Springsteen tape blasting over the speaker system.

Rhianna looked to her left, longing to take a dive into one of the tepid holding tanks. Even with her long hair caught up in a ponytail and the air conditioners pumping away on high, she was dying of the heat. And Dag was beginning to get ideas about taking off early. He'd been beseeching her for the past hour to accompany him out to the junction pond.

A trip to the pond, however, wasn't in her plans. At lunchtime, she was going to drive into town and take a look through the back issues of the Bremerhaven *Chronicle*. The east-end robberies had made headlines ten years ago. It was conceivable that the high-school senior had overlooked something that the private investigator could use to her advantage.

"Aw, c'mon, sweet thing." Dag tried again to win her. "You and me and all that beautiful, cool water. Wouldn't you like to take a dip?"

Rhianna slid from the workbench. "Not today, Dag." She ignored the fact that he was tugging off his shirt. Bulging muscles just didn't appeal to her. "Besides, what if Mark comes back?"

"Yeah, he would, too." Her ex-classmate grimaced. Unsnapping the clasp of his Timex watch, he removed that, as well. "Still, I don't think he'd fire you. Sam, maybe. She's been bitchy as hell lately, but never you."

"Oh, I don't know about that." Rhianna dusted off the seat of her shorts.

Dag snorted. "Well, I do. The guy's hormones aren't dead, baby. He used to make out with some pretty wicked women when he worked here. Don't kid yourself he's not thinking about moving in on you."

Rhianna offered no comment. She didn't like the sound of Dag's remark very much, but not for the reasons he was implying. If Mark did have an ulterior motive for wanting her here, it had nothing to do with sex.

She was hunting for her keys on the cluttered workbench and trying not to think about Mark when she caught a flash of metal in her peripheral vision. Dag had bent down to pick up the pliers, and as he did the Timex dropped out of his shirt pocket. The watch and something that looked suspiciously like a rolled silver bracelet.

She beat him to it by a good two seconds. "What's this, Dag?" she asked, scanning the inside.

A muscle twitched in his jaw, although his expression remained light. "Nothing much," he mumbled. "I've had it for years."

"Didn't Brodie have one just like it?"

Dag shrugged. "I guess so. An old lady up at the carny has been selling this kind of junk for years. Lots of people got suckered by her. Still do, I imagine."

Did lots of people also have numbers engraved on the inside of their bracelets? In Dag's case three numbers; in Brodie's six. Thoughtfully, Rhianna handed him the narrow band. Dag and Brodie had been friends. Maybe they'd gone up to the carnival together and bought the trinkets. It was hardly cause for suspicion... Except that Dag did have a faintly smug expression on his face...

Dismissing the matter, she stood and looked at her own watch. If she hurried, she could get to the *Chronicle* and at least make some headway in the stacks. She even knew the general dates for which she was looking. October through June, with a robbery occurring at random every fortnight or so.

Luck, it appeared, was on her side. The man who met her at the red-brick newspaper building was an old acquaintance of her father's. He'd been the managing editor there for years and had no qualms whatsoever about letting her loose in the back room.

"Got a computer these days, Rhianna," he announced proudly. "All I had to do was punch up the subject and bingo, you got your relevant editions. Numbers are right here on this sheet. Coffee's in the machine. Photocopier's in the corner." His eyes twinkled. "Don't know why you'd be interested in unsolved robberies, though. You writing a book or something?"

"Or something," Rhianna agreed. She waited until he had gone, then plunged into the reams of preserved newsprint. While the *Chronicle* wasn't a big-city operation by any means, the back issues of the paper had been stored in an orderly fashion. It took her only half an hour to amass a pile of headlined papers. Rather than waste time ferreting out individual articles, she copied whole pages and then returned them to their proper places.

Since she'd accomplished her mission so quickly, she decided to head over to the Copper Pot restaurant on Squire Street and have her lunch there.

In the sweltering heat of midday there was only a light stream of traffic flowing through Bremerhaven, mostly camera-toting tourists, she noted in amusement, who'd come to gawk at the old colonial buildings or to snap up an antique from the Brass Bell Farm just south of town.

Krista Franklin, the Copper Pot's most affable waitress, swished over to the window booth Rhianna had chosen, offering a plate of warm scones with one hand, fanning her flushed face with the other. "Whew, is it a scorcher out there today, or what? Did you hear the news yet? Poor old Mabel Parker fainted in the Bake Shoppe this morning. Right in the middle of ordering up a Boston cream pie. It took Doc Hannaman and three of the matinee ushers from the Gothic Theater to heft the poor old dear out to the ambulance. Can you imagine Doc in his bow tie and white skimmer being assisted by Frankenstein, Asmodeus and Quasimodo? It sure got the tourists going, I tell you."

Rhianna grinned. "The ushers still work in costume at the Gothic, huh? I bet it would have gotten old Mabel going, too, if she'd woken up and seen those three ghoulish faces leaning over her. Is she going to be all right?"

"Oh, sure." Krista laughed. "She'll be back gumming her way through the Bake Shoppe in no time." She leaned companionably on the edge of the butcher-block table. "I hear you're back working at the wax museum these days, Rhianna. How do you like the change in management?"

"No problems so far," Rhianna lied.

"Is Mark still a doll?"

Had he ever been? "I guess so."

"You guess so?" Krista looked shocked. "You must be walking around with your eyes closed if you're not sure. I used to see him sometimes when I was working over at the Heritage Inn. I swear, if I'd been the type, I'd have swooned, just melted right down into the crockpot of baked beans I used to cook up every Friday." She sobered a little then. "Say, I heard about Brodie. How they found his body behind that brick wall out at the wax museum. I imagine it's got business booming out your way, but it sure can't be easy for any of you."

"No, it isn't," Rhianna confirmed. "Actually, it's downright creepy."

"That's the truth. It's been all the buzz in town, right from the beauty salon on out to the Horsehead and Raven's Wing taverns. I'd love to hear what's flying around the west end right now."

So would she, Rhianna thought.

As a group of hungry diners forced Krista to move away, Rhianna turned to look thoughtfully out the window. She wanted to know what was flying around the town in general. Unfortunately, she didn't have time to indulge in any local gossip. Besides which, gossip wasn't going to help her solve this mystery. She could hang around town all day and likely pick up all sorts of juicy tidbits. But they wouldn't give her the answers she needed. They wouldn't tell her who'd murdered Brodie.

As she drove back to the museum, Rhianna's heat-dulled brain turned over those few articles that had caught her eyes at the *Chronicle*.

The thefts had been haphazard. No one neighborhood had been hit in its entirety, and several of the town's wealthier residents had been missed. From memory, she recollected that one of her own neighbors had been victimized, while numerous others had been overlooked.

Why only one family in a row of easier targets? Rhianna wondered, puzzled. The Dorsets' home had been equipped with an elaborate burglar alarm, and everything they'd owned had been branded with ID numbers. His job as loan officer at the First National

Bank of Bremerhaven had made Hiram Dorset a super cautious man. His house would have been one of the hardest to infiltrate, much harder than her parents' place or the Murrays' next door, neither of which had been touched.

And why, she wondered, had the thieves gone after Bill Burnett? He had no money to speak of. He ran a small wrecking company south of town. At best the man was a slightly above-average-income earner.

Rhianna was still pondering the dubious criteria used by the east-end robber or robbers as she climbed the stairs to Sam's apartment. She was greeted by a blast of "Rock Around the Clock" and a limp pink-poodle skirt when she entered. It was more than she'd expected.

"Fifties bash," Sam shouted, blowing the dust off a pair of well-worn saddle shoes. "Marion thought we needed a party to cap off the summer in style."

Rhianna deposited the stack of photocopies in her bedroom. Sam had been in a strangely downcast mood all week. It was nice to see her getting back to her old self. "Why the theme?" she called over her shoulder as she dragged out her Vampira gown.

"That was Joe's idea."

Instantly Rhianna's ears perked. "Is he coming?"

Sam tried a modified version of the twist. "Of course he is," she panted. "He used to work here. And anyway, he's Mark's friend. And he's cute. Besides, he's throwing a barbecue tonight, so why shouldn't we invite him to our party?"

"He's throwing a barbecue tonight?" It was the first Rhianna had heard of the plan, although that wasn't surprising, considering how testy Sam had been of late. "Who's going?"

"Well, you and me for two. Probably Dag. Mark, if he gets back from the city in time. Renee might hobble over, as well as the other guides who aren't working." She collapsed on the sofa, tugging on her spiky hair. "What's the matter? Don't you want to come? He lives in a terrific old house, you know. Spook City, U.S.A.—like that house they used in *The Amityville Horror*."

"Sounds wonderful." Rhianna stepped into her gown. "What time does it start?"

Sam waved an airy hand. "Whenever. Just haul your butt on over as soon as your last tours are finished. I'm on a half day, and I don't care what kind of a bribe I have to offer Sally Grogan; she's going to respike my hair this afternoon or find her own precious locks ripped out by their mousy brown roots."

A barbecue, Rhianna mused, at Joe's Banberry Crossroad home. Well, who knew? She hadn't had a chance to snoop around Mark's office yet; Joe's place might just be the next-best thing. After finishing up with her makeup, she descended into the cool shadowy environs of the wax museum.

The afternoon literally crawled by for her. The tourist visitors seemed to have brought five children apiece with them, and keeping chocolate-smeared fingers off silken costumes swiftly became Rhianna's primary job.

"Maybe you should threaten to dip that kid's Mickey Mouse ears in a vat of wax." One of the other guides offered Rhianna the suggestion after a particularly precocious little boy had slipped into Frankenstein's laboratory for the second time in less than a minute.

Rhianna smiled. "*His* mouse ears or his parents'? The whole family's wearing them. They must have come straight up here from Disneyworld."

"Lucky us." The guide motioned with his zombie head. "Hey, you'd better watch it. Mrs. Ears looks like she's about to give Lizzie Borden's head forty whacks."

Rhianna caught the woman only seconds before she leaned across the velvet-covered rope. "Our next display is over here, ladies and gentlemen," she announced firmly. "I'm sure you've all heard the tale of Jeanne d'Arc, or as she is more commonly known, Joan of Arc. We see her here on the stake after sentence has been pronounced, awaiting the torchbearer who will seal her fate and deliver her to the gates of hell ... or heaven. It's for you to decide where she will reside in her next life."

Although Mrs. Ears seemed determined to retrace her steps back to Lizzie Borden's abode, and Junior Ears was seeking to find a way to scale Joan of Arc's stake, Rhianna managed to keep the group together. She ushered them through the fairy-tale world of Sleeping Beauty, past the evil Malificent and on to Hecate and her sister hags in the witches' cave.

"Double, double, toil and trouble, fire burn, and cauldron bubble." From the pervading shadows of the cavern, Hecate's raspy, crackling voice spilled out.

Rhianna listened to the familiar incantation with only half an ear. The majority of her attention was focused on the young threesome who had formed behind Junior. They appeared to be in the midst of devising a plot that would gain them premature access to the neighboring Chamber of Horrors.

She should let them, Rhianna thought, amused but also a little tired of coping with a bunch of rambunctious seven-year-olds. If the guillotine lopped one of Mickey's ears off, Junior would undoubtedly quiet down for a while.

Quelling a sigh, she herded the tour group through the heavy oak doors and into the torture-filled chamber.

By seven o'clock she was exhausted, more inclined to fall into bed than poke around a crumbling old mansion. A glass of week-old Dubonnet and an icy shower revived her only marginally. She had to force herself to slip into a swingy print skirt and a black tank top. Leaving her legs bare and her hair loose and wavy, she picked up her car keys and staggered wearily down the stairs, only half aware of Billie Noble hovering in the underbrush. Accustomed now to seeing her around the museum, Rhianna didn't give the scraggly woman a second thought. She opened her car door and climbed inside.

It was easy enough to find Joe's house. Although she'd never actually been there before, she'd heard stories about it in her youth. Stories about a seventeenth-century witch and her mortal lover—and a burning that had supposedly taken place on the wooded cliff overlooking the town.

She braked her Scirocco at the side of the winding dirt road. Her first impression wasn't one of Amityville at all. This house had its roots in Edgar Allan Poe, her favorite and possibly too-often-read author. A solid stone foundation led upward to peeling white clapboard and badly warped window panes. That there were no other cars in sight was a fact she overlooked until her third knock on the plank door went unanswered.

Now, that was odd, she thought. She was sure Sam had said the barbecue was tonight. And there was no doubt about it, this was Joe's house. Twenty-seven Banberry Crossroad. His name was even emblazoned on the mailbox.

Sighing, she wandered around to the backyard. There she spied a broken grill standing in four rusty pieces atop a brick barbecue pit. And taped to the bricks was a huge sheet of paper with block printing on it.

> Welcome stragglers!
> Dinner's a bust, and so's the grill.
> Gone to the Raven's Wing instead. My treat!
>> Joe.

Rhianna was halfway back to her car when it suddenly occurred to her that she was blowing a heaven-sent opportunity to search the place. How much easier it would be to sneak around the old house alone, knowing that Joe wouldn't be back for several hours. True, it was also underhanded and a complete invasion of privacy, but if there was even the slightest chance that he was connected to Brodie's death, then his privacy deserved to be invaded.

Whirling around, she retraced her steps to the rear entrance. The door was locked; however, it was an old lock, simple to slip open with her American Express card.

Once inside the rambling kitchen, she dropped her purse on the counter. Where would be the best place to start, she wondered. If he had a den, that might be good. Desks were notorious hot spots for incriminating evidence. So were bookshelves.

She stumbled across both in a cluttered room just off the main living area. Rows of floor-to-ceiling shelves housed books of every description, from Smoky the Bear's *How to Prevent Forest Fires* to Nostradamus's ancient prophecies. The desk, she noted, was a rolltop, a genuine oak antique, riddled with pigeonholes and false-bottomed drawers.

Streaks of waning sunlight filtered through the paned-glass windows for the first thirty minutes of her search.

They faded out slowly as she reached into the bottom drawer, and almost in tandem with the evanescing rays, she felt a shiver of foreboding slide down her spine.

Her hand poised on a wad of papers, she twisted her head around to the open doorway. Even in near darkness, she could see that it was empty. And so was the house, she told herself firmly, shaking off her momentary attack of nerves. The sound of summer crickets and the steady tick-tock of a grandfather clock were perfectly natural...

And yet...

An unearthly stillness seemed to have invaded the house. It was almost as if she were the last living soul in town. The last person alive in a graveyard full of wandering spirits.

For no reason that made sense, she lifted her head and listened. She could almost hear the crackle of dry brush on the cliff beyond the window, could almost see the blaze of fire as yet another witch was burned. It was as though she'd been thrown back centuries in time. Back to the New England witch trials, to the burnings and the torture, all the judgments of a more fearful age.

With an effort, she banished the ghostly images. Almost. From somewhere in the house, there suddenly came the sound of a creaking floorboard. A horrible whining sound that sent a shaft of pure terror down her back.

Snatching her fingers from the drawer, Rhianna scrambled to her feet. This wasn't the seventeenth century, she told herself fiercely, and old houses had an aggravating tendency to settle. Maybe that was all she'd heard. A board groaning in protest as the ground beneath it shifted. Or maybe bats in the attic. But then the

low, ominous groan came again and it didn't sound like
a settling house or bats. It sounded like footsteps.

Try as she might, she couldn't stop her skin from
crawling. It was too quiet out here, too secluded. And
now she could feel someone's presence in the house.
Someone stealthy. Someone who'd doubtless heard her
shuffling papers.

Heart hammering, Rhianna bit down hard on her lip.
She could run for the door, but which door, front or
back? She listened for what felt like an eternity before the
next creak came. It sounded as though whoever was
creeping around was out in the kitchen. Front door, she
decided, tiptoeing across the carpet.

At the archway, she kicked off her pumps. If worse
came to worst she could gouge anyone who might try to
attack her with one of her heels. That would slow the
person down a bit and give her time to reach her car...or
so she hoped.

Holding her breath, she peered into the shadow-filled
hallway. Visions of white-robed crusaders bearing flaming torches flashed through her mind once more. Pushing them back, she made a desperate dash for the door.
She was wrestling with the most stubborn bolt she had
ever encountered and still combating the eerie demons in
her imagination when she heard the floor groan again.
And with that sound came a hiss she couldn't even begin
to fathom.

"Having fun, Rhianna?"

Oh, God, would she ever learn? Stealth was Mark
Reimer's middle name. And sneaking up on her had become his hobby of late.

Angrily, she swatted at the obstinate bolt. Then she
swung around to face him. "What are you doing here?"
she demanded in a waspish voice.

Mark raised an open beer bottle to his lips. "I came by to see Joe." He wiped his mouth with the back of his wrist, and his mocking expression irritated her.

"I thought you were in New York," she snapped in exasperation.

"I was. I came back."

"Well—why aren't you over at the Raven's Wing? Didn't you see the note on the barbecue?"

He grinned. "I saw it. I didn't feel like going." A wry brow arched in her direction. "I can't wait to hear your excuse."

Rhianna stared at him. It was hard to be defiant when she'd been caught in the act, like a common sneak thief. "Maybe I just happen to like old houses," she murmured, leaning against the door. "This one does have quite a history, you know. Who wouldn't be curious about a witch's house?"

He rested a shoulder against one of the rough support beams. "Find anything supernatural while you were tearing up the den?"

She felt like throwing her shoe at him. "If you knew I was in there, why didn't you say something?"

A flicker of amusement danced through his eyes. "I guess I just don't like to be a spoilsport. Besides, it was Joe's stuff you were going through, not mine. If I'd found those lovely hands of yours in anything that belonged to me, you'd be halfway back to Boston by now."

"Is that a threat?"

"Whatever." He tilted back the bottle, polishing off the contents in one long swallow.

She knew she should have stomped out right then, but she couldn't seem to move. She wasn't really sure she even wanted to. Mark, in a sleeveless black T-shirt and jeans, which hugged at slim hips and legs without being tight, was a dangerous sight to behold. He looked incredibly good with his tumbling blond hair and entrancing German features, so compelling with his clear blue eyes and indolent stance.

And his hands... He had beautiful hands. Long, tapered fingers, slightly calloused. They were the hands of an artist, and she couldn't help wondering how they would feel touching her skin.

Yes, she could help it, she thought, shaking herself. She had to help it. And she had to get away from him. Right now.

Spinning around, she began tugging on the bolt. It wouldn't give despite her best effort to move it. Then she felt the warm touch of Mark's fingers as he trapped her wrist in a firm grasp and turned her around to face him.

"It doesn't work, Rhianna," he said patiently. "It never has. If you want out, you're going to have to use another exit." He tilted her chin up until she was staring into his eyes. His knuckles grazed her jaw. "Of course, you could always stay for a while. Maybe we could... talk."

"I... wouldn't mind seeing more of the house," she murmured, lowering her lashes.

His lips twitched. "The house, huh?" He tapped her chin with his forefinger. "Sure, why not? The witch's house. I'll give you the grand tour if you'd like—starting with the basement."

He was trying to goad her. Amusement was evident in his voice. "Thanks, but I think I'll pass on that."

Mark's shrug was deferential. "Suit yourself, but you could just be passing up a private eye's dream. You never know how many bodies might be piled up down there."

"I'm not interested in finding bodies, Mark."

"Just a murderer."

"Yes, just a murderer."

"And you still think there's one here in Bremer-haven."

"Yes."

"But you're not sure who."

She met his eyes. "No." In that denial, at least, she felt she was being relatively honest. Throat lozenges not-withstanding, she couldn't quite convince herself that Mark was capable of murder.

She could be wrong, though. Tragically wrong. She was still learning her trade, learning how to tell the dif-ference between a slick acting job and the truth. Mark had grown up on the streets. He had years of experience on her—and a cool, unruffled expression that gave ab-solutely nothing away.

The eyes studying her seemed to reach right into her soul. She could almost feel him listening to her thoughts. It was time to say something—anything—before she was too transfixed by him to break the spell.

"How was your trip to New York?" she blurted out in a rush.

To her relief, he released her wrist and moved away to walk into the living room. There, he stopped at the win-dow to look out over wooded landscape. "It was fine. I'll probably have to go back in a couple of weeks."

For some reason, the news disappointed her. "More problems?" she asked.

A slow grin touched his lips. "Something like that." He averted his head slightly. "By the way, I found out where your bricklayer lives."

Wisely keeping her distance, Rhianna asked, "Where?"

"Out on the Cape."

"Have you talked to him?"

"No. I figured you'd want first crack at that."

She lingered by the wide fireplace, absently taking note of the hanging kettle and blackened stone work while a puzzled frown furrowed her brow. She didn't understand him. On one hand, she'd heard him talking to Joe about others whose identities were a mystery to her, about a woman who couldn't be trusted and a murder in which he claimed not to believe. On the other hand, he was now giving her a direction to take, a man to speak to who might very well be able to clear up a great deal for her.

Did he want her to get to the bottom of his cousin's death, or not? Had he been a part of it, or not? What did he really know about the east-end robberies? She decided to probe deeper.

"Mark, you remember that night behind the wax museum when I was waiting for Brodie?"

He nodded. "What about it?"

"Why were you there?"

His laugh was short and biting. "You aren't going to let this go, are you, Rhianna? You want a confession of some sort from me, don't you? Or at the very least a convincing alibi."

She gritted her teeth. "I just want an answer, Mark. A straight answer."

He shrugged. "I was on my way home."

"To the wax-museum apartment?"

"I used to live there," he reminded her, his tone sarcastic.

"I know that. Where were you on your way home from?"

He stared at her, impaling her with his blue eyes. "From the Pullman, Rhianna. And no, I wasn't alone out there."

A faint blush crept into her cheeks. "I didn't think you were," she muttered, dropping her gaze.

"Yeah, I'll bet you didn't." There was a thread of irritation in his voice now, a bitter edge she didn't care to explore. And then he left the window to join her by the hearth.

"Don't push me too hard, Rhianna," he warned softly. "It's in my nature to be defensive. You don't grow up in the west end of town without learning very quickly how to keep the wolves from snapping at your heels. Sometimes you tend to want to snap first."

She met his eyes calmly. "I don't think you'd hurt me," she said, startled to discover she actually believed that.

Evidently, Mark didn't. "Yeah, right," he drawled. "You trust those uncertain instincts of yours that much, do you?"

"I have good instincts," she countered defensively.

"Like hell you do," he said flatly. "You're impulsive and stubborn. You act first and think later, and trust me, that's a dangerous way to live."

Her eyes sizzled with fury. "You bastard," she hissed. "Who do you think you are?"

"I know who I am, Rhianna."

"Well, so do I," she retorted angrily. "I know exactly who I am and what I'm doing here. And if you think I'm going to stand here and listen to you preach, you're crazy."

He quirked a sardonic brow. "Maybe I am crazy. Did you ever think of that? And if I am, do you really want to risk that pretty little neck of yours any more than you already have?"

Not tonight, she didn't. But not because she was afraid of him. She was too angry to feel even a tiny scrap of fear. "You're right, I don't," she said whirling away from the hearth. In the entry hall, she paused to send a withering look over her shoulder. "Do have a nice night, Mark," she added frigidly. She let the back door slam loudly behind her as she exited the old house.

MARK HELD HIS TEMPER just long enough for the echo to die, then he turned and slammed the palm of his hand into the stonework. The pain felt good as it shot up the length of his arm. And it offset his irritation to some degree.

But even pain couldn't erase what Rhianna could do to him. She had a way of bringing his emotions out, of blasting right through his guard and shaking him up. Of melting him down. Another minute with her, and he knew he would have given in to his desire to take her in his arms and hold her, to give something of himself to her. He might have even been tempted to confide in her, to tell her what she wanted to know about the east-end robberies. And all for the sake of gaining her trust, he thought testily. God, he really must be losing his grip if he could actually consider betraying a confidence.

No doubt about it, Rhianna's effect on him was becoming far too strong. His self-control invariably crumbled when he was with her, and even four days in New York hadn't helped him there. All it had done was get him out of this town and back to the anonymity of big-city life, back to the faceless hordes, to a place where no one could even begin to touch him.

She thought he'd murdered his cousin. At the very least, he was right up there on her suspect list. But he was still only a suspect, he reflected on a thin note of humor. She hadn't convicted him yet. She was still hunting for proof, waiting for a chance to rifle his office. That she hadn't yet received the opportunity was due solely to the fact that he used a double combination lock on his office door, and those kinds of locks took time to crack.

She'd figure a way in eventually, though—for all the good it would do her. But he supposed she'd have to try, if only to satisfy that feline curiosity of hers.

Lost in his own troubled thoughts, Mark strode into the kitchen and pulled the fridge door open. He was shoving aside containers of Chinese food, chili and coleslaw when he heard a scream from outside—a checked scream that had him frowning with concern as he automatically made for the door.

Five seconds later he spied her, hovering indecisively on the wood-chip path encircling the house. From all outward appearances, she seemed to be uninjured. Nonetheless, he reached for her, allowing himself to enjoy the silky texture of her skin, the scent of her hair as a feeling of relief washed over him. Then, reluctantly, he pushed her away, his fingers retaining his steadying grip on her bare arms.

"What's wrong?" he demanded, certain there must be a body lying on the road. "Is there someone out there?"

She shook the hair away from her face. "Not someone, Mark," she gasped. "*Something*. There's a spider in my car."

"A spider?" He wasn't sure whether to be amused or shake her until her teeth rattled. She'd taken ten years off his life back there. "You screamed because of a spider?"

"It's a big spider." He felt the shiver that rippled through her. "A tarantula."

A big spider. Jesus, it figured. Anything over a tenth of an inch in diameter would probably be her idea of big. But when he recalled her fear of the eight-legged creatures, he relented a bit. Everyone was entitled to a fear of something. He should know. He had more than a few of his own to contend with. "Okay, where is it?" he asked her patiently.

"On the passenger seat. It was . . . staring at me."

Well, at least it had good taste. Suppressing a wry smile, Mark turned her around and gave her a gentle shove. "Come on, Rhianna. Let's just see how big this thing really is."

She dug her heels firmly into the path, shaking her head. "No! I'm not going back there. Not until it's gone. I'm sorry, Mark, I just can't. I don't like spiders."

Mark tugged on a lock of her silky hair. "I know you don't," he said. "And you don't have to be sorry about it."

The door of her Scirocco was wide open, and the keys were lying on the dirt road, along with her shoulder bag. Rhianna had ventured as far as the trunk of a gnarled elm at the end of the driveway, which at least proved she trusted him not to throw the creature at her. It was a slim vote of confidence, but a step in the right direction, he supposed.

He slid into the driver's seat. There was no sign of a spider on the passenger side, no sign of it on the floor mat or on the dash. Reaching down, he flipped the release lever to lower the seat back. Still no spider. Just a box of promotional pamphlets from the museum and a red Knirps umbrella.

Aware of the green eyes following his every move, Mark extricated himself from the car. "There's nothing here, Rhianna," he said mildly, resting his arms on the roof.

"Yes, there is," she insisted as she inched closer. "I saw it, Mark. I swear I did. It was huge."

Suppressing a sigh, he made a last sweeping search of the interior. As a last resort, he reached under both seats. But he found nothing except a window scraper and a clean cotton rag.

"Rhianna, exactly how big is huge to you?" he asked from a crouched position on the road. He spied the hem of her print skirt near the hood. She seemed so certain of what she'd seen. "Come here," he said, holding out his hand to her. "Look in there. Do you see a spider?"

She peered over his shoulder. "No—yes! Behind the box."

She was practically on top of him and that was far more distracting than what she was saying. However, Mark did manage to lean back inside and snatch away the box of pamphlets.

And then he saw it. A very large, very hairy bird-eating spider. A tarantula—poised on the edge of the upholstery.

Stifling a shriek, Rhianna jumped away from the Scirocco while Mark continued to stare at the motionless creature. Tarantulas didn't particularly bother him, but they sure as hell didn't make a habit of crawling around Massachusetts. Someone had planted the thing in her car. Likely someone who knew all about her fear of spiders.

"Rhianna, dump your purse and give it to me," he said, his eyes moving to the shadowy woods, to all the possible hiding places in there.

"Are you out of your mind?" she countered. "I don't want that thing in my purse."

"Would you rather I left it in your car?"

That got her going. The contents of her handbag promptly spilled out over the Scirocco's hood. "Here." She shoved the leather pouch at him.

It took only a few seconds to trap the spider, five times longer than that to zip the bag up properly. Mark said nothing as he carried it across the road and into the woods. Although he couldn't imagine her wanting it back, he brought the purse with him when he returned minutes later. Expensive leather was, after all, a pricey commodity.

"You can relax, it's gone," he said in response to her wary expression.

She wanted to back away, he could see that. Her pride, however, wouldn't allow her to budge. "Did you kill it?" she asked hesitantly.

Under any other circumstances, that would have been a loaded question. At the moment, though, it was probably innocent enough. He nodded. "I killed it."

"Are you sure?"

"Do you want to see the corpse?"

"No." She took a backward step and Mark lifted an oblique shoulder.

"Then I guess you'll have to trust me, won't you?"

He saw her features cloud over. "How did a tarantula get in my car, Mark?" she questioned him thinly, albeit without any discernible accusation in her tone.

He dropped the empty handbag onto the hood next to the jumbled pile of makeup, hairbrush and perfume, and shook his head. "I don't know. At a guess I'd say it was put there—by someone who knew you'd be going out tonight."

Her eyes strayed to the darkening woods. "I saw Billie in the bushes before I left the museum," she murmured thoughtfully. "She was watching me from the trees next to the lot."

Mark's muscles tensed. "Was she anywhere near your car?"

"I'm not sure. Maybe—while I was changing." Absently, she began collecting her belongings. "That doesn't make any sense, though. Why would Billie want to put a tarantula in my car? For that matter, where would she even get one?"

The latter was a fair question. And there was really only one answer. The carny owner was a spider freak. He had a collection of them on display in one of the less popular tents at the rear of the fairgrounds.

Mark glanced over at Rhianna. She was right in the middle of this now, and there wasn't a damned thing he could do about it, except wait and watch and hope she wouldn't do anything rash. It was a bleak hope at best. And Mark knew he'd have to keep a close eye on her.

Chapter Five

Under scrutiny from those intense blue eyes, it was next to impossible for Rhianna to scoop up the contents of her purse gracefully. She had no idea what he was thinking; she only prayed he wasn't zeroing in on the rusty box of Sucrets she had clutched in her hand.

After piling her wallet, hairbrush and compact on top of them, she risked adding a bottle of Ombre Rose. That was a mistake, she realized, biting her lip as the lozenges slipped through her fingers. The metal container landed with a dull thud on the packed dirt.

Seemingly lost in thought, Mark retrieved them for her. A faint grin curved his lips as he read the label. "Sore throat, Rhianna?" he questioned.

"No," she denied hastily. "It's . . . a souvenir."

He shrugged. "If you say so."

"I do." Taking the box from him, she tucked it under her perfume bottle. Since Sam's apartment was singularly lacking in hiding spots, her purse had seemed the safest place to keep them. How was she to foresee that the bag would be ultimately transformed into a spider trap?

It surprised her a little that Mark hadn't insisted on keeping the lozenges. But then she remembered that he'd admitted to Joe he hadn't known what she'd found down in the cellar. Maybe now that he'd seen the evidence for himself, he didn't feel it was worth making a fuss over— if the lozenges had even been his to begin with.

Using her skirt as a catchall, she let everything slide. Holding the hem exposed her bare legs, but at least that kept Mark's gaze from rising to her troubled features. He was perceptive enough to recognize indecision when he saw it.

"You want a bag for that stuff?" he asked.

She nodded, conscious of the rising heat in her limbs, in her throat, in her abdomen. "Anything but the one I came with," she replied, shuddering as she looked over at the Scirocco's hood.

Smiling a little, Mark reached around her to remove the offending crumple of leather. "Joe should have something usable at the house." He squinted up at the darkening indigo sky. "You feel like a trip out to the carnival?"

"To the carnival?" she echoed. "Why?"

"Just a hunch I have. Although you probably won't like it."

He'd been speaking over his shoulder as he walked to the house. When he slowed his stride on the porch, she grabbed his arm, then immediately ripped her burning fingers away from his skin. "What won't I like, Mark?" she asked, masking her reaction.

"The spider tent."

"That's disgusting." She paused, then managed a curious, "What's a spider tent?"

"Nothing, Rhianna," Mark said with a dismissive shake of his head. "Forget I mentioned it. I'll check it out myself tomorrow."

Check what out tomorrow? she wanted to shout. What the hell was a spider tent? And what was one doing at the carnival? For that matter, how did he know about such a thing when she'd never even heard of it?

For a moment, she considered forgetting all about her dubious clues. Too many things here just didn't make sense. Mark had told her about the bricklayer who lived on the Cape. He'd disposed of the tarantula in her car, and now he'd offered to help her find out where the horrible thing had come from. If that added up to murder, Rhianna failed to see the connection.

"Mark," she began once they were in the kitchen. "I think we should go out to the carnival tonight."

He handed her a tiny shopping bag he'd scrounged from one of the cupboards. "You sure you want to?"

"No." She controlled a shudder. "But I still think we should go."

With a nod, he picked up his keys from the counter and headed for the door. And Rhianna didn't think she imagined the flicker of concern in his expression.

IT WAS QUITE DARK by the time they reached the crowded fairgrounds. A myriad colorful lights glittered along the midway outlining the ticket booths, rides and concession stands. The pace, although slightly more languorous at night than it was during the day, didn't affect the festive atmosphere one bit. There was still plenty of pink candy floss to be had, and the thronging beer garden was alive with the sounds of a boisterous German oompah band.

Rhianna dreaded the thought of searching out the dark tents, the ones that formed a low ring around the perimeter of the fair. There was something utterly forbidding about them. Something that seemed to flow out from their dimly lit depths. In shadowy silhouette, they loomed like demon caverns, the sum total of every fear in the soul, the incarnation of pure evil in Rhianna's mind.

Mark glanced down at her as they approached one of the most ominous tents. "You don't have to come in with me," he said with more understanding than she felt she deserved from him. It was a nice gesture on his part.

"No, I'll come," she forced herself to say. "Somehow, I don't think standing around out here would be all that much better."

"No, I don't suppose it would be." Dropping an arm across her shoulders, he lifted the flap and led the way inside.

Although she kept her eyes trained squarely on the dirt floor, Rhianna knew instinctively that they were alone in this spooky place. Alone except for all the multieyed, multilegged horrors staring out from their Plexiglas abodes. "Do you see anyone we could talk to?" she asked, trying not to focus on anything but the floor or the black canvas walls.

"Uh-uh," came Mark's distracted response. "There's not much light in here, either. The display must be closed down for the night."

How could he tell? Rhianna wondered. Surely no one but a masochistic ghoul would ever venture across the threshold. "Maybe we should try again tomorrow," she proposed.

She felt rather than saw Mark's nod of agreement. "Come on," he said, pulling back toward the flaps. "As long as we're here, we might as well take in some of the more upbeat attractions."

That sounded like the best idea Rhianna had heard in years. She'd prefer taking on a swarm of cold-blooded murderers to stumbling across a stray daddy longlegs at this point.

It wasn't until they'd returned to the chaotic midway that she drew an easy breath. God, but she hated those revolting eight-legged monsters.

Shoving all thoughts of them firmly to the back of her mind, she looked up at Mark's entrancing profile. His arm was still draped warmly across her shoulders; his mood was easy and relaxed, and no matter how hard she tried, Rhianna couldn't summon up a single suspicion of him. It was a welcome change and one she was prepared to let ride for as long as she possibly could.

With his head, Mark indicated the bustling arcade ahead of them. "You want to test your marksmanship?" he asked, and she had to grin.

"You mean you'd actually trust me with a loaded weapon?"

"I think I can handle seeing you with a pellet gun."

Still grinning, Rhianna plunked a dollar onto the counter and took her place beside an enthusiastic twelve-year-old. She promptly flattened ten of the unsuspecting mallards cruising by on the conveyor belt.

"Impressive," Mark chuckled as she accepted her Kewpie-doll prize. "I take it you've had a few lessons."

"A few," she conceded. "But mostly I just hung on to what my father taught me. He used to set up targets in the backyard for my brother and me. He figured it was a good way for us to vent our frustrations."

"Did it work?"

"Uh-huh, only with a pellet gun, though. I never could get the hang of anything else."

An unreadable smile curved Mark's lips. Taking her by the arm, he propelled her to the next booth. Without so much as a second's pause, he rifled three baseballs at the farthest stack of cans, totally destroying them all.

"One of the perks of having an uncle who was a base-ball fanatic," he revealed over his shoulder as he lined up three more balls.

"You used to play baseball with him?" Rhianna was astounded. From the way he usually talked, she hadn't thought he'd had a moment of normalcy in his entire childhood. But when she looked at his face and saw him demolish three more stacks of cans, she did see something there. Something akin to the enthusiasm of the twelve-year-old beside her earlier. It wasn't as flagrant, but it was definitely present. So much for his radiant air of cynicism. He wasn't half as jaded as he professed to be. And suddenly, Rhianna wasn't sure of a single thing anymore.

A derby-capped man inside the booth came up to them then and Mark motioned to the array of stuffed animals lined up along the walls. "Go ahead and choose," he said. "Do you want Huckleberry Hound or Puff, the Magic Dragon?"

Still feeling a little shocked, Rhianna quickly replied, "Puff."

"The lady likes yellow dragons, does she?" the man noted in his nasal barker's tone. "Well, ladies and gentlemen, that just goes to show that you can win here. Step right up and try your own luck. You can win a dragon for someone you love..."

Determinedly, Rhianna tuned him out. "Do you want this?" she asked, holding up the winged animal.

Mark shook his head and dropped his arm back over her shoulders. "Nope. He's all yours. What I want is some food. Come on, let's grab a hot dog. Maybe it'll put you in the mood for a ride on the roller coaster."

That was doubtful; nonetheless, Rhianna accompanied him in thoughtful silence to the nearby stand. In her hands, she felt the fluffy little dragon and in her head she heard the Peter, Paul and Mary song, which was his theme. And somewhere in that, despite the throat lozenges and all she'd seen the night of Brodie's death and the strange conversation she had overheard last week, she saw Mark's name slowly fading from her suspect list.

"THE FRIDGE IS DEAD. Here, have a pop tart." Sam tossed the foil-wrapped bag at Rhianna, then came to join her at the kitchen table. "Damn, it's hot today," she grumbled.

Was it? Rhianna had scarcely even noticed the scorching heat. But then, she wasn't quite all here this morning, either, she realized distractedly.

After spending a good hour wandering around the carnival, eating every scrap of junk food they could get their hands on, and braving some of the moderately wild rides, she and Mark had gone over to the Raven's Wing to join the party in progress there. With Puff in her possession and Mark sitting beside her, looking relaxed and at ease in her company, her objectivity had taken a flying leap out of the tavern window. It had been quite late by the time she and Sam had finally gotten back to the apartment and even at that, sleep had been long in coming.

If she lived to be a hundred, Rhianna didn't think she would ever truly understand him. One minute, they'd been shouting at each other in Joe's living room and the next they'd been strolling around the fair like friends...if "friends" was the right word, she thought, still puzzled by the entire evening.

With a clearing shake of her head, she pushed Brodie's bracelet up on her arm and propped her chin on her hands. "I'm almost afraid to ask, but what time did we get in last night?"

"Four a.m., according to Heckyll the Magpie," Sam said. "I figure he's about half an hour slow, so all in all, I'd say we got in somewhere around four hours of sle—" She broke off abruptly, her eyes locked on Rhianna's left arm. "What's that?" she demanded stridently.

Instinctively, Rhianna jumped. Attack of the spider people, she thought blackly, relieved to see that there was nothing crawling on her. "What's what?"

"That...thing on your arm. That bracelet. Where did you get it?"

Startled, Rhianna glanced at the silver band. She'd slipped it on sometime during the evening and neglected to take it off again. "It's Brodie's," she revealed, puzzled by Sam's glazed eyes. "I..." She stopped. This was no time for truth. "I've had it for years. He...left it in the biology lab one day. I was going to give it back to him, but I never got the chance. I've just sort of made a habit of keeping it with me. And now that I know he's dead—I don't know—I felt like putting it on."

There was no mistaking the overwhelming easing of tension in Sam's body. Her shoulders slumped forward. "Thank God," she murmured. "I thought for a minute there... I mean—well, what I mean is, I'm glad you've had something to remember him by all these years."

No, she didn't. That wasn't what she'd meant at all. And Rhianna didn't like the implications behind that realization one bit.

Brodie's bracelet had visibly rattled Sam. And Dag had a bracelet just like it, a twin to the one she'd found a week ago.

So now it was Sam and Dag as well as Joe...and Mark. Dammit, there was still Mark and his perplexing conversation with Joe. There was also Billie hanging around the woods yesterday evening. Billie pleading with her to warn them. And there were throat lozenges and a huge spider and red stains on Mark's clothes the night Brodie had disappeared—the night he'd died.

God, there was so much; yet there was nothing at all. Nothing that fit together. No tie to bind the loose pieces. No answers. No proof.

Less than an hour later, she was sitting on a wooden stool in the museum booth at Bremerhaven's Annual Charity Bazaar, her chin propped on her hands, listening absently to the blare of carnival music close by. A crowd of people milled about, examining the old costumes and props that were for sale. Rhianna munched on Spanish peanuts, toyed restlessly with the bracelet on her wrist, accepted money for merchandise and wished she could be clairvoyant for about five minutes. Just long enough to read a few crucial minds. Then, she could be done with this mystery once and for all, return to Boston and immerse herself in a wonderfully anonymous client list. If that was what she really wanted, that is. She wasn't quite so sure anymore.

Marion came by the booth near one o'clock to drop off another box of merchandise. In a plain white blouse and gray skirt, she could have passed for the woman whose eyes she possessed. Bette Davis, a quarter of a century younger, right down to the stylish pageboy and freshly lit cigarette. Today, though, she looked tired and uncustomarily drawn.

Rhianna regarded the older woman thoughtfully. "Is anything wrong?" she asked.

Marion shrugged and exhaled a long stream of smoke. "You could say that," she drawled. "For some unknown reason Billie took it into her head to come out to the carnival yesterday. She's decided that the diner is still in operation. She was actually trying to drum up business by shouting, 'Come and eat at Noble's,' to the carnival goers."

"She was really upset about losing the place, wasn't she?" Rhianna asked, thinking back on Billie's white-hot fury in the aftermath of the bank's decision.

"God in heaven, yes," Marion declared. "She hated everyone who had any part in the closure. She was damn near homicidal in her threats. Many's the night I sat and listened to her rant. Now, though, she just spouts gibberish. Sometimes I even feel she thinks Mother's still alive."

Like Norman Bates in *Psycho*, Rhianna thought. That was so sad, so tragic. Unfortunately, it also provided Billie Noble with a strong motive for committing murder. What better way to extract revenge on Reed Morgan for buying her family's land than by killing his only child.

She mulled that theory over while Sam continued to sell and Marion left the grounds to return to her office duties at the museum. Rhianna was finishing off the last of her salted nuts when a jaunty male voice greeted her from the side of the booth.

"Second shift reporting for duty, sweet thing," Dag announced around a leer of appreciation for Rhianna's bare legs. "Care to keep me company for a few hours? Lots of room in here for both of us."

God, what a revolting thought. Dag with his sandy brush cut, pumped-up muscles, bulging thighs and swaggering smugness was exactly everything she didn't like in a man. To spend even thirty seconds caged up in an eight-by-five box with him was worse than contemplating the rack in the wax museum's Chamber of Horrors.

She shimmied out of the booth without touching him. "Sorry, Casanova. I'm officially off duty. Besides, I don't think Mark would appreciate your idea of a museum exhibition."

"Mark, huh?" He hitched his thumbs in his belt loops. "So you're into that west-end tough stuff, are you?"

Rhianna halted. "What west-end tough stuff?"

"That danger thing." He cocked his head. "Baby, if that's what you like, you missed the boat. I could tell you stories that'd make your hair stand on end."

"Yeah, and they'd be nothing but a pack of lies," Sam inserted gruffly, coming to join them. "Zip it up, Bluto. She's not biting." She regarded Rhianna. "You want a ride home, or are you going to stick around for a while?"

Rhianna hadn't missed the tension in Sam's voice, or the pointed elbow she'd shoved into Dag's rib cage. Neither did she miss the way Dag's mouth suddenly snapped shut. The sight of those cautionary gestures sent her spirits plunging. "No, I'm going to stay," she returned as lightly as she could. Spinning around, she left them to their shared secret and wandered away from the noisy bazaar into the noisy carnival beside it.

She'd seen Mark arrive not ten minutes ago. That he'd gone straight out to the spider tent, she appreciated. That he hadn't stopped by the bazaar booth, she found a trifle disappointing. Still, that was her problem, and she was going to have to learn to deal with it if she planned to stay around Bremerhaven for another three weeks.

She spied Mark emerging from one of the rear tents with a squat, balding man she recognized as the carnival owner. They talked for a few minutes, then the man slipped back inside—back to his creepy crawlers and the handful of nervy souls who'd braved the shadowy exhibit.

She paused on the strip of dirt track between the fair and the outer tents. Mark looked cool, she thought, unaffected by the cloying heat, and none the worse for wear after a late night at a local tavern. Lucky him. She felt tired and wilted in the beating sun.

As he approached her with that long, rangy stride of his, Rhianna deliberately blanked her expression. "Is he missing a tarantula?" she asked without preface, and Mark nodded. He was his usual aloof self today. Another disappointment for her to contend with.

"He's missing a tarantula and a black widow," he told her, his blue eyes unrevealing.

Rhianna's entire body went cold. "I don't want to hear that," she said flatly. "Does he have any idea who took them?"

"No, but he figures they disappeared sometime yesterday afternoon."

"Ah . . . Mark? Aren't black widows poisonous?"

He regarded her contemplatively. "Only the females, Rhianna. I wouldn't worry too much about being bitten if I were you. There are antitoxins available. A black widow's bite is seldom lethal these days."

Seldom lethal? Was that supposed to reassure her in some way? Especially now, when she wasn't altogether sure she could trust Sam, who had conveniently been off work yesterday afternoon. And what about Billie? The way her brain functioned these days, who knew where she might plant a black widow spider? Or Dag? Or Joe? What might either of them have in mind for her?

Mark walked past her to stare at the screaming people on the roller coaster.

Something of her turbulent feelings must have transmitted itself to him, for he averted his head to scan her features. "For your own sake, Rhianna, you should back away from this."

His tone was strangely gentle, yet even at that, she couldn't allow herself to be dissuaded. She squeezed her eyes closed. "I can't, Mark," she said quietly. "I can't just stand by and let Brodie's murderer walk."

For the longest time, Mark's gaze held her, probing her features, as a host of indefinable emotions washed across his face. The last one to register was the one he'd used so often in the past. That shuttered, remote expression she couldn't quite breach. The one he had to have learned in his youth. The one that gave her nothing except a feeling of unbridgeable distance.

But it was nothing more than a sham; and she knew that now. She'd spent much of last night with him. She'd glimpsed another side of his remote nature. And quite suddenly, she wanted to run. As fast and as far away from him as possible. Because he was a danger to her emotions, and because she wasn't at all sure she was capable of handling that danger.

Relief coursed through her when one of the off-duty guides bounced over from the arcade. Her perky appearance successfully diverted Mark's attention and gave Rhianna the opportunity she needed to make a graceful escape.

She could feel Mark watching her as she made her way toward the confusion of the carnival. And suddenly, she didn't think there were sufficient barriers in the universe to get her through this investigation.

MARK WASN'T DECEIVED by Rhianna's outward composure. She knew what was going on between them, the attraction that was very nearly past the point of control. Maybe she didn't want to admit it any more than he did; maybe she didn't even understand it completely yet, or him for that matter. But he wasn't all that complicated. And sooner or later, she'd find that out. Then, he'd just have to push himself away from her that much harder. The way he always pushed, and probably always would.

Tilting his head back, Mark let the sun wash over his face. He'd drunk too much last night, and the hangover hurt. It slammed in his head, along with a barrage of unanswered questions and hunches he could neither prove or disprove.

He could tell Rhianna the truth about the east-end robberies, he reflected dryly. But the truth contained a set of drawbacks all its own, not the least of which was the fact that he knew full well who'd been behind them. There was also the fact that she didn't trust him completely, and her mistrust still rankled a little, even if it was more or less justifiable. Those two points were negligible, however. It was the danger she'd landed in that bothered him most. God only knew what would happen next if this mess wasn't nailed down soon.

From among the press of midway gawkers, Mark saw Joe detach himself. He was in uniform and wearing a somber expression as he halted in front of the spider tent.

"I've been wandering around here since one, Mark," his old friend said in a strained undertone. "I almost thought you weren't going to show."

Mark's expression was bitter. "I almost didn't," he retorted. "Bremerhaven's finest are so screwed up right now that it took me two hours just to find out what they know. I had to call in a dozen favors just to scratch the surface."

Joe chuckled, relaxing. "Even so, I don't suppose you got much out of old Chief Gage, did you?"

"You can't bleed a corpse, Joe," Mark said with a wry sideways glance. "Besides, you know Harry Gage. He works with his head in the clouds most of the time."

"So, does he have anything or not?"

Mark tried to keep his eyes from the midway as he replied, "Only a body, and he's doing his damnedest to forget about it."

Joe perked up. "Well, that's something, anyway. At least we don't have to worry about him breathing down our necks."

Mark shrugged. "Forget about Gage," he advised. "What have you got on the others?"

"Same as before." Joe grunted. "Nothing. They've all clammed up." He paused. "You know, I can't make any sense of it, Mark. Why would anyone torch the north wing? Best I can figure is the arsonist had nothing to do with what happened ten years ago."

"You could be right," Mark allowed, unconvinced. He had a theory about the arsonist, but it was a questionable one at best, certainly nothing he could share with Joe. He arched a speculative brow at his old friend. "You feel like going fishing?"

An uncomprehending frown invaded the man's dark features. "Figuratively or literally?"

"Literally. I know a guy out on the Cape who has a boat. A couple days on the water, and Dag might just be willing to spill his guts."

"You want to do this one by one, hmm?"

"Divide and conquer," Mark agreed, grinning. "He's the weakest link, and that's the best one to start with."

"I can think of a weaker link," Joe stated with a pointed look southward on Blueberry Road. "Wouldn't she be an easier target?"

"Do you want to work on her?" Mark countered.

A slow smile spread across Joe's features. "Dag it is," he concurred. "When do you want to leave?"

"End of next week."

"Think he knows anything?"

Mark scrunched his eyes closed against the relentless glare of the sun. His head was pounding, and he was in no mood to play guessing games. He had a feeling he was overlooking something—or someone. And that someone was after Rhianna.

For perhaps the first time in his life, he wished he could go back and change the events of the past. It was a useless waste of time and energy, though, and he squashed the thought the moment it crossed his mind.

It wasn't hard to do. Not half as hard as it was to keep from thinking about Rhianna. Not half as hard and not half as disturbing.

He looked over at Joe. "I think Dag's the best place to start," he said. "And if he does know something, then it's time he shared his secret."

Joe shook his head. "I hope you know what you're doing, Mark," he muttered. "For everyone's sake, I hope to hell you've got all the angles covered."

Mark said nothing, just turned and walked over to the dirt lot where he'd parked his car. Joe was counting on him, and he didn't like that. He didn't want to be anyone's defender, anyone's savior. Then he glanced at the colorful line of booths, and he knew he would defend at least one person in all of this. Somehow, though, he didn't think Rhianna would appreciate the methods he might have to use to reach that end. And he wasn't at all sure how long he'd be able to hold out against the emotions that were threatening to overtake him.

THE APARTMENT WAS EMPTY when Rhianna got back from the fair, and Sam was out for the evening, over at her parents' place, so for three uninterrupted hours, Rhianna pored over newspaper accounts of the east-end robberies.

They appeared, to her, to be disconnected. The First National Bank's manager had been hit, as well as the loan officer, a well-to-do CPA and a Blueberry Road stable owner. No less than seven of the eleven town council members had also been victimized. But so, too, had a number of middle-class residents, including the demolition-company owner, a local baker and two teachers on staff at Bremerhaven High. The thief or thieves had even broken into the house of a police officer, a sergeant who'd purportedly patrolled the west end of town during those turbulent years.

Rhianna wrote down names, dates and occupations. What she wound up with was a list of people whose incomes ranged from just above the poverty line to six figures. Staring at the list was an exercise in futility. Robbing the rich made sense—but the poor? Why harass those people?

Time after time, she almost traced the thefts back to Billie Noble. Almost. Yet every time she thought she had it pinned down, a name would suddenly crop up that didn't tie in with the destruction of her family's diner.

With a disgruntled sigh, Rhianna set aside her handwritten notes to concentrate on some of the other frontpage articles she had incidentally copied. For the most part, they were dull, unrelated to her search. She did, however, spy a fuzzy picture of Marcie Noble under a caption reading: "Noble's Roadside Café Torn Down." She was just about to scan the smaller print when she heard the balcony doors slide open.

Cursing Sam's rotten timing, Rhianna made a grab for the scattered papers, shoving them under a bulky sofa cushion. She was bouncing on the cockeyed cushions when Mark came into the living room holding a set of car keys in his hand.

There was a certain amount of humor in his eyes as he regarded her. "New form of exercise, Rhianna?" he inquired in that lazy drawl of his.

She immediately stopped bouncing and stood up. "Don't you ever knock?" she demanded, annoyed to be the source of his amusement.

"Sorry," he murmured, but there was no trace of apology in his voice. "Force of habit. Rear-window ethics die hard in a small-town setting."

"Potential burglars can get themselves shot, even in small towns, Mark," Rhianna pointed out with no lack of sarcasm. "Why are you here?"

For an answer, he tossed her the keys. "I brought your car back. It needs a tune-up, but you'll be happy to hear it's spider free."

Maybe for the moment, but Rhianna still didn't like the idea of a black widow crawling around loose in or out of town. "Thanks," she muttered, ignoring his dig about the much-needed tune-up. She wished she could ignore everything else about him as easily. Heat or not, he had a leather jacket slung over his shoulder. The ends of his hair were damp and his eyes, his gorgeous, hypnotic eyes, were the ice blue of a winter pond. He was long and lean and so unfairly attractive in his faded denims that she longed to take a swipe at those remote features of his—

anything to alleviate the hot, scratchy feeling of desire clawing at her insides.

Beyond the glass doors, a train whistle blew, and the woods seemed to settle a little deeper into the sultry night. The summer song faded. The magpie cawed ten times. A distant hum of tires on the freeway south reminded her of the city—the one where she lived and the one where he lived. Two different worlds, both then and now. And this was likely the only moment in either of their lives when they would be in the same place at the same time.

Rhianna swallowed as Mark took a step toward her. The man was dangerous, she reminded herself forcefully. She couldn't let this strange attraction overwhelm her. The timing was all wrong to become emotionally involved with him. Besides, he wouldn't want to be involved. Not with her. Likely not with anyone.

"Was there something else, Mark?" she inquired calmly as his eyes skimmed the cushions on which she'd been bouncing.

"No." His gaze lifted to her face. "Just be careful with your dirt digging, okay?"

"Why?"

"Because you could be playing with fire, that's why."

He turned and walked to the balcony doors before Rhianna could think of another question to level at him. Mutely, she watched him leave. Like so many others around here, she sensed he knew far more than he was letting on. And she didn't think she liked that feeling very much.

THE TRAIN WHISTLE sounded again, a shrill, mournful blast that reverberated through the night air like the howl of a hungry wolf. He was watching her closely now, protecting her from the harm he knew would ultimately befall her. And she wasn't easily frightened, this woman, this threat from the outside.

Control, the murderer thought rigidly. Success lay in control. In total manipulation. Of people and events. Of opportunities, so precious and so very few.

It must stay that way. A dark shadow, disguised, yet not disguised at all. A mind too brilliant to truly be called twisted. A mind Brodie Morgan had come to fear. And soon she would come to fear it, too.

And then she would die.

Chapter Six

The weekend arrived in a rush of blistering heat and confusion. On Sunday, Marion dragged a group of off-duty employees up to the production shop's south-wing attic for a cleaning spree in preparation for the bang-up party being thrown to end the summer. She was vacillating now between the original idea of a fifties bash and an out-and-out masquerade dance.

"I vote for the masquerade thing," Sam said later that afternoon as she and Rhianna trudged over to the apartment. "You can come as Spider-Woman."

"Thanks, but I'll leave that outfit to someone else." Rhianna pushed her hair from her face. The air in the attic had been hot and dusty. It would be a great room for a party, but it hadn't been her first choice of places to spend a day off. She should have been hunting for clues around the wax museum, or at the very least looking for Billie Noble. Too many of the east-end homes targeted had belonged to people against whom the ex-librarian might have held a grudge. It couldn't have been mere coincidence that they'd been hit.

While Sam went into the bathroom to take a shower, Rhianna lingered on the balcony. She could see Billie's A-frame among the trees across Blueberry Road. Maybe now would be a good time to pay the woman a visit. Before it got dark and her nerve failed her.

Hastily she ran down the stairs. If she didn't do this while her impulses were in charge, she probably wouldn't do it at all.

The tiny yard surrounding the dilapidated old house was riddled with weeds and thorny bushes. Rhianna had to pick her way carefully along the dirt path leading to the front porch. Hidden high in the leafy limbs of the trees, a crow cawed down at her. Even the gaping windows seemed to be warning her to retreat.

But she couldn't do that. It was either concentrate on Billie or concentrate on Mark. And she just couldn't bring herself to believe that Mark was a murderer. No matter what the evidence implied, he simply wasn't capable of killing his own cousin.

She wondered a little about her objectivity, then dismissed her self-doubts staunchly. She was attracted to Mark, yes, but not so attracted that she would let him get away with such a heinous crime if he was indeed guilty of committing it.

Refusing to consider the foolhardiness of her actions, Rhianna climbed the rickety porch steps and knocked on the front door. There was no response, so she tried the knob. It was unlocked.

Dredging up every ounce of her courage, she ventured inside. The dingy, dusty hallway was empty. So was the cluttered loft above her.

Rhianna stepped tentatively across the threshold. "Billie?" She called the woman's name in a slightly unsteady voice. "Billie, it's Rhianna. Are you home?"

There was no answering cackle, no sound of scurrying feet. In fact, there was no sound at all except for a strange scratching noise from the rear of the house.

"Billie?" Leaving the door open, she crept toward the sound. Without a doubt, this was the creepiest place she'd ever seen. A thick patina of dust covered every stick of furniture. Cobwebs clung to the light fixtures. Rodents appeared to have gnawed holes in both the curtains and the upholstery. The only thing that wasn't filthy or dirt-caked was a collection of unhooked telephones atop the mantel in what Rhianna assumed to be the parlor. There were seven of them in all, ranging from an old-fashioned contraption with a hook receiver and broad mouthpiece to a more modern princess style. Her eyes shifted to the left of the mantel. And there, tacked to the peeling wallpaper, she spied a picture, or rather a group of pictures, mounted on a torn sheet of scrapbook paper, in the center of what appeared to be a replica of a telephone dial.

Rhianna's throat muscles constricted as she examined the photos more closely. There was one in every third round hole, four of them altogether. Joe, Dag, Sam and Brodie. And in the center, scrawled in bright orange crayon, was one word. One single, perplexing word: Mama.

A horrible chill skated along Rhianna's spine. She spun away from the picture—and found herself staring right into the beady little eyes of a mottled brown game hen.

A feeling of curiosity quickly overrode her reaction to the disturbing discovery. What the hell was Sam's yearbook picture doing in Billie's house? And Brodie's and Dag's and Joe's? She could think of only one plausible answer: maybe they'd been involved in the east-end robberies. All of them—and perhaps one other: Billie. The ringleader? Rhianna theorized ruminatively.

After a moment's thought, she grabbed the raggedy paper from its wall mounting. She would have run out with it then, but seemingly from out of nowhere, the scrawny ex-librarian suddenly appeared in the parlor doorway clutching a platter of fig newtons in her gnarled hands.

"Teatime," she announced, hobbling like an aged wood nymph over to the lopsided settee. "Won't you join me before you go back to school?"

Rhianna folded the picture, tucked it into the waistband of her shorts and pulled her shirt down over it, hoping against hope that Billie hadn't seen her doing it.

The olive-pit eyes, however, gave no indication that anything was amiss. The woman didn't even seem upset to have found an intruder in her home. In fact, she looked quite pleased to be greeting an unexpected visitor.

"Teatime, teatime," she chanted gleefully. "You and me and Mama makes three."

Rhianna swallowed. "Mama?" she rasped, edging away from the hearth. "Is your mother here with us, Billie?"

Thin lips drew back into a yellow-toothed smile. "Yes, yes," she tittered. "Mama and me." The smile faded slightly. "Oh, I forgot, Mama had to go to work today. She couldn't come for tea." Her voice took on a little-girl trill. "It's war, you know. Mama has to be at the town switchboard and I have to work at the diner. That's what she says. I work after class. Just like you and all my children."

Children? What children? Rhianna seriously considered making a dash for the door. It sounded to her like Billie was jumping all over the place in terms of the past. Mark had called her unpredictable and he hadn't been kidding. She was living in a world all her own.

"Have you come to join us?" Billie asked suddenly, sharply. "Are you playing hooky? Mama won't let me play hooky. She won't let me play on the switchboard, either." Her voice changed to a chirping singsong. "You load sixteen tons, and what do you get; another day older and deeper in debt. St. Peter don't you call me 'cause I can't go; I owe my soul to the family store." She giggled. "Do you like that? I changed the words. I owe my soul to the family sto— Oh!" She stuttered jerkily, and her black eyes were locked on the platter of cookies. A horrible, strangled screech suddenly burst from her throat.

Rhianna's blood turned to ice water. Billie had leaped to her feet and was hopping around the floor like a demented jackrabbit.

"Kill it! Kill it!" she screamed, clawing at her cheeks. "Kill it! Please kill it!"

Already halfway across the room, Rhianna had to force her feet to stop. Billie's eyes were still focused on the platter, on a moldy Fig Newton, which seemed to be moving. Eight legs worth of movement.

"Please, kill it," Billie begged, sobbing. "Please!"

Kill it! Was she crazy? Well, yes, of course she was. But she was doubly crazy if she thought for one minute Rhianna planned to kill a spider.

Still, the woman looked so scared and panicky. The least she could do would be to drop something on the horrible creature, Rhianna thought.

With fingers that felt lead weighted, she grabbed a ratty old travel guide and slammed it down onto the cookie platter. Then she turned and fled from the parlor, not slowing down until she reached the sanctuary of the front porch.

Giving her heart a chance to resume its normal pace, she started down the rickety steps, clinging tightly to the peeling rail. Had she not been so finely tuned in to every sound and movement around her, she might have missed the barely discernible creak of hinges from the ancient and badly rusted green Comet parked beneath the heavy fronds of the weeping birch on her right. She might have missed the flash of blond hair as Mark disappeared inside the battered vehicle. She might have, but she didn't.

She paused momentarily, then made her decision. Careful not to step on any of the tiny twigs in her path, she crept over to the old car. From inside the house, she could hear Billie wailing at the four walls—and probably climbing them, to boot, she reflected grimly. Her main objective, however, had nothing to do with Billie. She wanted to know what Mark was doing sneaking around out here. Sneaking was part of her vocation. Building contractors from New York City were usually less inclined to do things like that.

Although she was positive her sneakers had made no sound on the weed-infested ground, Rhianna saw Mark lift his head and motion her closer. Without any hesitation whatsoever, she joined him on the far side of the car.

He was crouched down by the open rear door and she knelt in front of him behind the dented green fender.

"What are you doing here, Mark?" she whispered rather accusingly.

He tossed the grimy rag he'd been holding into the Comet. "Checking out another hunch."

She frowned in confusion. "What kind of a hunch?"

His expression was grim. "One that has to do with arson."

Arson! Rhianna's gaze roamed to the production shop's burned-out north wing. "You think—Mark, you think Billie's an arsonist?"

For an answer, he pointed to a streaked metal container and a number of empty soup cans strewn across the floorboards of the car. "Kerosene," he informed her dryly. "I'd say it's a pretty good bet that Billie torched the shop."

Puzzled, Rhianna looked at the telltale mess inside the car. "No, that's—no," she murmured. "Why would she do that?"

"I don't know," Mark said wearily. "Revenge, maybe."

Revenge? Maybe . . . but where did that leave her burgeoning theory that Billie had killed Brodie and hidden his body behind the storeroom wall? It seemed to blow it wide open. And yet . . . Billie could hardly be described as a rational human being. There was no telling what kinds of things went on in her head. It was possible she'd forgotten where she'd put the body. Or maybe, Rhianna postulated, one of the "them" Billie had mentioned that day at the Pullman had been the killer.

As Mark pushed himself away from the car's door, Rhianna stood. Neither of them said a word until they were back across Blueberry Road. Then he sent her a humorously speculative glance.

"I don't suppose you'd care to tell me what you were doing over at Billie's, would you?"

Not really, no. "I thought I might find something in her house," she said, conscious of the folded paper in her waistband, wishing she could show it to him, knowing she didn't dare. Not yet, anyway. "I still think she knows more than anyone's giving her credit for."

"You could be right," Mark allowed. Then, to her surprise, he dropped the subject and murmured a lazy, "Why don't you go on upstairs and change."

"Change? What for?"

"For dinner, Rhianna. I think we can both use a break tonight."

No question about that. Looking up at him, she saw the solemn expression in his eyes, the patience, the strain of a long day—yet amazingly enough, not the detachment. Not the usual distance.

She made her choice swiftly. "Give me fifteen minutes," she said.

THEY ATE AT THE Pepper Mill in the heart of old-town Bremerhaven. It was a busy place on a Sunday night, filled to the rafters with colorful local patrons. The tablecloths were red-checked and padded booths lined the walls. Muted gas lamps strewn around the room provided just enough light to see by.

"You know, you can't be sure that Billie torched the north wing," Rhianna pointed out reasonably, after she and Mark placed their orders. "You certainly can't prove it."

"No, I can't," he agreed in a similarly reasonable tone. "But it seems a likely possibility."

"Only if you can come up with a good motive."

He sent her a dry look. "Do you seriously believe that twisted mind of hers couldn't come up with a viable motive for gutting the building that is presently standing on her family's old property?"

"But why wait ten years?" Rhianna persisted. "Why not burn the place when it was first built?"

Mark shrugged. "Maybe she wasn't quite so deluded ten years ago. Maybe she's only now getting around to blaming Reed for everything that's happened."

No, that didn't sound right to Rhianna. Not when she took into consideration the picture she'd found on Billie's parlor wall. The woman had to have been mixed up in the east-end robberies. Billie and her "children."

Still, that didn't tell Rhianna who'd actually murdered Brodie. And while the picture thankfully didn't implicate Mark, she still couldn't completely disregard the throat lozenges she'd found next to the body in the cellar. Damn, she reflected irritably, why did everything have to be so complicated?

Dinner was served to the beat of Jim Morrison on the jukebox. They were just finishing their meal when a group of leather-clad bikers parked their Harley Davidsons outside the window and sauntered in for a bite to eat.

One of them, a heavyset man with a beard, long braided hair and a gold key chain earring, stopped beside their table. "Hey there, Mark," he said in a voice somewhere between a growl and the rumble of a cement mixer. "Hear you're going to be stringing together a local construction crew soon. Think me and my buddies might sign on to do the job? Save you bringing your own people up from New York."

Mark looked up at the man. "Think seven of you can handle it, Logan?"

"I figure maybe we can round up a few others to help out."

"West enders?"

"Wouldn't have it any other way."

Mark glanced at Rhianna, who appeared to be absorbed in Logan's brass skull-and-crossbones belt buckle.

"What do you think?" he prompted her, fully aware that she wasn't paying the slightest bit of attention to the conversation around her.

"What do I think about what?" She tore her eyes from the huge buckle.

He suppressed his amusement. "Should I hire these guys to work on the production shop?" he repeated patiently.

She peered around Logan's bulky frame to the six other bikers at the bar. "As long as they know to check behind walls first, sure."

"Check behind walls?" Logan chuckled gruffly. "What the hell's that supposed to mean.?"

"Nothing." Mark drained his beer. "Rhianna has her own criteria for hiring construction crews."

"Rhianna, huh?" Logan's hooded eyes lowered a fraction. "Do you spell it like the Fleetwood Mac song?"

She shook her head. "No, like my grandmother."

"She a Welsh witch?"

"She was a suffragette."

"A what?"

"An Edwardian E.R.A. advocate," Mark supplied, rising to his feet and holding out his hand to Rhianna. "If you really want the job, Logan, come by the museum tomorrow afternoon. I'll be there for a couple of hours. I'm bringing a foreman up on Tuesday. You can start first thing Wednesday morning."

He practically had to drag Rhianna out of the Pepper Mill. She seemed fascinated by the burly bikers, which probably made sense, considering her predilection for trouble.

"Staring at a guy's belt buckle isn't really the smartest thing to do," he said mildly, once they were out in the parking lot. "A look like that could easily be taken the wrong way."

That brought a faint blush to her cheeks, but instead of defending herself, she opted to go on the offensive. "Where do you know this Logan from, anyway, Mark? Is he one of your old west-end cronies?"

"Yeah. He lives down on Rowe Street."

"Still?"

Mark sent her a mocking sideways glance. "Not everyone gets out of there, Rhianna," he said flatly.

And that was an understatement, he thought to himself as he shoved the car in gear and headed for the midtown drive-in. He'd been lucky to get out when he had. Logan hadn't made it. And while Joe may have clawed his way out of the west end, he hadn't quite managed to escape his past.

It was his own fault, though. His fault and his problem. Joe had escaped with his life, and that was more than Brodie had done. More than Rhianna might do, unless she was kept under close scrutiny.

He looked over at her. She was the problem here, he thought, his only real problem, or at least the only one that really mattered. He could push his emotions away all he liked, but it wouldn't change anything. Pushing wouldn't keep him from wanting her, from wanting to make sure that she was safe. And that was what it all boiled down to in the end, he decided grimly. He did care about her. A lot. And he wasn't about to let anyone hurt her. Not anyone. Not even himself.

THEY ARRIVED at the drive-in just as the cartoon began. While Woody Woodpecker was parading across the big screen, Rhianna went to the concession stand. It was nothing more than an excuse to get out of the car for a couple of minutes, but she just had to be away from Mark for a little while. His car was a sport model. Every time he moved, she felt it. It was like having hot oil poured over her body. She was ridiculously conscious of him—and all too aware of the groping teens in the neighboring vehicles.

Sighing to herself, she paid for her order of Cokes and fries and started for the car. She was sliding back into her seat just as *Invasion of the Body Snatchers* started up.

She noticed instantly that Mark wasn't paying any attention at all to the opening credits. He was pencil sketching someone's face on a paper napkin. With a start, Rhianna realized that it was her face he was drawing. Her face in full Vampira makeup.

She leaned over his arm. "You're good at that," she murmured, taking care not to spill the Cokes.

"I'm passable," he allowed. "I do characters better than real people."

"Thanks, but I like to think I'm real people even in costume."

His lips twitched. "You are, but I couldn't do you justice any other way. For that matter, I'm not really doing you justice this way." He tossed the completed sketch onto the dash and reached for a French fry. She felt his contemplative eyes raking her. "I figured you'd be married by now, Rhianna," he remarked thoughtfully, perhaps a bit wryly. "A married lawyer. Probably a public defender."

She scooped her hair over one shoulder to cool her overheated skin. "I went to law school," she revealed, running her fingers along her plastic straw. "I didn't like it very much."

"Too much bookwork?"

"Not enough action."

"You'd have made a good lawyer."

She grinned at him. "I still could. I've only been a full-time private investigator for about a year and a half. I was getting ready to take the bar when I decided to switch careers."

He chewed a catsup-covered fry. "What did your parents think of that?"

"They expected it. My brother did the same thing. He got all the way through medical school, then took off with a scientific team to explore caves in South America."

"Sounds interesting."

"It is." But Rhianna was curious about something else. "Mark, what finally made you decide to leave Bremerhaven?"

His smile was distant and a trifle jaded. "You'd have to have grown up in the west end to understand my reasons. The west end was like Kent State ongoing. After a while I got tired of watching my back and got out. When the police chief's on the take, it's time to leave."

"Gage?" Rhianna was genuinely startled. "You never mentioned that he was crooked. I always thought he was straight. Lazy but straight."

Mark leaned back in his seat, resting his arm on one upraised knee. "Baby, if he were straight, half the west end would be behind bars, and those east-end robberies you're so intent on resurrecting would have been solved years ago. Trust me, the people involved weren't pros. Any cop with half a brain could have caught the thieves."

Rhianna very nearly choked on her food. "How do you know that?" she demanded.

For an answer, he raised a mocking brow. "Come on, Rhianna, how do you think I know that? I'm hardly a paragon of virtue. I saw the inside of Gage's jail cells often enough to learn a few things."

"But you just said that Gage was on the take. What did he arrest you for?"

Mark munched an ice cube. "Just about everything he could think of," he said calmly, reflectively. "Disturbing the peace, attempting to incite riots, drunk and disorderly conduct, minor assault... Do you want me to go on?"

He was using sarcasm to daunt her, but Rhianna wasn't about to be daunted. It was time they got down to the truth. "Yes, I want you to go on," she said. "Did you really do any of those things?"

"Some of them." His restless gaze shifted to the flickering screen. "Most of them."

"So, you decided to go off to the city to start over. Is that it?"

"More or less," he agreed. "I had a reputation in this town back then. Part of it was real; a lot of it was nothing more than hype. But Gage didn't see it that way. If a fight broke out on Rowe Street and I happened to be in the middle of it, he'd haul me down to the jail just to prove a point."

"And what did Reed have to say about that?"

Mark shrugged. "What could he say? I wasn't exactly a responsive kid. If he pushed me, I pushed him back. In the end, we both wound up in a corner."

"And where did Brodie fit in?"

A slow grin crossed Mark's lips. He lifted a hand to touch her cheek. "About where you'd expect. Right in the middle of the ring. Right where any east-end brat would have fit."

Rhianna felt his thumb grazing her chin, the incredible warmth of his body and the steamy heat of the night air around her.

"I think you have the wrong idea about us east enders, Mark," she remarked as he shifted closer to her. "We're not all brats."

The lazy grin widened. "Just some of you, right?"

"Uh-uh. Just some of *them*." As Mark's fingers caressed her cheek, Rhianna slid her hand along the length of his arm, over sleek muscle and sun-warmed skin. She felt the heat he exuded, the strength, the power. And she saw in him more than she ever had before.

The noise on Central Street was a kinetic din in the background. The air was hot and damp. It seemed to close in on her, on the two of them, pressing, daring, heightening the static charge between them.

Rhianna felt the muscles in Mark's shoulders bunch as he shifted position again, facing her now, staring into her eyes, urging her on with nothing more than a look. And she ran her fingers through his long hair, marveling at how soft it was, how much like gold it seemed in the black-and-white light of the big screen.

In the middle of the crowded drive-in, the night pressed in. The night, the heat, the heavy moisture . . .

Mark could feel the need growing inside him. But it wasn't a need born of hunger or pain or even sheer physical longing. It was something more than that. Something only Rhianna could bring out of him. Something only she could make him understand.

Slowly, he drew her toward him. And she responded. Softly. Willingly. And when he kissed her, when her parted lips met his, he knew exactly what that something was. He fought it, but he knew.

Stifling a groan, he deepened the kiss, pressing his tongue between her lips, exploring her mouth, tasting her heady sweetness, wanting the one thing he'd never allowed himself to have. Wanting her... Needing her.

Over the speaker, the movie music reached a crackling crescendo. And with the gritty strains came a breathless feeling Rhianna was half afraid to acknowledge. Yet, even as she kissed Mark, even as he kissed her, held her, caressed her, slid his hands down over her sensitive breasts, she knew this wasn't the right time. Not for either of them.

She sensed the desire in him, a match for her own as his lips teased hers, as his moist tongue roamed deeper into her mouth. And it cost her an enormous effort to end that kiss, to pull away from everything she craved.

But she had to do it. And when she looked up into his eyes, she knew he felt the same way. It *wasn't* the right time. There was still too much unspoken between them, too many doubts, too many unanswered questions.

A small smile curved Mark's lips as he released her. There was a certain reluctance in his eyes, in his action, in the way he shifted his weight away from her.

"I think maybe it's time we left," he murmured, and Rhianna didn't have to be a mind reader to understand the reasons behind his quiet suggestion. He wasn't immune to her. In fact, he was every bit as aroused as she was. Even in shadowy darkness, she could see the taut lines bracketing his mouth.

Damn, it was all so unfair, her heated mind cried out. It could have been so perfect between them, so good. They could have been so close. She could have fallen so easily. If only...

Closing her eyes, Rhianna pressed herself deep into her leather seat. And she fervently wished she'd never gone down to the north-wing cellar. Never discovered those stupid throat lozenges. She desperately wished she'd never had any reason to doubt Mark's motives.

FAR BEYOND the towering drive-in screen, a figure sat in motionless silence. It sat and it waited and it hungered for a chance to break out. Just one more chance, that was all it wanted. One clear-cut opportunity to strike, to eradicate the problem. To recall once more the rich smell of vengeance...

Say **yes** to
romance

AND YOU'LL GET

- **4 FREE BOOKS**
- **1 FREE BRONZE-AND-ROSEWOOD LETTER OPENER**
- **1 FREE SURPRISE**

NO RISK • NO OBLIGATION
NO STRINGS • NO KIDDING

Say yes to free gifts worth over $20.00

Say YES to a rendezvous with romance, and you'll get 4 classic love stories—FREE! You'll get an elegant bronze letter opener—FREE! And you'll get a delightful surprise—FREE! These gifts carry a total value of over $20.00—but you can have them without spending even a penny!

MONEY-SAVING HOME DELIVERY!

Say YES to Harlequin's Home Reader Service® and you'll enjoy the convenience of previewing 4 brand-new books every other month, delivered right to your home before they appear in stores. Each book is yours for only $1.99—26¢ less than the retail price, and there is no extra charge for postage and handling.

SPECIAL EXTRAS—FREE!

You'll get our newsletter, *heart to heart*, packed with news of your favorite authors and upcoming books—FREE! You'll also get additional free gifts from time to time as a token of our appreciation for being a home subscriber.

Say yes to a Harlequin love affair. Complete, detach and mail your Free Offer Card today!

FREE—bronze-and-rosewood letter opener

As a bonus for saying YES to romance, we'll give you this beautiful letter opener as a GIFT! Elegant, with a lovely, supple blade, this bronze letter opener has a dainty rosewood handle. It will make your correspondence a romantic experience! This is FREE as our gift of love.

Harlequin HOME READER SERVICE®

FREE OFFER CARD

4 FREE BOOKS   **FREE DELIVERY**

Place YES
sticker here

FREE LETTER OPENER   **FREE SURPRISE**

Please send me 4 Harlequin Intrigue® novels, free, along with my free letter opener and surprise gifts as explained on the opposite page.

180 CIH RDAX

Name _____
(PLEASE PRINT)

Address _____ Apt _____

City _____

State _____ Zip _____

Offer limited to one per household and not valid for present subscribers.
Prices subject to change.   PRINTED IN U.S.A.

Chapter Seven

"Well, that about does it, Mark." Joe burst through the jangling door of Barhard's Sporting Goods Shop, a brand-new tackle box in his hand. "What do you think? Should we grab a bite to eat over at Wanda's Café?"

Mark looked around at Central Avenue from behind the lenses of his dark glasses. He saw old Mabel Parker dragging her lopsided grocery cart across the middle of the road, her swollen ankles impeding her progress, her fleshy cheeks reddened from the laborous trek. She puffed her way onto the sidewalk, then through the door of the Bremerhaven Bake Shoppe.

God, some things just never changed, he mused reflectively. Old Mabel still shuffled around all day sticking her nose into everyone's business and filling her face with jelly doughnuts. And poor old Stu Wormer just kept whittling away on his dried birch strips, waiting for someone to come by and toss him a spare coin.

Dragging his mind back to Joe's question, Mark nodded. He'd down a quick bowl of Wanda's thick clam chowder, then go back to the museum and find Rhianna. He had to tell her he was leaving town for a few days. And he had to make a point of speaking to Logan, as well, he reminded himself, flipping a handful of loose change at Stu in passing. If he couldn't be here, he had to know that someone was keeping an eye on the lovely Vampira.

Squinting behind the shield of his dark glasses, Mark made one final sweep of Bremerhaven's main street—the street that separated the east and west ends of town. Funny how different it all struck him, he noted dryly. When he'd been younger, he hadn't ventured over here very much, preferring the earthier atmosphere of the Rowe Street Pool Hall to the jumping Burger Palace on the corner of Central and Eighth. Now, though, the whitewashed shops and stores on the border road seemed perfectly ordinary to him.

His glance rose above Wanda's Café, lingering there for a thoughtful moment. Although the distant rooftops of the affluent east-end homes didn't inspire a feeling of resentment in him, neither did they particularly impress him. Not anymore. This was a small town, plain and simple, he decided, watching as Joe crossed to the café doors. It was run down in some spots, well-tended in others. And it was a part of him now, he realized, a little shocked by the force of his feelings in that area. The town, the wax museum—and most of all, Rhianna. Rhianna, who didn't even live here, his mind prodded sarcastically. At least not yet.

Smiling to himself, Mark cut across Central and joined his uniformed friend on the other side.

"NOW, LADIES AND GENTLEMEN, if you'll please follow me, we'll move deeper into the realm of darkness." With a sweep of her ebony gown, Rhianna led her enthralled tour group through the eerie black-screened maze, halting silently beside Dracula's dungeon. Around her, floating like invisible vapors of the night, the shadows flickered and changed. Several of the bats hanging from the rafters inside the diabolic abode opened their marbled eyes, and Count Dracula's evil grin seemed to grow more malevolent.

"Legend has it," she began in a low, deliberately emotionless voice, "that Prince Vlad, from whose life the story of Dracula later grew, was born in the fifteenth century, in a remote area of the Carpathian Alps known as Transylvania. There, he ruled his loyal Romanian subjects. And there, he received his nickname, Vlad the Impaler."

"Where did the nickname come from?" one of the wide-eyed tourists whispered.

Rhianna lifted slightly one black-clad shoulder. She kept her tone low and unimpassioned. "Prince Vlad was a notorious man. Notorious and cruel. It was his custom upon encountering an enemy to impale that person's head on a wooden stake. Among his numerous atrocities, it is said that he would drive a nail through the head of any nobleman who failed to raise his hat in passing."

A young boy in the front row of the group promptly snatched the Red Sox cap he'd been wearing from his head. Biting back a smile, Rhianna continued with her narrative. Luckily, this was the last display on her tour, for out of the corner of her eye, she saw Mark moving soundlessly in her direction, stopping to lean on the richly paneled wall just behind the tourists.

He waited until she'd made her closing remarks and ushered the group back to the main doors before approaching her.

It was Friday afternoon, the first time she'd seen him since they'd been to the drive-in. Which was probably just as well, Rhianna thought, since she was still having trouble sorting out her feelings for him. Not to mention sorting out the confusion surrounding Brodie's death.

"I'm heading out to the Cape tomorrow," he told her, when they were alone. Both his voice and expression seemed strangely distracted. "Dag and Joe and I are going fishing."

"What?" She couldn't have heard him correctly. He couldn't possibly be planning to drag Dag out onto the bay. Dag Nichols had to down Dramamine just to swim in the junction pond. Her brow furrowed. "Why are you telling me this, Mark?" she asked him a trifle warily.

"Because your bricklayer lives in Wellfleet."

She regarded him with a small frown. "Are you going to talk to him?"

She didn't think she imagined that Mark swayed a little on his feet. She was sure she wasn't imagining the shadows beneath his eyes. He wasn't sleeping, and he probably wasn't eating, either. Damn, but she wished that didn't concern her quite so much.

In response to her question, he produced a slip of paper from the pocket of his jeans. "I don't have time to talk to him, Rhianna," he said without particular inflection. "This is his phone number. You can call him if you want to."

She was slipping the folded sheet into her Vampira gown when Marion glided through the side entrance, a harassed look making her angular face appear more drawn than usual. "There you are, Mark," she exclaimed. "I've been searching all over for you. Who in heaven's name are those thugs down in the production shop? They look like Hell's Angels refugees."

Mark's eyes gleamed with faint humor. "You're close," he replied. "They're going to be working on the north wing."

"Surely you can't be serious." Marion rolled her eyes skyward and groaned. "Lord, what did I ever do to deserve this? First Gage's men, now this."

Rhianna's ears perked. "Gage's men? What do you mean, Marion?"

The older woman waved an exasperated hand. "Oh, they've been hanging around all morning. Bloodsuckers, all of them, if you ask me. They've even been harassing Billie, for God's sake."

"Rhianna, your next tour's waiting," one of the guides whispered to her in passing.

"Go ahead," Mark said. "I just wanted to give you that number."

Of course he did. Why else would he have come here?

Rhianna left Mark and Marion to their candid exchange and walked to the main entrance. She was familiar enough with her spiel to be able to think while she recited it. Unfortunately, thinking wasn't going to expose Brodie's murderer. Only a great deal more digging on her part would accomplish that feat. If digging would even work here.

She'd have to talk to Sam, she decided at length. As soon as she possibly could. Then, maybe, some of the scattered pieces of this puzzle would begin to make some sense.

THE OPPORTUNITY TO SPEAK with her old friend didn't arise until Tuesday evening. As far as she knew, Mark was still out fishing. The tours had been relatively light that night and only Sam was working late. Rhianna heard her stiletto heels tapping across the plank floor as she walked in the direction of the side entrance.

The wax museum was deserted. The cleaning crew had not yet arrived, and the night watchman was making his rounds in the production shop. Rhianna waited patiently by the door until she spied Sam's filmy Lily Munster shroud and spiky hair.

"I have to talk to you," she said bluntly as the smaller woman rounded one of the black-screened partitions. "It's important," she added at Sam's dubious expression. "We can go into the Chamber of Horrors."

Mouth thinned to a straight purple line, her friend accompanied her to the torture-laden chamber. It was a macabre setting. Wax skeletons hung in iron shackles on the stone walls. Draped over the wheel was a less bony wax figure, its features contorted into an agonized mask. There were cages filled with loose straw, an evil-looking hook, a guillotine, a bed of nails, a large pendulum suspended over a flat butcher-block slab, and the inevitable rack. In black light, the displays looked doubly menacing, but Rhianna was so accustomed to the twisted limbs and ravaged faces that she scarcely even noticed them.

Neither did Sam. She marched directly over to one of the straw piles and extracted a cheap jug of burgundy from beneath it. "One of the cleaners is a closet lush," she announced, although there wasn't a trace of humor in her voice. "He makes his own stuff. It bites a little but it serves its purpose."

Rhianna leaned against the door. "I don't want to drink home brew, Sam," she said flatly. "I want to know why your picture is in a frame along with Joe's and Brodie's and Dag's."

Sam dropped onto the straw, uncapped the bottle and took a long swing of the contents. There was no surprise or denial in her expression. "I don't really think you do," she returned tightly. "I know I sure as hell don't."

"You were all mixed up in the east-end robberies, weren't you?"

"That's none of your business."

Rhianna moved to the door of the shadowy cage. "Would you rather I went to Chief Gage with my suspicions?"

"It wouldn't do you any good," Sam snapped, but there was a scathing twist to her lips. "He's selectively blind, always has been. As long as someone is willing to slip him a healthy bribe, he'll close those pudgy little eyes of his and play bat for all it's worth."

"Is that what one of you did? Bribe him?"

"One of *us*?" Sam took another swig. "Don't try to trap me, fancy britches." And Rhianna winced a bit at the use of a high-school tag she'd never liked. "You and I are friends. Let's keep it that way, huh?"

Rhianna ventured into the dimly lit cage. "There's a statute of limitations on robbery, you know," she said calmly. "Even if there wasn't, my father's a lawyer, and I know people in the State capitol."

"Yeah, I'll just bet you do," Sam sneered. "Pretty little fancy britches. Probably have half the politicians in the state panting at your heels, don't you? But what do you know about hard times? You never needed money. Daddy was always there with a big fat allowance for you and a Ferrari on your sixteenth birthday."

"It was a Mustang, and I paid the insurance on it." Rhianna sat down cross-legged in front of the other woman. She wasn't prepared to be labeled a rich snob. She also had nothing to justify here. She'd be damned if she'd let Sam force her into a defensive posture. "Are you going to answer my question or not?" she demanded, reaching for the wine bottle.

"I already did."

"No, you didn't."

"I told you to stay out of it. Listen to me, Rhianna, just stay out of it."

"I can't." Rhianna struggled not to cough as the horrible wine slid down her throat. Despite her sniping tone, Sam was weakening visibly; another prod and she might just come clean. "Look, Sam," she tried again, "I know you didn't kill Brodie, but—"

"How do you know that?" Sam interrupted her. "How do you know I'm not a murderer?"

"I just do. I know you. You could no more have killed Brodie than I could. That's not what I asked you, anyway. I want to know what Billie was doing with a picture of you."

Sam glanced sullenly at her. She seemed to be debating with herself. "If I tell you the truth," she said finally, "you have to promise that it won't go any further. Do you swear?" At Rhianna's affirmative nod, she swallowed a bitter mouthful of the wine, then drew a deep, bolstering breath. "Okay," she admitted slowly, heavily. "I was one of the robbers. So were Joe and Dag and Brodie. Billie recruited us right after the bank took over the diner—after Marcie Noble died. She offered us a deal. She'd get a measure of revenge, and we'd get a kick and some extra cash." Sam's features clouded a little. "It was hard for me back then, Rhianna. All I cared about was getting my hands on some money. Brodie and Dag were in it strictly for the thrill. And Joe—well, I don't know what he was thinking about. I guess he just wanted a ticket out of the west end."

Rhianna handed over the jug. "What made Brodie decide to get out?" she asked, disappointed but not shocked by Sam's disclosure. "He did want out, didn't he? Isn't that why he called me?"

Sam shook her head, her stony features softening slightly. "I honestly don't know what set him off. He did want out, that much I'm sure of. We both did. We even talked about it a couple of times. But I have no idea what made him suddenly up and call you out of the blue like that."

"He said he knew who was behind the east-end robberies," Rhianna murmured. "And why."

"Well, hell, we all knew that," Sam retorted.

"Then why did he sound so—desperate?"

Her friend lifted an uncertain shoulder. "All I can say is I had this gut feeling that something was going on behind the scenes. Like maybe Billie wasn't telling us everything. It could be he felt the same way."

"What do you mean?"

Sam sighed. "I can't explain it. It was just this feeling I had. At times, Billie just acted so strange—stranger than usual, that is. Sometimes I got the feeling that she was two entirely different people. Weird, huh?"

Weird, yes. "How was she after Brodie disappeared?" Rhianna pressed.

"I don't know," Sam admitted. "The robberies stopped right about then. We all went our separate ways. End of story."

No, not quite the end, Rhianna brooded, taking another sip of wine. Brodie was dead and his murderer was still out there somewhere.

For a good forty minutes, the two women mulled over a handful of different theories about the murder—none of which really made much sense. Now that the truth was out in the open, Sam appeared to have no qualms about helping Rhianna search for the answers. As they talked, they drank. It wasn't long before neither of them was capable of forming a coherent statement, much less coming up with a solution to the mystery.

"I say Billie's our man," Sam declared fuzzily.

"Woman," Rhianna corrected her, tipping over the now-empty jug. "But I agree. It could be she thinks she's her own mother. And Billie always did what good old Marcie told her to do, right?"

"Just like Pushover Smurf," Sam agreed. Groping for the stone wall behind her, she climbed to her feet. "Hey, is this room moving or what?"

Still shaking the jug, Rhianna looked around at the exhibits. Either her head was vibrating or the pendulum was beginning to swing. Back and forth and back and forth... For the longest time, she simply stared at the gleaming orb. Watching it, half mesmerized by the play of changing shadows on its silvery surface. Until it finally dawned on her that her eyes were moving. Along with the pendulum and every other eerie display in the chamber.

She scrambled to an unsteady standing position. "Did you touch the switch, Sam?" she demanded, trying not to tilt as she forced her eyes to focus on the panel by the heavy door.

Her friend giggled. "Hey, I'm Lily Munster, remember? Not Rubberman. You're the one with the witchy name."

Somehow—and she wasn't quite sure how she managed it—Rhianna reached the heavy door. It was bolted from the outside. Worse, the control panel appeared to be locked into the on position. The override switch was in the production-shop pit. The machinery could only be shut off from down there.

She made herself concentrate. It was possible that someone could be playing a practical joke, but she didn't really buy that. No one knew she and Sam were even here. Not unless . . .

No, she wouldn't let herself think that. The murderer would have no way of knowing about this impromptu chat. Not unless the intercom was on . . .

"Oh, hell!" Rhianna banged her fist against a panel she simply couldn't bring into focus. "I think we're locked in."

Sam paled, but not with fear. "We can't be locked in," she wailed. "We can't be. I have to go to the bathroom. We just can't be locked in!"

But they were, and every single one of the grotesque displays had ground to life behind them. A series of eerie moans rose above the clanking, rattling chains. In near darkness, the room had indeed been transformed into a medieval dungeon.

Rhianna endeavored to peer into the shadows. She had a horrible, giddy feeling that there was someone else in the vicinity. Maybe even in the chamber itself. A wax figure that perhaps didn't belong there.

Her eyes strayed to the tunnel on the far wall. "Can we get out through there?" she asked Sam.

"I . . . think so." Sam squinted into the pervading darkness. "It . . ." She hiccuped. "Excuse me. It should lead to the MacBeth exhibit. To the witches' cave. That's an animated display, though. It might be sealed off at the other end."

Well, if it was sealed, it was sealed, Rhianna thought with an amazing lack of alarm. She willed her feet to move toward the spooky tunnel. Everything would be fine, just as long as none of those witches were alive.

Together, she and Sam groped their way to the tunnel entrance. After prying open the trapdoor, Rhianna got

down on her hands and knees and began crawling along
the stone floor.

It was pitch-black inside the tubular space. Echoes of
a thousand tortured souls followed them along the narrow corridor. Cobwebs snagged at Rhianna's hair, but for
once, she disregarded them. The wine glow was awfully
strong. But so was the feeling that some third person was
close by. Someone who had no intention of helping them.
Jitters, she told herself fiercely. She was letting the eerie
atmosphere get to her. There was no one here but she and
Sam.

Brushing her hair away from her face with one hand,
she continued to crawl. "Is the cave closed up?" Sam,
hampered by her shroud, hissed over her shoulder.

"No, it's open," Rhianna told her, wondering why she
could no longer seem to feel her fingers. Then her entire
body went rigid.

One of the witches was moving!

THREE AND A HALF DAYS of blistering sun and sea air had
baked film sweat and salty grime onto Mark's skin. He
felt gritty and hot and just cross enough to snap at Marion, who was presently letting herself out of the offices.

"It's eleven o'clock, Marion." He frowned at her.
"What are you doing here?"

She flashed an ancient prescription pill bottle at him.
"I left this in my desk," she explained quietly. "It's Billie's. If I don't get it refilled first thing tomorrow morning, God knows how agitated she'll become." She
glanced up at him, then over at the parking lot. "When
did you get back?"

Mark flexed an aching shoulder. "A couple hours ago.
And if you're looking for Billie, she's hiding in the trees
across from the museum."

"Where else would she be?" Marion sighed. "Did she seem upset?"

"I don't think she was too happy to see me, but other than that, she looks all right." He lifted his eyes to the lighted apartment. "Have you seen Rhianna or Sam tonight?"

Marion blinked in surprise. "No. Should I have?"

"Has anyone other than Billie and the work crew been hanging around?"

"Not that I'm aware of, dear." Marion tucked the bottle into her purse. "But then, I only just got here a few minutes ago myself. I did see a light on in the pit, if that's of any importance to you."

Mark's muscles tensed. "I'll check it out," he muttered, then with his head he indicated Billie's cringing form. "Take her home, will you? I don't want any more 'accidental' fires breaking out around here."

Marion hastily lowered her eyes. "Oh, God, Mark," she whispered, as if she'd been struck. "You've known all this time, haven't you?" At his brief nod, she squeezed her eyelids closed. "I should have told you myself, but I kept hoping I could get her under control. When I found out myself, I was too sick with worry to tell you the truth. I thought you might blame me for letting her run around loose." She drew a deep, painful breath. "How did you find out?"

"That the fire had been deliberately set? Joe told me."

"Will you go to the police now?"

"Joe's already done that, Marion," he told her. "But as for pinning the fire on Billie, he doesn't have any proof of her involvement. Just keep a closer eye on her, huh?"

Relief washed over Marion's angular face. Relief mixed with gratitude. "I plan to, Mark. And thank you," she added, laying a sturdy hand on his arm. "I appreciate this, more than I can say. I'll watch her very closely from now on."

Mark waited until she had Billie in tow and was leading her back across Blueberry Road before he went over to the pit. Marion's confession hadn't surprised him. She wasn't blind to her sister's faults, not by a long shot.

As he bounded down the stairs, he felt the groaning protest from his muscles. He'd spent most of his time out on the bay hauling Dag up from the side of the boat, wrestling with the green-faced kid who outweighed him by more than thirty pounds.

When he hadn't been throwing up over the side, Dag had been surly and amazingly tight-lipped. The only thing Mark had gotten from him was a vehement denial that he'd had anything to do with Brodie's death, which wasn't really worth a damn, as far as Mark was concerned.

When he reached the pit he spied Dag hunched over the master control panel, scratching his head as he pondered the myriad switches.

"What are you doing here?" Mark bit out, and the younger man started violently.

"Jesus, Mark, you scared me," Dag quavered. "I saw the light on down here and came down to investigate."

"Oh, yeah?" Mark stole a glance at the panel. It appeared to have been activated in selected spots. "You alone?"

"Far as I know." Dag pointed to one of the flashing buttons. "That's the lock on the Chamber of Horrors, Mark. It shouldn't be on at this time of night."

"Then turn it off."

"Well, I was going to, but I could have sworn I heard voices in there coming over the intercom."

"Whose voices?"

"I'm not sure. I think there were two of them."

"Male or female?"

"Female. Stragglers, you figure?"

Mark punched up the sound. He couldn't hear anything except a lot of wailing and rattling shackles. "Why did you come here tonight, Dag?" he repeated as he listened for anything out of the ordinary.

The younger man shifted his weight nervously. "I...uh...came by to see Sam," he mumbled. "She wasn't home, so I came downstairs to check on the light."

Mark's eyes narrowed. "Are you sure she wasn't home?"

"Positive."

"Did Rhianna tell you that?"

"Rhianna? No. I thought she and Sam must've gone out somewhere... Hey, where're you going? Mark?"

His shouts fell on deaf ears. Mark was already halfway up the stairs via the offices.

"Rhianna!" He shouted her name as he slammed his way in through the side entrance. "Are you in here?"

A muffled shuffling sound emanating from the far end of the building proclaimed the presence of someone other than himself. He took off toward it, cursing the winding, black-screened maze that impeded his progress.

"Mark—over here." Logan's gruff voice hailed him from the MacBeth display. "I think we're in a cave of some sort."

The witches' cave. "Logan, what the hell do you think you're do—" He stopped speaking abruptly at the sight that greeted him as he skirted Lady MacBeth's castle chamber. Sam's shroud was impossibly twined around Hecate's scepter. She sat there pinned to it while Logan and Rhianna struggled to free her without ripping the wisps of costume.

"Oh, God, not you, too," Sam moaned when she saw him. "This is so humiliating. I feel like a trapped rat."

Rhianna grinned. "You wouldn't if you hadn't decided to play leapfrog in the tunnel."

Mark crouched in front of them and raised a questioning brow. "You were in the tunnel?"

"It's a ridiculously stupid story," Sam warned. Then she hiccuped. "We got locked in the torture chamber. Sherlock Junior, here, decided we should crawl out through the tunnel. When she stopped crawling, I thought she must have seen a spider, so I climbed over her and landed smack on top of Hecate, who promptly proceeded to zap me with her wand."

"Her arm moved," Rhianna supplemented lightly. "I forgot the witches are linked to the chamber's animation system."

"Yeah, she forgot, and I wound up getting the shaft, so to speak." Sam sniffed. "Some deal." She glowered at Mark. "The least you could do is put a john in this cavern."

"I'll think about it," Mark murmured, distracted. He rose to check the chamber door. It was indeed bolted.

Logan gave the shroud a final tug. "There you go, Sammy." He grunted and wiped a film of perspiration from his bushy brow. "Man, this is some spook show you got here, Mark. I'm banging away in the cellar, and suddenly I hear what sounds like someone howling at the moon. So I come up to the lot, and what do you think I find?"

"Billie." Rhianna mouthed the name and Mark nodded.

"I find Olive Oyl screeching her lungs out," Logan continued. "She's yelling for her old lady, and then damned if I don't hear someone else yelling away in here." He tapped Sam's ghoulish cheek. "Knew it was Sammy right off, though. No one else can swear like her."

"Thanks for the ego boost, Logan," Sam retorted disdainfully, gathering up her tattered hem. "Now if you'll excuse me, I think I'll go invent a few new four-letter words."

Mark ensnared her wrist, preventing her from leaving. "Do it at your parents' place, okay?" he suggested.

"At my what?" She stared at him as though he'd sprouted horns. "Why?"

"Because I'm asking you to."

She considered the request for a long moment. "Oh, all right," she agreed at last. "You can give me a lift, Logan." She hiccuped again. "I think I'm over the legal limit."

"We're gonna have to go on my bike."

"We can go piggyback, for all I care. But let's go now. One quick pit stop, and you can drive darlin' Lily to her old stomping grounds."

Sam shot off to the apartment, and Logan followed, grumbling all the way. That left only Mark and Rhianna in the museum, and she seemed to be trying very hard not to laugh. He'd have to clean out those straw pallets more often, Mark reflected. Then again, maybe he should just leave them alone. On her, a wine glow looked good. And it had probably kept her from becoming frightened in the chamber.

"Come on." He took her by the hand. "Run upstairs and get your things."

She didn't budge. "Why? Are you firing me?" She grinned at him. "The tourists won't like that, you know. Vampira has a way with them."

"The men, anyway," Mark concurred, tugging on her hand.

"Actually, the kids like her best. Especially teenagers. They think she's punk. Way cool, Mark."

He had to bite back a chuckle. "How much of that hooch did you and Sam drink?"

She tried to measure out the height with her free hand. "A little brown jugful. Hardly anything. But you know, Mark, it's really not bad stuff once you get used to it. Sam drank most of it, though."

"I can tell."

He watched as she made a tentative fist. "Are your fingers supposed to go numb from homemade wine?"

"Let's just say you'd better not plan on using them for a while." He pulled her to her feet. "Come on, we're going over to Reed's. Do you need anything from upstairs?"

"Uh-huh," she said, accepting the situation without question. And she proceeded to rattle off a list that would have filled a trunk.

After settling her in his Corvette and locking the doors, he went up to the apartment to fill her order. Logan was there, picking his way through the fridge while he waited for Sam.

"I don't see anything dangerous here," he announced around a mouthful of cold lasagna. "I gather you're getting rid of your tenants because you want me to spend the night."

Mark nodded. Logan was a lot sharper than he looked.

"You wanna tell me what's going on? Why I've been bulldogging Rhianna for the past three days?"

"Nope."

Logan grinned. "I figured as much. Well, if it's worth anything to you, Mark, she looks great in those black threads.'' He offered over the tray of lasagna. ''You want some of this?''

Mark shook his head. His hunger had nothing to do with food—and everything to do with the woman out in his car. For her own protection and his peace of mind, he'd take her to Reed's tonight. Somehow, though, he didn't think he was really doing either of them a favor. Stifling a sigh, he went into Rhianna's room.

IT WAS DARK AGAIN. Dark and hot, like Satan's fiery furnace. And in that pervading darkness, in that heat, a black widow spider crawled silently around its temporary home. Waiting for a chance to strike. Waiting for the freedom it had yet to gain. Waiting to claim its next victim...

Chapter Eight

For the duration of the short ride to Reed Morgan's home, Rhianna held her tongue, fascinated by the sight of Mark as he drove. It was a simple enough task, which he managed to make look incredibly sexy. He didn't say much, but she could feel the heat of his frequent sideways glances.

She thought he looked wonderfully messy after his fishing trip. Obviously, he hadn't taken the time to shower and change before going to the wax museum. She wondered, hazily, if that was good or bad.

She also wondered why she'd agreed to accompany him to his uncle's place. Since he'd been staying with Joe, she'd assumed Reed's home had been sold. Apparently, that wasn't the case. It wasn't what bothered her, either. She didn't understand why he'd insisted that both she and Sam spend the night away from the apartment.

Too absorbed by him to pose the question, Rhianna continued to stare. She didn't realize they'd reached their destination until he'd braked his Corvette to a halt in the carport. Then she felt maybe she should say something.

"Why did you bring me here, Mark?" she asked, cautiously sliding from her seat. "And why did you send Sam to her parents?"

He extracted her carryall from the trunk. "The crew I hired is going to be working tonight," he replied easily. "I thought their banging might keep you awake."

"Oh." She tried not to sound too disappointed.

A cobbled path led from the carport to the back porch of the large colonial house. It was tricky walking with all the wine she'd consumed, but Rhianna did it. She had no intention of sprawling flat on her face in front of him.

On the veranda, Mark reached around her to unlock the door, and the scent of his skin and hair swept over her. It reminded her of the sun and the sea and the hot summer night. She longed to back up and press herself against him, to feel the taut muscles of his body digging into her flesh.

That was the effect of the wine, she realized. It had stripped away her defenses and her logic and now it was urging her to do something she knew full well she shouldn't.

"Do you want some coffee?" Mark questioned her once they were in the quaint kitchen.

She shook her head and began to prowl the spacious room. For all his money, Reed's tastes had remained amazingly unpretentious. The old house still smelled of dried apples and spices, despite the fact that it hadn't been occupied for several months. It practically shouted home to her.

In her bleary peripheral vision, she noticed that Mark was still standing in the doorway, watching her every move. "Do you mind sleeping in Brodie's old room?" he inquired in a distantly polite tone.

She hesitated. "No, that's fine," she murmured, suddenly feeling very tired.

Without a word, he propelled her up a steep flight of plank stairs to a bedroom at the far end of the hall.

Rhianna took absent note of the oak bureau and desk and the miniature mock-up of Dracula's Carpathian castle strewn across them. The bed was made, and that was all she really cared about. The wine might have sparked a number of tantalizing fantasies, but it had also made her extremely sleepy. Right now, all she wanted to do was climb between the sheets and dream the night away.

As she sank into the bed, images of the torture chamber floated through her head. She and Mark locked inside a darkened room. Only Mark hadn't been there with here, had he? He'd been off fishing with Joe and Dag.

He'd been fishing, and so had she. In his absence, she'd spoken with the retired bricklayer, who had told her about the wall in the north-wing basement, a wall he'd left unfinished that Friday afternoon ten years ago. It had been seven feet high—two feet from completion—with a scaffold conveniently set up beside it. What a heaven-sent opportunity for the murderer. Hit Brodie on the head, dump his body over the wall and let someone else brick him in the next morning. A calculated risk that had worked perfectly. In the meantime, she'd been right outside—waiting for a rendezvous that could never have taken place...

She felt her thoughts slipping away from her. Slipping into the shadowy world of her dreams. She saw herself in her Vampira gown, felt the gown being removed from her body. And then she was being laid to rest, deep inside Dracula's waffle-shrouded coffin.

The last thing she remembered was the coffin lid closing above her as she sank further into a peaceful realm of oblivion...

MARK MADE CERTAIN that Rhianna was sound asleep before he left her to her dreams. Something wrenched brutally inside him when he closed the door to Brodie's room, but he knew better than to try to analyze it. Tiredly, he walked out onto the second-floor terrace to throw himself onto one of the wicker lounges.

A dozen different emotions clawed at his insides, feelings that should have been long gone by now. And every one of them, it seemed, centered around Rhianna.

Propping his feet up on the railing, Mark stared broodingly at the glow rising from the center of town. He was wrong for her, as wrong for her as she was right for him. He'd realized that from the start, and still he'd been unable to fight the overwhelming attraction he felt for her.

Avoiding her sure as hell wasn't the answer, he thought darkly. He'd done his damnedest to keep his distance from her after that night at the drive-in. He'd even stayed out on the Cape longer than necessary. But neither of those ploys had worked. Deep down, he'd only wanted to find her again, to be with her, to tell her the truth about everything, to make love to her until he was too exhausted to think.

A rush of heat in his lower limbs forced him to shift position on the lounge. In the back of his mind, he knew that someone had deliberately locked Rhianna and Sam in the Chamber of Horrors tonight. Maybe neither of them realized that yet, and maybe it was just as well, since nothing had happened. But there was definitely someone stalking her, someone who was afraid that she was coming too close to the truth. Someone who was doing his or her damnedest to scare Rhianna. Or worse, to kill her.

Shuddering violently, Mark extricated himself from the chair and went back inside to check on her.

MORNING BROUGHT WITH IT a stream of brilliant sunshine and an agonizing return to consciousness, which sent Rhianna's dreams scurrying into oblivion. It took her several minutes to figure out where she was, several more to realize that she was wearing nothing except a pair of bikini briefs and a bra.

With a start, she levered herself onto her elbows, then fell back against the pillows as a bolt of pain streaked through her head. She'd been bludgeoned just like Brodie, she thought dismally, closing her eyes against a rising surge of nausea. Bludgeoned or hit by a truck, she wasn't sure which.

Cautiously, she reached for her watch, which had magically found its way onto the nightstand. Eleven o'clock! Her eyes widened in disbelief. How could it be that late? She had a tour at nine. It couldn't be eleven. Her watch must have stopped.

But it hadn't. The position of the sun in the sky confirmed that.

Groaning, she lifted her head from the pillow. Mark had brought her here last night, that much she did remember. Had he also undressed her? God, she hoped not. Still, it seemed likely, since she couldn't recall doing it herself.

A knock, which resembled a sonic boom, sounded on the bedroom door while she was endeavoring to slide from the bed. If indeed Mark had removed her clothes, there seemed little point in a show of modesty. Nonetheless, she dragged on her oversize cotton shirt before responding.

"Welcome back from the grave, Vampira," he drawled with more mocking humor than Rhianna cared to hear just then. "How do you feel?"

"Go to hell."

"That good, huh?"

She managed a baleful glare. "I'd appreciate it if you wouldn't shout, Mark. I happen to have a headache."

He crouched down in front of her. "I've seen you look healthier," he murmured, "but I think you'll live."

"You're too kind," she muttered, then winced as the throbbing in her temples intensified. "At least I won't need much makeup today."

"You won't need any," Mark informed her, too dangerously close for her liking. "Just to prove I'm not totally heartless, I'll let you have the day off."

For a moment Rhianna had thought he was throwing out a nasty insult. It mollified her a bit to know that he wasn't being deliberately cruel.

Shuddering slightly, she pushed her hair away from her face. "Is it my morbid imagination, Mark, or were Sam and I locked in the Chamber of Horrors last night?"

His expression didn't alter a fraction. "That's the story I heard," he said evenly. "By the time I got there, though, you'd already crawled out through the tunnel."

"And now I'm here." She frowned in confusion. "Why am I here?"

"The night construction crew," he reminded her patiently. "Do you want an aspirin?"

"Please."

When she was alone, Rhianna dragged on her jeans. She'd shower when she got back to the apartment, and she'd never touch a drop of anything alcoholic again, she vowed. Not ever.

Splashing water on her face helped, and so did brushing her teeth. She felt marginally better by the time she emerged from the bathroom. However, she still couldn't make a very good fist, she noted dryly.

Mark met her at the foot of the stairs with a couple of coated aspirins and a glass of tomato juice. "It'll help, Rhianna," he told her as she eyed the red liquid distastefully. "Drink it, and I'll take you back to the apartment. You can sleep all day if you want to."

That was precisely what she planned to do. Of course, it didn't work out that way, but at least she felt semi-human after a few more hours of sleep.

A cool shower revived her further. By five o'clock, she could actually face her reflection in the bathroom mirror.

"Oh, God, get away from me," Sam groaned from the sofa where she'd been lying spreadeagled since Rhianna had staggered in. "You don't look a tenth as bad as I feel. Where did you get to last night, anyway?"

"Reed's." She made it to one of the armchairs before collapsing.

"Mark take you there?"

Rhianna nodded. "He said the night crew would've kept us awake, but I don't know if I believe that."

Sam cracked her eyes. "I do. Every time they drop a nail down there, my head explodes. I think they must have come up here and raided the fridge just for good measure. If you want to make yourself really sick, take a look at the dishes in the sink. There's a mountain of them, all covered with disgustingly sticky bits of food."

"Thanks, I'll pass." Rhianna forced herself out of the chair. Sam had turned the air-conditioning system off and opened the sliding doors to admit the afternoon breeze. As hot and humid as it was outside, the air was fresh and wood-scented. Maybe if she breathed some of it into her lungs, she'd wake up completely.

Because movement seemed to help, she wandered down the balcony stairs and over to the production-shop offices. She still hadn't had a chance to look through the personnel files. Maybe today would be her lucky day in that regard.

Marion wasn't at her desk when Rhianna went inside. A number of the other employees were finishing up their work, preparing to leave for the night.

"Schedule's out for next week," one of the women said as Rhianna sank onto Marion's padded desk chair. "I think it's in Mark's office."

"Is he still here?"

"Nah. He left around three... Unfortunately," she tacked on with a dreamy look Rhianna had seen before. "I sure hope he decides to stay here," the woman continued. "Bosses like him are few and far between."

"One in a million," Rhianna agreed.

She waited until the building had cleared, then slid from the chair and crept down the corridor toward Mark's office. The door was wide open, for a change. She hadn't had to break in, after all. How simple that made her quest.

"Oh, hell," she muttered, annoyed with herself for even contemplating searching his files. It was deceitful, dishonest and totally unscrupulous. But she wasn't trying to pin Brodie's death on him, her brain rationalized. She only wanted to find out which of the others, besides Billie, might have had a motive for killing Brodie.

She sighed in exasperation. They'd all had a motive, hadn't they? And they'd all been working at the wax museum back then. All except Billie Noble.

Could Billie have known the details of the construction work? Known about the nearly completed brick wall? Had she perhaps lucked out in discovering the perfect hiding place for a body?

As her mind toiled, Rhianna's feet carried her toward the large metal filing cabinet in the corner of the Spartanly furnished room. Sucking in a deep breath, she gave in to temptation and tugged open the bottom drawer, where logically the oldest files should have been stored. It was empty.

She went to the next drawer. This one was filled with manila envelopes: insurance policies, bills of sale for outgoing wax figures, shipment receipts. Nothing worth wasting precious time on.

In the next two were the current personnel files. Dag's revealed an appalling absentee record and a salary far above the one he'd been earing as a part-time custodian. Sam's was much the same. Her absentee record was good, her salary beyond reproach. Nothing to be learned there, either, Rhianna decided.

She started to close the top drawer. A dull gleam in the very back, however, caught her eye. Reaching in, she wrapped her fingers around something cold and metallic. Something that struck a discordant note in her mind.

Her heart slammed violently against her ribs. The cold metal object was a gun. A gun like none she'd ever seen before. At least, she'd never handled one of its type before. It looked to have come straight out of *Lethal Weapon*. And it was loaded.

"Put it down, Rhianna."

Mark's low-voiced command from the doorway had her momentarily tightening her grip. But then she released it and dropped the weapon back into the drawer.

"I told you not to go through my things," he said, and Rhianna knew he was directly behind her now. Behind her and angry.

"Why do you have a gun, Mark?" she asked him without turning around.

He curled his fingers about her arm and turned her around to face him. There was leashed fury simmering behind the icy blue of his eyes. His jaw was set in an uncompromising line. If there had ever been a moment to fear him, it was this one. Regardless, now was no time to panic.

He glared at her steadily for several interminable seconds. "This is my office," he informed her in the coldest, most dispassionate tone he'd ever used on her. "You have no business snooping around in here."

"But that's a . . . I don't even know what that is. What is it?"

"It's a gun," he snarled. "Nothing more. And don't act like you aren't familiar with them. I'm sure you've handled one or two in your life."

"I've handled all sorts of them," she countered belligerently. "Just never one like that. Where did you get it?"

The grip on her arm tightened. "Forget it," he said. "I'm through with questions for today. You want answers, go play with the computer. Or better yet, find yourself another case to work on."

She met his glacial eyes. It cost her a tremendous effort, but she didn't flinch. "Not until I find out who killed Brodie."

"Right." He set her free so abruptly that she almost stumbled against the filing cabinet. She stayed where she was while he strode over to his desk. He glowered at her. "Go ahead, Rhianna," he snapped. "Go play Sherlock.

Go on out there and solve your damned murder. Just get out of here, and let me get on with my work.''

Just like that? Wasn't he even going to fire her?

Rhianna opened her mouth to say something, then decided not to bother. He wouldn't believe her anyway.

So she left, without uttering another sound. Without a backward glance. She marched through the offices, across the lot and up the stairs to the apartment. And she thought she'd never felt so empty in her entire life.

ALL AFTERNOON AND EVENING, she paid the price for her compulsive snooping, for the previous night's wine, for her own stupidity.

Finally she couldn't stand it anymore. Sam was asleep on the couch. There was no one to talk to, nothing to do except flog herself for her foolishness.

She couldn't sit still, and she didn't feel like driving into town. A swim out at the junction pond might help. At least it would give her an outlet for her pent-up frustration. If she was lucky, the solitude might even provide a few of the answers she sought. Answers to questions that had little to do with Brodie's death.

Before common sense could prevail, Rhianna exchanged her shorts and top for a one-piece black swimsuit and threw on a pair of cutoffs and a large T-shirt. Then, determinedly, she made her way to the moonlit tracks.

Never once did she notice the shadowy form in the woods behind her, or feel the piercing eyes that trailed her movements down the overgrown path. Nor did she see the black-cloaked figure that ducked into the woods, gloved fingers holding tight to the handle of a large butcher's knife...

Chapter Nine

A good two hours passed before Mark moved from the chair behind his desk. Two solid hours before he even let himself think about Rhianna.

She'd been snooping through his files, for Christ's sake. Even after all that had grown between them during these past few weeks, she'd still felt the need to rifle his office. Damn her, he swore bitterly to himself. Damn her suspicious mind and the mistrust she just wouldn't shut away.

What the hell had she been hoping to find in here anyway? A confession written in his own hand? A blood-stained brick with traces of Brodie's hair on it? A videotape of the murder? What?

Stifling a curse, Mark pushed himself out of his chair, strode to the tiny oak liquor cabinet in the far corner of the room and dug out a half empty bottle of Scotch. He considered pouring himself a stiff measure of the stuff, then shrugged and decided to drink it straight from the bottle.

The amber liquid burned as it slid down his throat, and its raw bite took the irritated edge off his anger. It wasn't really Rhianna's fault that she'd felt compelled to search his things. God knew, he hadn't given her much of a reason to trust him. And he had shown up at the wax museum the night Brodie had died—probably within a few minutes of his cousin's death, in fact. He'd seen Rhianna, and she'd seen him. Maybe it was only natural that she should doubt him.

Dangling the open Scotch bottle between his fingers, Mark wandered back to his desk, and for a moment just stood and stared into the darkened woods beyond the parking lot. The problem was, he wanted her to trust him completely. He wanted that, but he had no idea how to make it happen—short of dumping the murderer on her doorstep, that was. And, of course, he could hardly hand Brodie's killer over to her when he had absolutely no proof of who the killer was.

Running a weary hand through his hair, Mark flexed the aching muscles in his shoulders and turned away from the window. Getting drunk wasn't going to solve a damned thing, he reflected, eyeing the bottle he still held. Neither was brooding in his office. What he needed to do was to find her, first to make sure she was all right, then, second, to talk to her, to make her understand that he hadn't had a reason in the world to harm Brodie.

After a moment's consideration, he capped the Scotch bottle and started for the door. Rhianna's car was in the lot, he noted as he left the office complex, which probably meant that she was up in Sam's apartment, no doubt letting her suspicions run wild over the discovery of the gun in his filing cabinet. That gun for which he had a license. All legal and aboveboard, and yet he could well envision her sitting there, assuming the worst. Damn, he swore again.

In front of him, he saw Sam descending the balcony staircase like she was walking on eggshells. The apartment above was dark, and that had Mark frowning as he intercepted the woman.

"Where's Rhianna?" he demanded in a voice just loud enough to rise above the clatter in the north-wing cellar.

"I haven't seen her since five or so."

"Do you know where she went?"

"Keep it down, will ya, Mark?" she beseeched him. "I haven't the foggiest idea where she might've gotten to. I only know that I have to go over to my mother's. I gather she accidentally set fire to the kitchen curtains while she was cooking dinner, and now she wants me to help her clean up the mess."

The word fire had Mark glancing sharply across Blueberry Road, to Billie Noble's flaking A-frame. But her place, too, was shrouded in darkness. With an absent nod to Sam, who had begun to teeter over to her car, he sought out the museum's side entrance. There was tourist action in the eerily lit maze, but still no sign of Rhianna and not one of the guides he questioned had seen her around the place that evening.

Okay, so where the hell was she, he wondered, returning to the lot. Over at Billie's? He seriously doubted that. She might be willing to brave the woman's home in broad daylight, but he couldn't see her trying it at night.

His troubled gaze traveled to the woods behind the production shop. The Pullman then? Yeah, that was a possibility. A good possibility. She hadn't taken her car, so she couldn't have gone very far. And she had made the trek to the junction once before. It was worth a shot.

Above his head, Mark spied gnarled tree limbs silhouetted against the silvery orb of the moon. Wispy tendrils of cloud gliding across the lunar surface gave the night a supernatural air, an air of foreboding like none he'd ever felt before. And with that disturbing sensation, there came a howling cry. It echoed through the sultry night, then was gone.

Clamping down on the angst that rose from the pit of his stomach, Mark bounded up the incline to the ancient railway tracks. He had to make sure that Rhianna was safe.

SOFT MOONBEAMS REFLECTING off the surface of the junction pond had a tranquilizing affect on Rhianna's disruptive state of mind. She cut cleanly through the mirror-smooth water, her sleek strokes dissolving to a lazy crawl as she neared the mossy land's edge.

From the woods, the chirping of a thousand crickets provided a random cacophony to fill her senses. Over the Pullman a swarm of fireflies lit the night sky. Rhianna watched them, savoring the cool, wet rivulets that slid down her back and limbs as she twisted the excess moisture from her hair.

She felt better, even if she had forgotten to bring a towel. That oversight was negligible, however, and hardly likely to matter, since the temperature had to be in the high eighties. She'd be dry enough by the time she reached the old rail car. Unless, of course, it decided to rain. From the south a low rumble of thunder reverberated through the night sky.

Beneath Rhianna's bare feet, the mossy ground was spongy and damp. Farther along the tracks, a small campfire burned, a flickering testament to the hapless transients who preferred the wooded tracks to the raunchy west-end bar scene.

For a split second, she thought she heard the underbrush crackling, as though someone—or something— had parted one of the thorny vines. She fought the nervous shiver that brought goose bumps to her skin, chiding herself for her jumpy attitude. There was no one out here, she told herself firmly. She'd heard a rabbit or a squirrel or some other equally harmless animal.

Willing her qualms to abate, she swung herself into the dusty coach. The drone of heat-crazed flies accompanied her to where she'd dropped her sneakers and cutoffs. Pushing them to one side, she dragged on her T-shirt, flopped onto the worn velvet seat, propped her feet up on a broken chair and tugged Brodie's bracelet from her wrist. Idly, she reread the numbered inscription: 627466. She also recalled Dag's bracelet: 324. A number for each letter of their names, she presumed.

She wondered if the bracelets really had come from the carnival. It seemed likely. Maybe Dag and Brodie had bought them when they'd been younger, before they'd gotten mixed up in the east-end robberies.

Silvery beams tumbled lazily through the Pullman's dirt-encrusted windows. Rhianna slipped the bracelet back onto her wrist and picked up her cutoffs. The nearly full box of Sucrets she pulled from the pocket looked so harmless, so innocent.

And maybe they were innocent, she postulated optimistically. At least innocent in so far as Mark was concerned.

So where, then, did that leave her investigation, she wondered, emitting a tiny sigh. So far, the only facts she'd been able to ascertain were, one, that Billie Noble belonged in a padded cell, and two, that Sam and Dag, Joe and Brodie had helped her rob a number of east-end residents ten long years ago. Beyond that she knew virtually nothing. Nothing except her feelings for Mark—a flood of tangled emotions she was afraid to examine and, at the same time, unable to ignore. She stuck the throat lozenges back in the pocket of her shorts. For several drowsy minutes, she sat there trying to recall all that she'd seen and heard at the wax museum the night Brodie had died. Was it possible she was overlooking something? Some crucial little detail that could supply the key to this confounding puzzle?

Preoccupied by the jumble of recollections somer-saulting fuzzily through her head, Rhianna failed to take notice of the parting underbrush near the tracks and the shadowy black-swathed figure that crept from the shelter of the tangled vines. Creeping, crouching, moving ever closer to the crooked steps of the Pullman. Not a sound did it make as it stole across the clearing and into the coach, as it skulked in shadow across the littered floor...

More asleep now than awake, Rhianna heard nothing, saw nothing. Until a pair of gloved hands suddenly shot out and clamped themselves around her wrists.

For a split second she was too stunned to react. It took only that second for the shadowy figure to jerk her out of her sleepy reverie. With lightning swiftness, it also yanked her violently to her feet and out of the dappled moonlight.

Rhianna couldn't see the face of her attacker, couldn't see anything except inky blackness and two leather gloves, the kind of gloves worn by construction workers or possibly wealthy gardeners.

She didn't bother to examine them for very long. She didn't really have the chance. The figure was behind her so quickly that she barely had time to wake up fully and realize what was happening.

When alertness returned, her heart lurched sickeningly into her throat. One thing was certain, this was no vagrant. It was pure evil. The Ghost of Christmas Future shackling her wrists, issuing no words, only guttural grunts as it succeeded in slamming her over one of the velvet seats.

Setting her teeth to keep from crying out as her left arm was wrenched behind her back, Rhianna allowed her muscles to relax. Then, suddenly, she wondered what the hell she was doing. Suppressing her screams wouldn't help her. Besides, she was a terrific screamer. If ever there had been a time to prove that, it was now.

A bony hip dug cruelly into her backside. Man, woman, she couldn't establish a gender. Only pain and rising fear and a few scattered remnants of hand-to-hand combat registered in her brain. She was in an impossible position. Her only hope was to make some noise.

Pulling in a deep, difficult breath, she let the screams fly, fully prepared to continue screaming until the hammerlock on her wrist was broken.

The hip dug into her flesh again, and her left arm was forced higher. Gloved fingers inched along her forearm, but still her attacker didn't speak. And still Rhianna screamed. And when the black figure finally bent over her, doubtless to shut her up, Rhianna deliberately flung her head back.

It was a vicious hit. The resounding crack of skulls slackened the iron grip on her right wrist just enough for her to free it. Automatically, she spun around, lashing out into the pervading darkness with her foot.

And she did hit something with her heel, she was sure of it. Perhaps the bony hip, perhaps an arm, perhaps some more sensitive part of her attacker's anatomy.

Whatever she'd kicked, however, she hadn't inflicted serious injury. In a swirl of black, the figure darted for the door of the coach at a surprisingly fast, hobbling gait. It didn't pause or falter on the crooked steps. By the time

Rhianna realized that she should be pursuing it, it had vanished into the woods.

"Dammit!" She swore out loud, kicking the metal doorframe in vexation. She'd let her attacker get away. Damn!

From the neighboring underbrush, a muffled thrashing brought her silent reproach to a screeching halt. Heroics be damned, she thought, scrambling out of the old coach. She was unarmed, unnerved and totally unprepared to do battle with a demon of darkness. Not out here in the middle of nowhere, in the middle of the night.

This was no roll down the stairs with a kidnapping spouse. This was malevolence in its purest form. And you couldn't fight that with clever kicks and jabs.

Heedless of the uneven terrain, Rhianna took off at a dead run. It was about a mile back to the wax museum. All she had to do was follow the tracks, and she'd be fine. Too bad for her lungs if they didn't like the pace. She'd gulp air when she reached the apartment, not before.

Well—maybe just a little before. She had covered approximately half the distance when a cramp in her side forced her to slow up. Unless the demon shadow was hot on her heels, she knew she was going to have to stop for a minute.

It wasn't, and she did. Wincing, she collapsed on one of the steel rails. Her breathing rate wasn't bad, but the cramp hurt, and so did her head where she had smacked the intruder—the intruder she'd allowed to escape, she reminded herself caustically. In all likelihood, Brodie's murderer. Damn, why hadn't she chased it into the woods?

In the cricket-filled stillness of the night, a tiny twig snapped, and Rhianna's head shot up. One fluid movement brought her to her feet.

This was getting ridiculous. She was running from an unknown entity, possibly the very entity she sought to expose. The least she could do was stand up to it. In a sprint there were few enough people who could catch her. If she had to, she could always rely on speed as a last resort.

From the south, a long shadow fell across her. It seemed to be coming from the wrong direction, and that confused her for a moment. No way could her attacker have passed her; therefore, the shadow should be falling from the rear—shouldn't it?

Oh, God, who cared anymore? In a burst of anger and adrenaline, she spun around. But the shadow was gone. Only the tracks remained, and they were clear as far as her eyes could see.

She began to scan the surrounding area. Trees, bushes, vines, weeds. There was no sign of human life. Nothing except . . .

For the second time in less than fifteen minutes, a pair of hands reached out to grab her. And for a second time, Rhianna twisted her body around to lash out with her foot. She was wide awake now and sick to death of being grabbed. This time, she was going to scratch and claw her way to a few answers.

Or not . . . These hands, unlike the first pair, weren't gloved, and her kick didn't seem to faze this shadow in the slightest. All her well-aimed lunge got her was a muffled curse and a twirl on the ties, which landed her flat up against someone's firm, lean body. A man's firm, lean body. A terrifyingly familiar one.

There was no mistaking the arms that held her or the fingers that were wound around her wrists or the hair that brushed across her cheek. No mistaking the angles and planes of the man against whom she was pinned.

"Are you through, Rhianna?" Mark demanded, his stony voice a balm to her beleaguered senses. That he'd caught her from behind, from the direction of the Pullman, was of no consequence. He was here, and she knew he wouldn't hurt her.

A feeling of overwhelming relief flooded through her. Of their own volition, her struggles ceased. "Yes, I'm through," she breathed, closing her eyes against the belated weakness invading her limbs.

In the back of her mind, she was aware that Mark's jeans and her bathing suit provided a thin to nonexistent barrier between the two of them. The heat from his body warmed her in a way that caused an all-too-familiar ache to her senses. She'd come to love that feeling—maybe a little too much.

When he spoke again, his tone, though impassive, held a note of concern she'd finally learned to recognize. "Was someone chasing you?"

She opened her eyes as he turned her around to face him. All muscle and bone, not an ounce of spare flesh. Thankfully, no lingering trace of anger. God, but he looked good in the fading moonlight. "I'm—not sure," she admitted. "Someone grabbed me in the Pullman, someone wearing leather gloves and a black..." She choked back the rest of her sentence. Mark was wearing black—a loose-fitting black sweatshirt. But his hair was blond, she reminded herself. Long and blond. Even hooded, she would have seen his hair had he been the one to assault her.

His eyes hardened ever so slightly. He knew what she was thinking. She hadn't masked her expression quickly enough. "A black what, Rhianna?" His hands dropped to his sides. He looked distant and aloof once again.

"A black..." She hesitated, furious with herself, uncertain now about what she'd seen. "I don't know. A black something. A black-all-over something. Mark, this is going to sound silly, but whoever it was was covered up like a monk. Or a *Star Wars* Jawa."

"A Jawa?"

"Yes." She sighed. "I can't explain it any better than that. I kicked it, and it hobbled off into the woods."

Mark's brows lowered. "It hobbled?"

Rhianna dropped her lashes. "Well, I'm not exactly sure where my foot landed," she explained, squirming a little. "It might have been hobbling for a reason."

"Yeah, I'll bet it was." An oblique smile quirked the corners of Mark's mouth. Then his eyes darkened. "I gather this 'it' could have been male or female. Do you have any idea how tall he or she was?"

"Ah...no. Not really. As tall as me, I suppose. Maybe taller. It was hard to tell where the person stopped and the darkness took over."

Reaching out thoughtfully, Mark trapped a strand of her hair between his fingers. "Do you know what your Jawa was after?"

Entranced by a touch she could scarcely even feel, Rhianna shook her head. "No, I don't. It...uh, didn't say what it wanted, and I didn't really think it would do much good to ask. It wasn't exactly talking up a storm."

His face was an inscrutable mask in the wisps of waning moonlight. "Are you hurt?"

"No."

"Have you had enough of the woods for tonight?"

"Yes."

With one last distracted twist of her hair, Mark released her. "Come on, then," he murmured. "I'll walk you back to the museum."

Walk? Half a mile? With bare feet? On rough ties and gravel? Running for her life had been one thing. Walking was something else again. Besides which, she was still hot and trembly from the touch of his fingers on her hair.

Nevertheless, she did what she had to, hopping from tie to tie in an effort to avoid the broken glass and sharp pebbles in between. Beside her, Mark moved with the ease of a panther. How nice for him to be wearing hard-soled work boots, she thought a trifle spitefully. The least he could do was slow down a bit.

They'd gone perhaps fifty yards along the tracks when, to her amazement, he actually did slow down. More than that, in fact; he stopped. "How the hell did you get all the way out here with bare feet, Rhianna?" His frowning gaze traveled down the length of her legs, bringing a rush of heat to her skin and a cramp that ran right through the center of her.

"I was wearing a little more than this earlier," she told him. "Midnight attacks have a tendency to make me forget about the way I'm dressed."

Wrong thing to say, she realized, snapping her mouth shut. His indolent surveillance burned right through the fabric of her thin T-shirt and swimsuit. For all the cover they provided, she might as well have left them piled on top of her cutoffs and sneakers.

A horrible thought struck her, then. Her cutoffs! The throat lozenges! They were inside the Pullman. How could she have been so stupid as to have left them there?

"I have to go back," she announced suddenly. "I just remembered; I left my things in the Pullman."

"Tough, Rhianna." Mark grasped her arm before she could move. "You can get them tomorrow."

"No, I can't," she protested. "I need them tonight."

"Too bad. I'm not going all the way out to the junction just for a few clothes."

If only he knew. "Fine," she retorted, hunching her shoulders. "I'll go by myself."

"Yeah, right," he drawled. "You do that, march on back there, and get yourself killed."

Killed? Who'd said anything about getting killed? "You think someone's trying to kill me?" she questioned him, startled.

"Don't you?"

Well, yes, now that she thought about it, she probably did. Somehow, though, it had been less nerve-racking to ignore the possibility. She preferred to believe that someone was simply trying to frighten her. The word "kill" was restricted to the fate that had befallen Brodie. It had no business associating itself with her.

"You're right. I should wait until tomorrow," she said, and tried to look unruffled.

Without another word, Rhianna began tie-hopping. She had taken perhaps half a dozen steps when she felt Mark's hands encircling her waist, lifting her effortlessly onto one of the steel rails.

"Try a balancing act for a while," he suggested mildly. "You should be an expert at walking fine lines by now."

"And you're not?" she rallied, willing the hypnotic spell he cast to abate.

His reply was noncommittal, a deferential evasion. "I prefer to choose one side and stay there."

"I guess that would simplify things," she conceded.

Because the track was slippery in spots, she was having trouble holding herself upright and talking at the same time. Naturally, she chose to talk and take a chance that she wouldn't topple from the metal rail. Her curiosity was too great to be quelled.

"Why did you really go fishing, Mark?" she prompted him. "And don't tell me you like to fish. If you did, you wouldn't have dragged Dag along for the ride."

His enigmatic eyes swept over her. "I wanted to get away from here for a couple of days; it's as simple as that."

"Just you and the guys?" She shook her head. "I don't believe you."

"That's your problem."

No, it wasn't. *He* was her problem. Her conscience was her problem. She glanced over at him. "You didn't have to hire me to work at the museum, you know."

One of his shoulders lifted, brushing her arm as it did so. "Why wouldn't I have hired you? We were short-staffed, and you're a good tour guide."

"Doesn't it bother you that I'm also a private investigator?"

He regarded her blandly. "Should it?"

She sighed. "No, I guess not." She wished he wouldn't walk so close beside her. She couldn't think straight when he was this close, when every incidental contact between them ignited a brushfire from breast to thigh inside her.

It was all she could do to keep her hands to herself. They were just itching to explore every inch of him. Too bad she wasn't brazen enough to give in to the wanton desire.

The half mile passed in companionable silence. Where the tracks were broken, Mark swooped her into his arms and carried her, and Rhianna enjoyed the smooth texture of his skin and hair beneath her fingertips. There was a certain erotic intimacy that came from simply touching him. Touching him, wanting him, wishing he would let that guard of his down long enough for her to get close to him.

The incline, when Rhianna reached it, was mossy and easy to traverse. She had to let go of Mark, of course, and that she didn't like, but at least he was behind her, showing no signs of disappearing like a vapor into the night.

The apartment, she noticed immediately, was dark. Either Sam had gone to bed early or she'd gone out somewhere.

In contrast, the lighted north wing cast a brilliant glow over the parking lot. From the cellar, she could hear drills and hammers and a great deal of swearing. Sam might not be around, but no less than fifteen other people were. It looked like another noisy night.

She began wondering if Mark would insist she accompany him to Reed's again, paying no attention whatsoever to where she was stepping. It therefore came as no great shock to her when she put her foot down on the edge of a rather large, wobbly stone. And it didn't really surprise her that Mark reached out to prevent her from falling. What shook her was the way he held her, almost frantically, for a second. Then, in his usual indifferent fashion, he set her down an arm's length away from him.

"Go on up to bed, Rhianna," he said without inflection, having deposited her at the bottom of the balcony staircase. "These guys will be gone inside an hour."

Deflating though that statement was, Rhianna refused to move. "Aren't you going to come with me?"

He sent her a wry look. "To bed?"

She could think of worse ideas. "No, not to bed," she retorted hotly. "Upstairs to the apartment."

"You figure your marauding Jawa might be up there, huh?"

"It might be." Which should have proven that she didn't consider him to be her assailant.

Mark stared at her for a long, probing minute. His features in the luminous flux of moon and starlight were vaguely ethereal. He was so long, so lean, so hypnotic. And if he wasn't going to move, she certainly was. Just near enough to absorb the heat he radiated.

He continued to stare as his hand slowly rose to brush her cheek, as his knuckles grazed lightly along the side of her jaw and his slightly calloused thumb stroked her chin.

A shiver of anticipation shimmered through her. Schoolgirl romances had nothing on this moment. Past encounters faded into obscure insignificance. This man could seduce without moving a muscle. His eyes, his beautiful blue eyes, were more potent than any mind-expanding drug could ever be. More compelling, more addictive, infinitely more spellbinding.

Rhianna thought her lungs were going to burst from lack of oxygen. But she didn't want to breathe. It would take so little to resurrect that rigid control of his.

From the production shop a stream of raunchy workers flowed back and forth, ignorant of the twosome in the shadows of the wax museum. It was like Grand Central out there, a distant surge of activity to heighten Rhianna's awareness of the man in front of her.

"You really don't want to get involved with me," Mark said, his fingers sliding beneath her hair to the nape of her neck. "I wouldn't be good for you."

Maybe not, but it was a moot point right now. "I think I can take care of myself, Mark," she returned. "I never was a pampered ingenue."

He seemed unconvinced. A small smile flickered across his lips. "Yeah, you were. You just weren't a snob about it."

She let her own hands roam over the soft cotton of his sweatshirt, over his waist to his ribs. "Is that bad?"

"Depends on your point of view, I suppose." His fingers tightened just a little around her neck. And slowly, agonizingly slowly, he inclined his head to cover her mouth with his.

Rhianna had no idea what she'd expected from his touch. Yet the second his tongue probed beyond her lips, she knew she wasn't going to come out of this in one rational piece.

Something deep inside her exploded. The scent of soap and warm skin enveloped her. The heat and the taste of the texture of him made her long to draw him right into her. To assimilate him. Into her body, into her heart.

She relished the sensations as she slid her questing hands over the taut, smooth muscles of his back. She felt the trembling dampness of her response, the searing flood of heat in her limbs, the hardened nipples of her breasts crushed against his chest. She felt her own aching need where he pressed into the soft flesh of her stomach. Mark's hands caressed her, molding her hips to the rigid contours of his lower body. His fingers splayed across the small of her back. And he drew her closer still, his hungry lips caressing hers. Demanding, exploring, tasting. He taunted, and she responded. He took and she took—until her head began to swim, and she felt too drunk to stand.

She didn't want to let him go; she wasn't ready to end the intoxicating kiss. He knew what he was doing to her; she could feel what she was doing to him. His mouth was like liquid fire on hers, the thrust of his tongue a promise of something more, something primeval, an ancient alchemy she was only beginning to reach out and touch. And she thought she might have almost touched it when a thunderous clatter of beams and bricks from the north-wing cellar intruded on the moment, dissolving it, dragging her back to reality.

She could feel the warmth of Mark's breath on her lips and the sultry night air on her skin. She felt the heat from his body and the penetrating weight of his stare, heard the thunder rumbling threateningly in the distance. And then she heard Logan and the construction foreman bellowing in the distance and she stepped away.

There were people in the lot now; the situation had been taken out of her hands. And perhaps it was just as well. There was no way Rhianna could deny her response, no way she could control the trembling in her limbs, the hardness of her nipples, the breath in her throat that came in uneven spurts.

She stared over at Mark and saw the smoldering intensity in his eyes, the cryptic expression on his face. And when Logan bellowed again, diverting him, she turned and ran up the stairs to the wax museum apartment.

IN THE SHELTER of the neighboring trees, a figure cloaked in black stood and watched. Helplessly. Bitterly.

Failure again. Opportunity lost—again. Because she was young and strong and lucky. So very lucky.

The murderer looked up at the lighted apartment. A moment of lost control and the knife had disappeared into the undergrowth. And with it, all hope of ending her life. Tonight. But there was still tomorrow. Time enough to retrieve the evidence, to make her pay for her interference. Time enough to watch her die....

Chapter Ten

Thunder resounded across the blackened skies for much of the night while Rhianna tossed and turned restlessly in bed. Her dreams were filled with visions of wax figures suddenly come to life—gruesome caricatures that emerged from their various shadowy abodes to stalk her through the dimly lit museum. She awoke the next morning to air made wet and heavy by the rain and a pounding headache that kept her subdued on her early trek with Sam out to the Pullman.

Throughout the day, she was sure she could feel someone's eyes watching her. Although she told herself repeatedly that she was imagining things, she couldn't seem to shake the sense of foreboding that haunted her. Whoever had attacked her in the deserted rail car was somewhere in the vicinity, plotting, dogging her every move, waiting for another opportunity to strike.

But why? What had she done to elicit such a vindictive response? Or was it simply that she'd been prying into Brodie's death, stirring up memories that at least one person in town didn't appreciate?

Well, whoever this mysterious person was, Rhianna knew he or she wasn't watching her openly. It was a cold, evil presence, she perceived, someone lurking in the shadows, preparing to pounce the moment her guard was down.

"That's exactly the way I was staring to feel," Sam told her Saturday afternoon out on the terrace. "Like some creepy cloud was hanging over my head. I figured it was my conscience. That's why I decided I wanted out."

"I wonder if Brodie felt that way, too," Rhianna remarked.

"Beats me. I don't suppose we'll ever know, either." Grimacing, Sam popped the top on a can of 7-Up. "Time to change the subject, Rhianna," she announced flatly. "You feel like coming out to Mark's tomorrow?"

Rhianna controlled her surprise. "Mark's?" she repeated, frowning. "What for?"

"Nothing special. Joe's just rounding up a bunch of people to give him a hand packing up Reed's stuff. I gather he's going to donate some of it to the Salvation Army, and the rest I guess he'll put in storage for a while."

"Does Mark know about Joe's idea?"

"Oh, sure. He's all for it. Why wouldn't he be? It's pretty hard to heft a colonial dining-room suite into a U-Haul by yourself. Mark said he'd supply the beer and steaks for a barbecue afterward. So, what do you say, fancy britches? Can you handle working up a sweat for one day?"

Rhianna thought for a minute, then moved her shoulders. "Okay, I'll come," she agreed, rising and gathering up a bundle of laundry. "Just to prove I'm not afraid of work."

"Uh-huh." Sam's expression was smug and knowing. "Well, to change the subject again, as long as you're going to the Laundromat, give me half a sec, and I'll make the trip worthwhile for you. Oh, and on your way back, pick up *The Blob* from the Video Depot, will you? If we've gotta work on our fifties outfits tonight, we might as well feel fifties."

Feel fifties? Okay, she could do that, Rhianna supposed. It was infinitely preferable to dwelling on the murderous eyes she knew damned well were trailing her.

As she walked across the lot to her Scirocco, she heard "The Boy From New York City" wafting through the windows on the third floor of the production shop. The museum decorating committee was up there hanging posters for the Labor Day weekend party; Billie was hunched quietly on the porch of her dilapidated A-frame; Dag was sprawled on the grass beside the wax museum, soaking up his daily dose of sun rays.

And when she drove away, with her car doors securely locked, Rhianna again had the uneasy sensation of being watched.

THERE HAD TO BE a good forty people swarming around Reed's old house Sunday afternoon. Downstairs, Marion and one of the tour guides were struggling with a set of damask curtains. Several others were carrying furniture out to the U-Haul truck in the driveway. Pots and pans clanged noisily in the kitchen, and Sam had been rummaging through the front-hall closet for the past thirty minutes.

Through the windows in Brodie's bedroom, Rhianna spied Mark and Joe, both hot and perspiring, levering a baby grand piano up the ramp of the truck. Of course, Mark looked wonderful, all sweaty and dirt-stained, in his customary jeans and T-shirt. And, of course, he'd said very little to her since she'd arrived.

But Rhianna wasn't overly upset by his lack of attention. He'd sent her one blistering gaze in the driveway earlier, and that had been more than sufficient to drive her up to the second floor for a couple of hours. Maybe it was a cowardly retreat, but it was better than analyzing the surge of emotions that single look had evoked.

Turning from the window, she channeled her energy into packing up Brodie's belongings. Sam joined her just as she was finishing with his clothes.

"You do Dracula's dungeon, and I'll tackle the desk," her friend proposed, pulling open a drawer. "God, will you look at all this junk? The kid was a pack rat. A damned cute one, though." She tossed Rhianna an old family photo. "Remind you of anyone?"

Rhianna caught the framed picture. "Mark," she stated without hesitation. Then she studied the snapshot more intently. This one, unlike the head shot she'd found at Billie's, portrayed Brodie in a relaxed stance. Physically, he really had borne a striking resemblance to his cousin.

"He's come back..." she murmured thoughtfully, still studying Brodie's features.

Sam lifted her head. "What?"

Rhianna shook off the odd feeling that had suddenly assailed her. "Nothing. I was just thinking..." She paused. "Sam, if you'd seen Mark or Brodie for just a minute ten years ago, would you have had to look twice to be sure who was who?"

"I suppose so—if they'd been standing still. Brodie was a lot more of a clown than Mark. But yeah, if they'd been dressed alike, I might have gotten them mixed up for a second. Why?"

"I'm not sure. I was remembering something Billie said to me one day. Something about 'him' coming back."

"Who? Mark?"

"Or Brodie." She bit her lip musingly. "It's probably nothing."

"Only another wild hunch, huh, Sherlock?" Grinning, Sam returned to her task. "I wouldn't take anything Billie might have said to heart. She still calls me Samantha, like she did in high school. Far as I can tell, she half lives in the past. I doubt if she ever really got a good look at Mark back in those days. He wasn't exactly fond of cruising the east end."

Determinedly, Rhianna shoved the disturbing thoughts to the back of her mind. It was ludicrous. Even Billie couldn't be so deluded as to have mistaken Mark for Brodie... Could she?

Distracted by her implausible conjectures, Rhianna began carefully dismantling the miniature mock-up of Count Dracula's dungeon. A small part of her brain had to agree with Sam. Brodie had been a pack rat. In the count's mahogany coffin, she unearthed all sorts of little mementos he'd squirreled away throughout his high-school years. There was his class ring, his twelfth-grade student card, the ticket stub from a Doobie Brothers concert, his lucky rabbit's foot—and...

Rhianna's brow furrowed at the last object she extracted from the coffin. It was a bracelet—a rolled silver bracelet, identical in every way to the one on her left wrist.

Automatically, she scanned the inner rim. Sure enough, there were six numbers engraved on it: 276343.

Hastily, she shook the bracelet from her arm. The numbers were different: 627466. Something was very, very wrong here.

To her disappointment, she was given no chance to ponder the possible ramifications of her discovery. The chatty wife of one of the production shop workers came in to give her and Sam a hand, and Rhianna was forced to drop the newest bracelet deep into the pocket of her shorts.

When the room had been stripped, she left them and stepped out into the hall. Her timing couldn't have been worse. Mark chose that moment to mount the stairs, apparently en route to the bathroom.

His right wrist, she noticed instantly, was wrapped up in a red bandanna. Even so, she could see the smears of blood on his hand and forearm.

"What happened?" she questioned him, momentarily blotting out the turbulent jumble in her head.

He moved an unconcerned shoulder. "It's just a scratch. I sliced myself on one of Reed's wire skeletons."

"Do you want me to clean it for you?"

A small grin touched his lips. "Florence Nightingale and Sherlock Holmes rolled into one? Sure."

He hoisted himself onto the counter while Rhianna unwrapped the bandanna. The cloth was blood-soaked, more so than she'd first thought. The cut was deep and jagged, just this side of requiring stitches.

"I hope you're ambidextrous," Rhianna murmured as she cleansed the wound. "You aren't going to be writing much for a few days."

Mark shrugged. "I'll get Marion to review her shorthand."

He was so close and the bathroom was so confined that Rhianna was finding it difficult to breathe. The heat of Mark's body supplemented by the perspiration from a day's hard work made her feel a little light-headed. And the fact that he was staring at her with those hypnotic blue eyes of his didn't help matters, either. She longed to touch far more of him than just his arm.

Somehow, she managed to maintain her thin veneer of composure. She swabbed the cut with antiseptic, then bound his wrist with a gauze bandage. By the time she'd finished, the bathroom seemed to have compressed itself to the size of a cracker box.

Mark kept his eyes on her as she washed her hands and dried them on a thick towel, and she knew he felt the constriction taking place in here as surely as she felt it herself. She could tell by the way he looked at her, by the expression on his face and the way the muscles in his jaw tensed.

Her fingers curled around the carved towel bar behind her. When he hopped from his perch, he was only inches away from her. The loose cotton of his T-shirt couldn't disguise the supple lines of his body, and his jeans seemed to cling to him in all the right places.

Every pulse in her body throbbed as hot little streaks of fire shot through her. He smelled of sun and soap and physical exertion. And he was staring at her again, through the veil of his lashes this time. Staring at her like a cat—a hungry, roving feline whose motives could not be discerned.

With his good hand, he stroked the hair from her cheek. She felt the heat he exuded, the radiant animal magnetism, the smoldering desire.

She could have swayed close to him right then, bridged the few inches separating them, slid her arms around his neck and pressed her mouth against his. She could have— but it would have been too dangerous. And things were far too dangerous for her as it was.

Somehow, she held onto that thought, just long enough to straighten away from him. "I'd better go help Sam," she murmured in a low but relatively composed voice.

Mark made no move to stop her as she pulled open the bathroom door. He just let his hand fall back to his side and watched as she walked along the carpeted corridor to Reed's old bedroom. Then, expelling a heavy breath, he rested his forehead against the tiled wall, letting the smooth surface cool his heated skin.

FOR THE NEXT SOLID HOUR, Rhianna worked with Sam and three other people on tearing apart Reed's bedroom. She didn't speak to anyone. She couldn't, not when her mind was still thinking about Mark.

A whoop from the backyard terrace around six signaled an end to the day's labors and the beginning of the evening's festivities. The enticing aroma of scorched charcoal drifted through the upstairs windows, and breathing a relieved sigh, Rhianna trailed her co-workers to the lower level.

"Water polo," Dag shouted to her from the shallow end. "Come on, sweet thing. Let's see some skin."

Why not? she decided, tossing off her tank top and shorts, throwing them onto the grass beside the fence. It was far too hot to think straight, and her nerves were still tingling from her steamy encounter with Mark in the bathroom.

A full hour later, drenched and tired and panting, she emerged from the kidney-shaped pool to join Sam on the lawn. The strenuous exercise had done wonders to alleviate her inner tension. She could even smile at Sam's spiteful expression.

"Go away," her friend ordered, scowling at her from the shade of a sprawling oak. "You look like you belong on the Riviera. How can anyone get such a nice tan in such a short time? It's revolting."

"It's in the genes," Rhianna retorted, dropping to the grass and squeezing the water from her long hair. "My mother's half Italian."

"Your mother should be shot." Sourly, Sam regarded her own fair skin. Fifteen minutes of waning sun had brought out a light dusting of the freckles she'd despised since childhood.

Looking at Sam in her bathing suit cover-up reminded Rhianna sharply of her own clothes. She leaped to her feet.

In all the confusion, she had managed to forget about the bracelet she had unearthed in Brodie's bedroom. And that was foolish on her part, since the discovery of it could really only mean one thing. The bracelet in Brodie's room had to have belonged to Brodie; therefore, the one she'd been wearing for the past three weeks must belong to someone else.

A frightened tremor tore through her as her mind continued to move forward. She'd found a box of throat lozenges and a silver bracelet next to Brodie's body, and of course, in thinking that the bracelet was Brodie's, she'd assumed that the box of lozenges was her main clue. But what if it wasn't a clue at all? What if the bracelet she'd prised from the rubble had been on the murderer's wrist the night that Brodie had been killed? What if the murderer knew it had been lost that night?

Shivering violently now, Rhianna crossed the grass to the fence and picked up her shorts. But even before she could check the pockets, her eyes strayed to the gate—the gate that was ajar, open just enough for her to see into the nearby hedgerow. And there among the lush green fronds, she spied a scrawny cowering form. Billie Noble was staring straight at her, watching as Rhianna's hand slid into four empty pockets. Smiling obscurely as Rhianna made the inevitable discovery.

Brodie's bracelet was gone!

IT WAS CLOSE TO DAWN when the murderer finally stopped pacing. Damn that girl to hell for her trickery! She had no right being so clever, no business being so deceitful.

A rolled silver bracelet bounced off the nearest wall. It was the wrong bracelet. The little bitch had scored her final victory. Drawing a deep breath, the murderer struggled to regain control. Then a sudden crafty smile flitted across cruel lips.

Spiders and snakes, the murderer thought on a black note of amusement. Yes, that was it, spiders and snakes. Both were deadly, and either method would work. And that was the most important thing of all. For one way or another, Rhiannan Curtis had to die. One way or another, she *would* die. Just as Brodie had died... Only not quite so quickly. Not quite so painlessly...

Chapter Eleven

"Look, if I agree to hunt up my bracelet, will you agree to come to a movie tonight? I've got free passes." Sam offered the exchange as she and Rhianna finished their last tours for the day.

It was early Thursday evening, hot and pouring rain outside. Even in the climate-controlled wax museum, the air felt stuffy and damp, heavy with humidity. Rhianna pushed back the sleeves of her black gown and regarded her friend evenly. "What's playing?"

"*Murder in the Wax Museum*," Sam replied, grimacing. "A little macabre, considering what's been going on around here, but at least the script's different. I think the victims get dipped in wax rather than bricked up behind a storeroom wall. Come on, Sherlock," she cajoled. "It'll be better than sitting around the apartment all night knowing that Billie's right across Blueberry Road dreaming up ghostly visitations from her dear departed Mama."

"True," Rhianna conceded, albeit dubiously. "I suppose it wouldn't hurt to get away from here for a while."

Sam halted by the witches of New England exhibit, digging deep into the pocket of her Lily Munster shroud. "In that case, Ms Holmes, here you go: one ancient sil-

ver bracelet. My special present from Billie. Now give me
a hint. Why the sudden interest in jewelry?''

Rhianna's eyes skimmed the inside of the band. There
were eight numbers engraved on it. Eight numbers; eight
letters in Sam's name. Well, for what it was worth, her
theory that the numbers translated to letters seemed to be
holding up. And earlier that day, Sam had confided that
each of Billie's recruits had received one of the bracelets.
''Actually,'' she said, pointing to the inside rim, ''I'm
more interested in the engraving than in the bracelet itself. Do you know what the numbers mean?''

''Uh-uh. Billie never told us. All I know is she gave
similar bracelets to everyone in her family years before
she gave us ours. She said they were symbolic, that they
joined us—you know, united us for a common cause.''

''The common cause being revenge?''

''Yeah, I guess so.'' Sam shrugged. ''Hey, no one ever
said Billie was all there to start with. I mean, let's face it,
Rhianna, the woman collects telephones, for Christ's
sake. Coins, stamps, records, even campaign buttons or
stuffed animals I could understand. But telephones? I
think she's been out to lunch for a long time, way before
the doc started her on pills to calm her down.''

''Pills . . .'' Rhianna repeated. ''What kind of pills?''

''Downers, mostly, I think. Marion would probably
know—Marion?'' Sam hailed the older woman, who was
just letting herself out of the custodian's office. ''What
kind of medication is Billie on?''

Marion tapped out a Virginia Slims but didn't light it.
Smoking was strictly prohibited in the museum. ''I'm
afraid I'm not really sure, dear,'' she replied, then emit-
ted an aggrieved sigh. ''I only hope that, whatever they
are, they'll stop her from having so many wild fantasies.
The poor thing has such a vivid imagination.'' A wry

smile crossed her mouth. "She's convinced that you, Rhianna, are Linda Darnell. She envies you having worked with Tyrone Power."

Rhianna digested that tidbit of information. It wasn't the worst delusion Billie could have had, but it raised a very intriguing possibility—one she'd only touched on briefly last Sunday.

If the woman was really as crazy as everyone seemed to think, then drugged on top of it, she might very well have seen Brodie when she'd looked at Mark. Stranger things had been known to happen. Certainly, that would help to explain why she had torched the north wing, what she had meant when she'd said that he had gone away and then come back.

Brodie had died—he'd gone away. To Billie's confused mind, he might have appeared to return from the grave—a ghost seeking revenge on whoever had killed him.

But if Billie had burned the shop to make Brodie's ghost go away again, that had to mean she'd known where his body was hidden, didn't it? And if she'd known, it stood to reason she'd put the body there in the first place.

Something about that theory, however, didn't feel right to Rhianna. Mark had been in Bremerhaven for two months before Billie had up and decided to set the building on fire. Why had she waited so long? Why hadn't she done it when he'd first arrived?

In the background, she heard Sam and Marion chatting about the Gothic Theater, where *Murder in the Wax Museum* was playing, but she didn't pay much attention to the conversation. She was too busy trying to solve her own wax museum murder. And she had a feeling she was getting very close to the solution.

"I hear the ushers and concession workers dress up much as our guides do," Marion remarked, and Rhianna forced her mind back to the present. "You girls will have a good time. I only wish I could join you."

"Why don't you?" Rhianna asked her.

"That's very sweet of you, dear." Marion smiled. "But I'm afraid I'll have to stay with Billie tonight. She doesn't care for thunder, and the weatherman's forecasting quite a storm. I've just got time to clean up a few things on my desk, then it's off to battle I go. Have fun, you two. Do make sure your dresses are ready for the party Saturday night."

"Fifties cool." Sam grinned, gathering up her tattered hem. "Come on, fancy britches; let's you and me blow this joint and go check out the Gothic's ghouls. I hear a couple of them aren't bad at all underneath their costumes and masks."

Unless Mark happened to be moonlighting as a Gothic Theater usher, Rhianna wasn't especially interested in delving beyond any costumed facades. A large part of her was greatly relieved by the way the evidence seemed to be stacking itself up against Billie. But there was still that box of throat lozenges to account for, plus the fact that Mark's name—Markus—just happened to have six letters in it.

Nonetheless, her stubborn instincts insisted, there had to be a logical explanation for the presence of the lozenges next to Brodie's body. And as for Mark's name having six letters—well, he wasn't the only person guilty of that. Billie had a six-letter name and so did Joe, or rather Joseph. And both of them had taken part in the east-end robberies.

The apartment was stifling when Rhianna and Sam reached it. The magpie cawed once to announce seven-thirty. Crossing to her room, Rhianna shed her gown and donned a pair of cotton pants, a white camp shirt and her sneakers. She was strapping on her watch when she heard the phone ring. Two minutes later, Sam appeared in the doorway.

"We're gonna have company at the movies," she said, not bothering to hide her satisfied smile.

Rhianna almost hated to ask the question that sprang to her lips. She forced it out anyway. "Who?"

"Mark and Logan... And don't yell, it wasn't my idea," she added, tugging on her spiked hair. Then she chuckled. "I don't think you really want to yell, though, do you? Let's face it, Mark's a sexy man. You're only worried that you might fall for him, aren't you?"

Rhianna made a pretense of lacing up her sneakers. "I have no intention of falling for him," she stated in a re- markably bland voice.

"So, you don't mind that he's coming to the show?"

"No."

"Liar," Sam accused, but fortunately she didn't be- labor the point. She simply turned and marched back to her own room, leaving Rhianna to shove the murderer's silver bracelet into her purse.

As an afterthought, she slid Sam's onto her wrist and added her .45 automatic to the collection of makeup, credit cards and perfume in her shoulder bag.

No sense taking chances, her brain cautioned her. If the killer was watching—and she could still feel an evil presence somewhere close by—she'd be wise to at least try to cloud the issue with yet another red-herring bracelet.

They met Mark and Logan in the lobby of the Gothic Theater. Rain was still bouncing off the pavement, and an already murky, premature darkness had begun to spread over the town.

In black pants and a pale yellow cavalry shirt, Mark looked incredibly good. The ends of his blond hair were curling a bit from the high humidity, but despite the oppressive heat he was wearing a black leather jacket and boots.

Logan paused only long enough to greet her before hauling Sam into the jam-packed main seating area. "Front row." Rhianna heard him grunt at the vampire usher while Mark lounged against a poster-covered wall and stared at her through enigmatic eyes.

"Balcony or main floor?" he inquired, once the other two had vanished into the mobile throng.

Her gaze traveled up the carpeted stairs. The closed sign was in the process of being taken down. It would be a lot less crowded upstairs. "Balcony," she said at last.

A slow smile tugged at the corners of Mark's lips, but he made no comment, just followed her to the wide staircase. "Make-out city," he drawled when they'd reached the rows of double seats. "You've never been up here before, have you?"

"Of course I have," she lied, tempted to bolt back to the lobby. Defiantly, she held her ground.

She had to talk to Mark. Aside from a group of four giggling teenage girls and a man wearing an Indiana Jones hat and munching on a bag of Fritos, there was no one up here.

She sat down beside him and watched as he propped his booted feet up on the balcony ledge. It was next to impossible to concentrate with his thigh grazing hers and the warm, clean scent of him washing over her. He really was a sexy man, frighteningly sexy. She'd come to accept the fact that she'd never be able to think straight when she was with him.

Faking an insouciance she definitely didn't feel, Rhianna glanced at his entrancing profile. "Why have you been avoiding me?" she asked him bluntly, although she had no idea why. She hadn't planned on asking that particular question.

His grin was laconic, not in any way revealing. "Is that what you think I've been doing?" he returned, easily. "Avoiding you?"

"It's true, isn't it?"

"Nope."

"Then why haven't you been around the museum for the past days?"

"Because I've been busy."

She could believe that, even if it was a little bruising to her ego. She still thought he'd been avoiding her, though—and not necessarily because of the turbulent attraction between them.

A werewolf usher escorted a young twosome past them to the rear of the balcony. Over the theater's speaker system, "The Monster Mash" set the mood for the upcoming feature. The teenage girls erupted into a fresh round of giggles, and suddenly Rhianna didn't want to skirt the subject anymore.

"You think I still consider you a suspect, don't you, Mark," she demanded in a voice kept deliberately low.

He sent her a wry sideways glance. "Now why would I think that?"

Rhianna sighed. "Look, Mark," she began. "Whatever you do or don't think, I know you didn't kill Brodie—even if your full name does have six letters in it."

"My what?" He stared at her openly now. "You're starting to sound like Billie. What does my name have to do with anything?"

She hesitated for a second. This was not the best place to launch into a detailed account of her bracelet theory, or how she'd chanced upon it in the first place. But then again, her brain argued, perhaps here was as good a place as any to get everything out in the open. It wouldn't prove much, since she still couldn't decipher the bracelets' coded inscriptions, but it might go a long way toward clearing the air between her and Mark.

Briefly, she explained about the discovery she'd made in the north-wing cellar. She left out the part about the throat lozenges and concentrated instead on the bracelet.

When she'd finished her story, Mark eyed her consideringly, maybe a trifle irritably. "You think you found the murderer's bracelet next to Brodie's body, and you've been parading around with it on your arm all this time?" His gaze hardened. "What the hell kind of logic is that? It's no wonder the killer's after you."

Now he was angry. She could see the telltale glimmer of fury in the depths of his ice-blue eyes.

"If I'd known it was the murderer's bracelet, I would hardly have taken it with me to the junction pond," she retorted. "And if you're going to get mad, Mark, I'm not going to tell you the rest."

"Jesus." He swore violently under his breath. "There's more?"

She nodded. "To start with, I originally thought the bracelet was Brodie's. He wore one exactly like it all through his senior year. It never occurred to me, though, that the murderer might have owned a similar bracelet, or that there was any connection between it and the east-end robberies."

Mark clamped down on the sudden urge he had to reach out and shake her. He would only have wound up holding her instead, and that was something he wasn't prepared to deal with right now. First and foremost, he wanted Rhianna safe. She'd become tremendously important to him, despite his best efforts to maintain his distance from her. He couldn't and wouldn't lose her to a deranged murderer.

He turned brooding eyes to the wide screen, which was now beginning to crackle. The lights had been dimmed, and a slow hush had descended over the crowded theater. The werewolf usher moved silently past them, waving his flashlight from side to side. In his peripheral vision, Mark saw Rhianna lean back in her seat.

If her theory was right, the bracelet might very well be the key to Brodie's murder. Possessing such a key, however, automatically made her a target, and for a moment Mark considered demanding that she hand it over to him for safekeeping. Then he squelched the idea. She wasn't likely to give it up, and he couldn't very well force the issue.

He shifted uncomfortably in his seat. A cool draft of air wafted down from the air-conditioning vent over his head, chilling his skin but unfortunately not his blood. His lower limbs were pulsing warmly, and there wasn't a damned thing he could do about it.

He shifted position again. Except for the black-and-white figures on the screen, there was very little activity in the large theater. The crowd had settled down. Now might be a good time to disappear to the washroom, to try to pound some sense into his own head. It wouldn't do much good, but at least it would get him away from her for a few minutes. Rhianna should be safe enough here while he was gone.

"I'll be back in a second," he murmured, standing and squeezing past her. She said nothing, and he bounded down the wide steps.

Just outside the double door, he noticed one of the werewolf ushers standing next to a sand-filled ashtray, head bent down as he flexed his furry fingers. Jamming his hands into the pockets of his jacket, Mark strode to the men's room and banged his way inside. If this was any indication of the way the night was going to go, he'd probably do well to find Logan and Sam and haul them up to the balcony. On the other hand, he could always drag Rhianna out of the balcony instead and take her home with him. And not simply in an effort to ensure her safety.

A bittersweet smile crossed his lips as the washroom door swished shut behind him.

NOT FIVE SECONDS after Mark left his seat, all four of the teenage girls streaked out behind him, giggling and casting Rhianna covert glances as they left. She smiled in the wake of their Chloe perfume, snapping gum, purpled lips and oversize T-shirts. They were cute and bubbly, and they reminded her of another time in her life—the first time she'd seen Mark.

He'd been straddling a motorcycle down on Rowe Street in the heart of the west end. Beautiful, blond Mark with his wintry eyes, his Bohemian dreadlocks and oddly contrasting black leather jacket. God, that all seemed so long ago now...

Out of the blue, a sudden chill skidded along Rhianna's spine. The feeling of being watched was back. And it was incredibly strong.

She looked around at the nearly deserted balcony. The Frito muncher was dozing under his Indiana Jones hat, and the twosome in the corner seemed to have vanished into thin air. There was no one else up here—and she felt somehow there should have been. The main floor was packed. Why hadn't some of that mob dispersed to the upper level?

She saw the werewolf usher stroll past her. Out of deference to the moviegoers, his flashlight was doused. In the flickering light radiating from the large screen, his white fangs gleamed with a malevolence that unnerved her a little.

She hunched deeper into her seat. She couldn't rid herself of the horrible feeling that someone up here was staring at her. Maybe that was due in part to the eerie movie. Still, she couldn't dispel the sense of pervading evil that suddenly overwhelmed her.

It was more than just the movie, she realized, involuntarily clenching her fists. It had to be. There was someone up here. Someone evil. Someone who knew she was alone.

Behind and to the right of her in the carpeted aisle, she caught a glimpse of the werewolf usher. He seemed to be hesitating, staring at her through ferocious, dark eyes.

Her entire body broke out in a cold, clammy sweat. He was an usher, she told herself firmly. This was a theater, for God's sake. No one would dare attack her in such a public place. Besides, Mark would be back any minute now—wouldn't he?

A terrified scream erupted over the speaker system, and for a split second, Rhianna glanced at the shadow-filled screen. It was a mistake, and she knew it the instant she lost sight of the werewolf. He was behind her before she could twist her head around... And then she felt an icy cold cord wrapping itself around her neck.

"The bracelet," a terse, guttural voice growled in her ear. "Give it to me." The cord bit viciously into her throat, cutting off her air supply. "Give it to me, Rhianna. Now!"

Somehow, she managed to wedge her fingers beneath the coated wire. But she didn't have the strength to snap it, and the pressure increased.

Contrary to popular belief, her life failed to flash before her eyes. She was being choked to death and all she could see was blotchy darkness.

"Give it to me," the werewolf rasped in a voice too coarse to be identified.

A hairy hand reached around in front of her. To her horror, something was dropped into her lap. Dropped out of a brown vial.

Still maintaining a strangling hold, that same hairy hand forced her head forward.

And she saw it in the snatches of light from the movie screen. She saw black and a single spot of red. Crawling on her leg, over her thigh. Crawling on eight spindly legs.

Dragging in a ragged half breath, Rhianna gave a mighty tug on the cord. It gave just enough for her to fill her lungs. Then in sheer desperation, she reached behind her and twined her fingers in the werewolf's bristly hair. One jerk and the mask was ripped free. She used it to sweep the horrible black and red spider from her leg.

In the same instant, she was miraculously set free. Through a spotty haze she spied two of the teenage girls on the stairs, heard one of them proclaim loudly that the balcony was indeed open.

"I told you," the girl announced disdainfully. "That sign's a lot of bull. Whoa! What's going on up... Hey, watch it, buddy!" This as the werewolf, head dipped low, eyes averted, darted past the teenager, jostling her arm.

Gasping for breath, Rhianna scrambled to her feet. A wave of blackness swirled around her, and she had to brace herself on the balcony wall to keep from falling to her knees.

"What's going on?" the girl demanded, a trifle edgily. "This is fully weird, you know."

Rhianna swallowed, pushing herself upright. Her legs still felt treacherously weak, but she couldn't just stand here all night. For one thing, there was a black widow crawling around on the floor somewhere. For another, there was a murderous werewolf on the loose.

She almost screamed when she saw someone bound up the stairs. But this person wasn't wearing a werewolf's costume and he didn't have eight legs. Her entire body went limp. But only for a second. Then Mark was holding her, comforting her, and her forehead was pressed against his shoulder. And she felt safe and calm and secure in the warmth of his arms.

The ends of his hair skimmed her temple as he pulled her closer. "What happened, Rhianna?" he asked in a low voice.

She lifted her head to confront his steady gaze. "Someone tried to strangle me." To her own ears, her voice sounded toneless and dull. In the background, the film was still rolling forward. Eerie music caused a shaft of remembered terror to rip through her.

Mark must have picked up on it, for his fingers tightened around her upper arms. "Did you see who it was?" he grated, and Rhianna had no idea what he was thinking.

Her eyes lowered. "It was a werewolf," she told him.

He frowned. "A what?"

"A werewolf," she repeated, then sighed. "Look, I know this sounds ridiculous, but someone dressed up like a werewolf tried to strangle me.'' Suddenly, another memory assailed her. Her heart began to slam against her ribs, and she broke free of Mark's comforting grip, gasping. ''It dropped a spider on my leg, Mark. A black widow spider. I . . . it must still be up here.''

''A black widow spider!'' This from the stunned teenage girl who'd been devouring Mark with her eyes. ''For real?'' She started backing away. ''Did you kill it?''

Rhianna shook her head, battling down the urge to run for the stairs. She tugged on Mark's hand. ''We have to tell someone,'' she declared staunchly.

''Yeah, I guess so.''

His distracted expression puzzled her, but she wasn't prepared to stop and analyze it. Not with a venomous spider waiting in the wings to spring on her.

And it would jump on her, too, she thought on a satirical note of humor. The damned thing was probably drawn to fear like a magnet.

Mark picked up the discarded mask and handed it to her, along with her shoulder bag. Then he found the sleek length of cord, which had been wrapped around her neck, and shoved it into his jacket pocket.

''Get the girls out of here,'' he instructed her quietly. ''Take them to the lobby and try to keep them quiet. I'll talk to the manager.''

''But what about the werewolf?'' Rhianna protested, shaking the hairy mask for good measure. ''Shouldn't we go after it?''

Mark's lips thinned. ''Your werewolf's long gone by now. We wouldn't have a chance in hell of catching . . . it.''

Although she noticed a slight pause, Rhianna didn't bother to question him about it. Unlike her, he probably wanted to give the murderer a definite gender. For whatever reason, she couldn't quite bring herself to do that. The guttural threats could have been issued by a member of either sex. And the furry costume had very nicely covered up any distinguishing characteristics.

It required little effort on her part to shepherd the two young girls down to the lobby. Their friends were just emerging from the washroom when they got there. While the more vocal of the pair launched into an embellished version of the balcony scene she'd half witnessed, Rhianna glanced over her shoulder. She saw Mark standing outside the men's room talking to the theater manager. Then, she noticed the placard on his right. It had been reversed. The balcony, it said, was closed.

THE MURDERER DROVE the aging car carefully through the pouring rain. Taut fingers gripped the vinyl steering wheel. Agitation was evident in the strained features of the driver.

Spiders and snakes... Another failure. More blind luck for Rhianna Curtis.

But that luck couldn't continue forever. Not forever, it couldn't. Sooner or later it would run out. And when it did, her death would follow. Her slow, lingering death would follow...

Chapter Twelve

"Brandy?" With the phone pressed between his shoulder and ear, Mark held a glass of dark red liquid out to Rhianna. He turned his attention back to the receiver almost immediately. "Let me know if they turn up anything, Joe," he said, tossing off his jacket. "Yeah, I'm at Reed's. Rhianna's here, and Sam's with Logan. I don't want either of them in the apartment tonight."

Rhianna sipped the hand-warmed blackberry brandy. It burned pleasantly down her throat, numbing any residual aftershocks in her system. Now, there were only the bruises on her neck to remind her of what had happened, and they were nothing considering what might have been.

After speaking with the theater manager, Mark had urged Rhianna firmly out to his Corvette. She didn't know whether the black widow had been captured or not, and she could only guess where the murderer might be right now. But then, she didn't particularly want to delve into that at the moment.

The house had a closed-up feel to it, she mused, pushing the entire incident to the back of her mind. Tossing her hair over one shoulder to combat the heavy heat, she took her brandy and wandered into the living room. With the exception of a large ghetto blaster, a stack of cassette tapes and a pile of hardcover books, the room was empty. Her feet made no sound in the plush cream carpet as she crossed to the bay window.

The view of the town was spectacular at night. She could pick out the spire on the Gothic Theater and the angled drive-in movie screen in the distance. A myriad silver and gold lights winked upward, reassuring her that not everything in Bremerhaven centered around murder. Life, it appeared, went on. She only hoped the same would be true of her life.

She carried the ghetto blaster over to the window seat and began rummaging through the tapes. She didn't feel like listening to contemporary rock or anything mean-ingful. She wanted to feel the music. A soul sound, per-haps. Maybe the Supremes, or better yet, Sam Cooke.

She slipped a cassette into the machine and switched it on. The rock classic brought back memories of hot sum-mer fun and easy times. Of schoolbooks and weekends and the aging jukebox at the Burger Palace on Eighth Street.

Rhianna took another sip of brandy. Sam Cooke was singing about the sounds of men working away on a chain gang. Outside, the rain continued to fall, and well in the background, a mutinous peal of thunder rolled through the darkened night sky.

She was glad Mark had brought her here, relieved, too, that Sam wouldn't be staying alone in the apartment. The more she reenacted the scene in the theater balcony, the more convinced she became that her attacker had been a woman. Billie Noble? Well, perhaps, but she hadn't been able to tell whether or not the disguised figure had been hobbling. It *had* been hunched over, though. And it had been remarkably fast on its feet.

Billie as Mama Noble, then? It seemed more and more likely. Sam had told her that Billie had given her mother one of the silver bracelets. No doubt she'd also owned one herself. Which might very well mean that either Billie's or Mama's name was spelled out numerically on the inside.

Damn! She swore impatiently. What was the key to the code? What did the numbers mean?

A tiny sound from the doorway had Rhianna averting her head. Mark had apparently finished talking to Joe. He brought the bottle of blackberry brandy and a plate of purple grapes over to the window seat.

She thought he'd never looked better than he did at that moment. The pale yellow cavalry shirt made his blond hair resemble spun gold. Bavarian gold. Prince Charming with a twist, she reflected wistfully—a rough edge that only seemed to heighten his dangerous appeal.

"You okay?" Mark asked her, sitting down on the cushion and placing the grapes between them.

Rhianna nodded. "I'm fine. Did they find the spider?"

"Not yet. They're looking, but it could take a while." He lifted his legs to rest his forearms on his knees. Consideringly, he swirled the contents of his brandy snifter. "The killer tried to strangle you with a long piece of telephone cord," he revealed slowly. "Did you know that?"

"Telephone cord?" she repeated. "Are you sure?"

"Positive."

"Billie Noble collects telephones," she murmured, vaguely.

"So I've heard." Mark's eyes hardened. "She also starts fires."

And her name had six letters in it. Rhianna wished she could feel a bit better about all of this. The evidence was pointing squarely at the woman. Certainly, she'd had sufficient motive to murder Brodie. And yet, she'd just never seemed like an aggressive woman. It was true, she was mentally unstable, but murder struck Rhianna as completely out of character for the dominated ex-librarian. But what about Marcie? she wondered. What about Billie's beloved Mama?

"Let it go for tonight, Rhianna," he advised her softly. "You've been through enough."

Not as much as Brodie, she thought cheerlessly. However, he was right. She'd be as well to give her curious mind a rest.

It wouldn't be hard to do, not with Sam Cooke crooning about a wonderful world and lightning bolts splitting the angry heavens. Not with Mark sitting directly across from her on the window seat, staring at her through veiled eyes. Still, there were questions she had to ask, answers she needed to hear.

"You knew Joe was involved in the east-end robberies, didn't you?" she queried point-blank, and Mark made no attempt to evade her.

A humorless smile quirked the corners of his mouth. "Yeah, I knew. And I ignored it."

"How could you do that?"

"Because that's the way it is in the west end. You mind your own business and stay out of everyone else's. Joe did what he did. I wasn't in any position to pass judgment on him."

Rhianna's stare was slightly accusing, although probably not for the right reasons. "That's what you two were talking about out at the carnival, isn't it? You knew all about the robberies and the others who were mixed up in them.''

''Yes, I knew.'' He arched an indolent brow. ''Does that make me an accessory after the fact, Sherlock?''

She ignored his sarcasm. ''Who's the she you felt couldn't be trusted?''

''Billie.''

''Billie!'' Rhianna echoed, startled. Somehow, she hadn't expected that. ''I thought—oh, never mind.''

Mark regarded her dryly. ''You shouldn't eavesdrop, angel,'' he said mildly. ''You're bound to screw up the facts.''

''You knew I was listening?''

''Not until just now, no. But it doesn't really surprise me to find out that you were.'' He popped a grape into his mouth. ''Billie's been a problem right from the moment Brodie's body was discovered. Joe was afraid she might start babbling to the wrong people about the robberies.''

''You mean the police?''

He shrugged. ''There are a few good cops on the Bremerhaven force. If they were to find out about Joe's past, he could lose his job.''

''Then you don't think he killed Brodie.''

''I wouldn't put him at the top of the suspect list, no.''

''And you've been trying to help him.'' Rhianna lifted her head. ''You really do care about someone other than yourself, don't you, Mark?''

For an answer, Mark reached out and took her by the wrist. He didn't appear angry or even slightly annoyed by her candor. In fact, she wasn't sure he was really listening to her at all at this point. She had a feeling mere words didn't have much of an effect on him. He had his own way of thinking; he wasn't likely to change his whole point of view simply to counteract her blunt observations.

"You could be right about that," he murmured, surprising her a little. But then he was pulling her forward resolutely on the padded seat, tilting her head back with his forefinger, staring at her so intently that Rhianna's breath caught in her throat.

"I think it's time we both stopped playing games, don't you, Rhianna?" he asked her gently.

Biting her lip, she offered him a reluctant nod. It was time for that. Way past time, in fact. She just wasn't sure where to begin.

He made it a little easier for her when he queried, "Did you think the bracelet was mine? Is that why you were suspicious of me?"

"No, that wasn't why." Sliding from the window seat, she walked over to the hearth. It was easier to think when she was away from him. "The bracelet wasn't the only thing I found down in the cellar, Mark. I also found a box of throat lozenges."

She glanced over her shoulder to see what reaction, if any, her confession might elicit. Mark's only response, however, was to smile that slow, wry smile of his.

He swallowed the last of his blackberry brandy, then came to join her by the empty stone fireplace. "So you found a box of throat lozenges," he drawled. "And you figured they had to be mine."

She lifted her chin a fraction. "Well, it was a logical enough conclusion, wasn't it? You told me you had a cold. And as far as I'm aware, Brodie was perfectly healthy."

Mark grinned. "I'm sure he was."

"Well—there you go, then. You can't blame me for jumping to conclusions. I hardly knew you ten years ago.

And I certainly didn't know you any better the night I found Brodie's body.''

"No, you didn't," he agreed resting his shoulder on the stones and lifting a hand to stroke the hair from her cheek. "So what made you change your mind?"

She shrugged. "Little things, mostly."

"Such as?"

"Oh, I don't know, Mark. Just little things. Things you said—and did. No matter how I tried, I couldn't make myself believe that you would have murdered your cousin."

His fingers trailed a path along her throat, down to the line of her collarbone. "So you just explained the lozenges away, huh?"

"Something like that," she murmured.

Amusement danced in his eyes. "Ah, Rhianna, you're a gift from the gods. No one but you would have kept on digging."

"I'm still digging, Mark," she reminded him, although it was difficult to concentrate on an investigation when all she really wanted to do was feel his mouth on hers. "The murderer hasn't been caught yet."

"No, but just to ease your mind, I'll tell you now that those throat lozenges probably were mine. Brodie dumped a can of dye all over both of us late that afternoon. He said he didn't have time to go home and change, so I let him borrow a pair of my jeans. The box must have been in the pocket."

"Now I wonder why I didn't think of that explanation?" she said, unable to resist a smile.

"I wonder," he murmured. And then he was urging her into his arms, leading her away from the hearth and into the center of the room.

Outside, the thunder rebounded through the pitch-black sky. Inside, Sam Cooke continued to croon his classic melodies. Crooning while Rhianna and Mark moved to the soulful beat.

She lifted her eyes to look up at him, meeting his eyes made dark by the muted light filtering in through the windows. She'd made her choice and so, it seemed, had he. Slowly, exquisitely slowly, he inclined his head to seek out and cover her mouth with his. His tongue rimmed her lips expertly, parting them, leaving her in no doubt as to his sexual prowess.

A sweet, consuming flame of desire began to spread outward from low in her abdomen, and willingly, she gave herself up to pure sensation. If there were to be repercussions, she would deal with them later. For now, all she wanted was to touch Mark, to explore him, to savor this longed-for moment and let emotion take over from logic.

The air in the empty room was hot and wet, tinged with the scent of dampness and dense summer vegetation. Rain pelted against the lead-paned window, and the humidity seemed to rise another ten percentage points. Already, Rhianna could feel the blood rushing through her veins, urging her to return his kiss and then some.

Her fingers skimmed over the taut, smooth muscles of his shoulders and back beneath the thin material of his cavalry shirt. He was so sleek and warm, so persuasive. His lips strayed provocatively to the corners of her mouth, to her jaw and down her throat to the faint bruise near the base.

He lifted his head to survey the slight discoloration left by the telephone cord, and his eyes clouded. Then, gently, he pressed his lips to her throat, running his tongue over the soft, reddened skin.

Lightning sizzled through the roiling clouds, illuminating briefly the tenderness in his eyes. An enigmatic smile curved his lips and Rhianna's lashes lowered as his fingers worked to unfasten the buttons of her camp shirt.

A slow flush rose beneath her skin, then she gasped as he pushed the silky material of her bra aside and ran his thumb lightly over her hardened nipples. This was what she wanted. To feel and enjoy and absorb all that she could of Mark's touch—of Mark himself.

Still smiling ever so slightly, he tugged her from the narrow seat, chuckling a little when she landed on top of him on the deep pile carpet.

It was an erotic position, and Rhianna made no attempt to shift her weight from his lower body. Her knees were wrapped suggestively around his hips. All she had to do was lower herself to meet him.

Pressing her palms to his shoulders, she let her shirt fall forward. Only a hint of bare cleavage and tanned skin remained visible to his smoky blue eyes. She felt his hands on her waist, sliding up over her rib cage. And she worked eagerly at the buttons of his shirt, pulling the tail from the waistband of his pants, quivering with anticipation when he suddenly swept her down beside him and captured her mouth in a hungry kiss.

His tongue delved deeply beyond her lips, coaxing, demanding. Thunder crashed outside and the rain pounded like a steady drumbeat against the roof.

The raw passion that surged and swelled inside him astounded Mark. This feeling went far beyond physical desire. He didn't just want Rhianna's body; he wanted all of her—and not for only one night.

Quite suddenly, he felt vulnerable, hot-blooded and intense, like a groping teen in danger of allowing his hormones to take over. But he didn't want that to happen. He wouldn't let it happen. He would make love to her slowly, deliciously, completely, and to hell with the consequences.

He shuddered deeply as her hands closed around him and the pounding of his blood intensified. Groaning inwardly, he scrunched his eyes closed. She couldn't possibly have understood the emotions that were tearing at him, ripping him to pieces, destroying the wall of resistance he'd erected so rebelliously in his youth. He wasn't sure he understood it himself.

It was time to let go, he thought hazily. He'd long ago decided that Rhianna was the one person who was worth the risk. And God only knew, he wanted her to be that person. Someone he could give to and trust and love.

He stared in fascination at the slender lines of her body, drank in the beauty of her firm breasts and narrow waist and the creamy gold texture of her skin. God, but she was lovely, strong yet so delicate and fine-boned. She enchanted him totally, challenged him in ways he had never thought he would be challenged. Physically, mentally, emotionally. It was all he could do to keep from tearing off the rest of her clothes and jumping on top of her.

With a tenderness he had thought long dead, Mark unzipped her pants and drew them down over her hips and legs. Her silky bikinis followed, and he swallowed hard as his heated gaze traveled the length of her beautiful body.

Clenching his teeth, he allowed her to help him shed his own clothes. Another shudder enveloped him, and he lowered his mouth to one hardened nipple, grazing her slowly with his tongue, absorbing the taste of her, the exotic scent.

This wasn't something that would go away in a frenzied moment of release and fulfillment. His rigid control was gone. He had nothing left inside to bolster it—nothing except a longing he could no longer hold in check.

Streaks of lightning tore through the night sky, an electric supplement to the fever building between them. Rain splashed against the windows and thunder shook the very foundations of the old house. Sam Cooke went into repeat, and the beat of "Chain Gang" provided a soothing background rhythm for the rising tempo of their lovemaking.

Rhianna felt Mark's mouth, hot and moist, on hers. His fingers roamed to her inner thigh, caressing her, entering her, filling her with a thousand errant thoughts. She urged him on, arching against him as wave after wave of shimmering pleasure washed through her.

His body was slick with perspiration. The ends of his hair skimmed her breasts while his mouth continued to tease her sensitive flesh. His tongue rasped over her abdomen and lower, causing her to moan deep in her throat.

She ran her fingers through his hair, inhaling the clean, male scent of him, allowing her most primitive instincts to govern her responses. An earthy magic coursed through her, like a tinder fire of pure heat and passion. She wanted him so badly that she actually hurt inside. When he shifted position to raise himself over her, she saw the full extent of his desire and her heart jolted fiercely against her ribs.

For a moment he hesitated, his beautiful, lean body poised above hers, his eyes dark and smoldering, his features taut and strained. With his thumb, he brushed her damp lower lip and a rueful smile touched the corners of his mouth.

"Moment of truth," he murmured, and Rhianna didn't know if he was talking to her or to himself.

Her lip trembled where he touched it. Then, conscious thought dissolved into the rain-washed darkness as Mark caressed her once again, feeding her desire, replenishing it. She slid her hands across his shoulders, down his hair-roughened chest to the flat plane of his stomach. Blood pounded in his thighs as her fingers tightened around him. She felt him shift position again, lifting her, holding her... And then he was inside her.

Her breath caught painfully in her chest and her nails bit hard into the bunched muscles of his buttocks. Gasping his name, Rhianna wound her legs around him, pulling him closer still, deeper and deeper inside her. So deep, she thought she would never again feel as fulfilled.

A sigh of longing escaped her as she arched her body to meet his. She heard the low moan that accompanied his rhythmic thrusts, felt the slick film of perspiration on his skin, on her own, and the burning spasms of release as the moment and the night exploded around them.

Rhianna could have sworn that a sensual netherworld reached out to grab her. Nothing seemed real except Mark's presence inside her and the awesome forces of nature that allowed for such a total shattering of conscious thought. All the magic that existed flowed through her. Giving, taking, bursting into a shimmering cloud of white lightning and ecstasy.

They collapsed together on the carpet in a wonderfully painful tangle of heat and limbs and exhaustion. The erratic beat of his heart was a match for hers. And in the background, the music played on...

Rhianna couldn't move, so stunned was she by the strength of their lovemaking. She couldn't think; she didn't want to. She simply wanted to relish the vaporous tendrils of delight, to hold them for as long as possible, to savor the feel of Mark's warm, male body and the hair that trailed like damp silk along her collarbone.

But somewhere, deep in her heart, she realized a new and sinking fear, one that had been with her for days now, one she'd managed to deny until just this minute. It couldn't be denied any longer. It wasn't a feeling she could fight or ignore. It was real and as tangible as Mark himself.

She'd let herself fall in love with him. Totally in love.

A startled tremor of panic unleashed itself with the next bolt of lightning. Tears of frustration and futility welled up in her eyes, threatening to fall, to betray her. She choked them down along with the raw burning in her throat.

Mark had warned her not to become emotionally involved with him, but she'd failed to heed the warning. She'd let her heart rule her actions, and now the consequences were glaring at her—the reprecussions—and it was all she could do to keep herself still.

Mark stirred then, and Rhianna had to struggle for composure. She was thankful for the shadowy light in the room. With the back of one hand, she hastily dashed away a few traitorous tears that had spilled onto her cheeks.

But not hastily enough, it appeared. Mark's sharp eyes missed so very little. A frown touched his lips as he lowered his head to kiss the salty dampness away.

There was no irritation in that frown. Nor was there any in his voice when he spoke.

"Don't cry, Rhianna," he said softly. "Yell at me if you want to, but don't cry."

"I'm not crying," she denied, then halted to lift her troubled eyes to his. "Why would I want to yell at you?"

"Because yelling hurts less than crying." In one sweeping motion, Mark broke the union between them, leaving her more despondent than ever. He didn't move away from her though. Instead, he pulled her even more securely into the warmth of his arms.

She looked up at him. He was staring at her almost painfully. Intensity made his blue eyes deepen to navy. His features seemed vaguely celestial.

Having recovered somewhat from the initial shock of her discovery, Rhianna reached up to touch the hollows below his cheekbones. Whatever was causing him to push himself to the limit couldn't be healthy. He was purposely burning himself out, and suddenly she was far more concerned for Mark than for her own disruptive feelings.

He didn't jerk away from her touch, just let her explore the fine contours of his face. His lashes lowered, and she heard the ragged breath he expelled when her fingers slid to his left shoulder, to the tiny scar just below the bone. It looked to be the result of an old injury, perhaps a painful reminder of his youth, and she bit down hard on her lip to keep from asking him about it.

Grinning a little, he caught her with his unfathomable eyes, then slid his own hand around her waist. Tenderly, he stroked her hair. "No more tears, please?"

She shook her head. "I could yell, though, if it would make you feel better."

"I don't think so." His expression was one of wry amusement. "There's no way I could feel any better."

She lowered her eyes to his newly aroused state, illuminated for a second by a flash of forked lightning. "No way, Mark?"

His mouth reclaimed hers in a longing kiss, which sent all of her fears and doubts spiraling into the night. "Well, maybe there's one way," he murmured. And he pulled her close against him once more.

MARK AWOKE NEAR DAWN to a groaning stiffness in his muscles and an urgent physical need he could no longer ignore. He managed to ignore it for a moment, however, just long enough to gaze at Rhianna in sleep. Beautiful in sleep. Bewitching and exotic.

They'd moved to a mattress in the studio sun room sometime in the night. And sometime in the night, Mark had more or less come to terms with his own warring emotions.

It was very simple, really. He loved her. And he wasn't going to let anyone hurt her.

He slid naked from the mattress and reached for her purse, for the incriminating bracelet she'd found next to his cousin's body. For now, he decided, he would hold onto it, and he'd damn well let the murderer know he had it. If nothing else, that would divert any immediate attention from Rhianna... Or would it?

A strangely disquieting feeling settled over him. Rhianna had an excellent memory for numbers. She'd been a whiz at algebra. She would have memorized those numbers by now, and the murderer would no doubt realize that.

No, taking the bracelet wasn't the answer. Neither was making a display of it. He'd have to think of a way to trap the killer—and there was only way that stood a chance in hell of working.

He thought grimly about the werewolf usher he'd seen in the theater. The usher who hadn't been an usher at all. The costume, he knew, had come from the wax museum—proof of something, perhaps, but not proof positive.

Proof positive... He glanced at the bracelet in his hand. This was the hard evidence. Coded evidence that the murderer was desperate to retrieve. Evidence that could be used to nail its owner. This was the key to the murderer's identity.

Mark swore silently to himself as he went into the bathroom. He glanced at his reflection in the mirror, trying to ignore the bleary eyes that stared back at him. He looked like hell. Yet he didn't really feel bad. How could he feel bad after last night, after making love with Rhianna for most of it? Again, the answer was simple. He couldn't.

But he had to hold himself together, he thought, tensing his muscles. Do that for just a little while longer, and maybe he could end this nightmare once and for all. And maybe then, he and Rhianna could make this thing between them work.

Maybe... Mark still wasn't entirely convinced that he was the right man for her. He did, however, know one thing: nothing was going to harm her. Nothing and no one.

Chapter Thirteen

Rhianna didn't like the fact that Mark had stubbornly decided to hold onto the murderer's bracelet. She knew she could have argued the point and gotten it back, but after careful consideration, she chose to let him keep it. She might as well. To risk losing the valuable clue now would be extremely foolish. If the murderer were to get the bracelet back, the truth might never come out. Besides, the last thing she felt like doing on Friday was fighting with Mark. It was hard enough to go back to the museum and do her tours.

To her surprise, the day passed relatively quickly. Mark came by the apartment at eight while she was poring over the photocopied articles about the east-end robberies. She might have been tempted to do a striptease as Vampira had Logan and Joe not tromped through the balcony doors directly behind him.

"I want you to do me a favor, Rhianna," Mark told her straight out, his expression somber.

She didn't think she liked the sound of that very much. Nonetheless, she was prepared to hear him out. "What kind of a favor?" she asked, conscious of Logan rooting through the fridge, more conscious of Mark crouched down beside her.

"I want you and Sam to stay here tonight. Logan and Joe and I will keep an eye on the apartment. The murderer might just try something if you two are alone."

A strange tightness invaded her chest. She could still feel the telephone cord wrapped around her throat, cutting off her air supply. But that was over, she reminded herself. Shaking away her momentary apprehension, she nodded. "Does Sam know?"

Mark inclined his head. A vaguely reminiscent smile touched his lips. "Yeah, I talked to her downstairs," he said absently. His eyes turned a smoky shade of blue. "Trust me, Rhianna," he murmured, sliding his fingers around the nape of her neck. "I won't let anyone get up here. No one's going to hurt you." Bending his head, he dropped a quick, hard kiss on her lips. Then, as Sam burst into the apartment via the side entrance, he rose reluctantly to his feet, calling out to the men in the kitchen.

With a cheerful, "Bye, guys," Sam came to sit beside her friend on the shag rug. A smirk lit her piquant features. "I take it you had fun last night, fancy britches."

Rhianna abandoned her search through the pile of photocopies. "Before or after I was attacked in the balcony?" she countered dryly.

"Take your pick." Sam grinned; then she sobered. "God, what a panic it was when the lights went up. One of the ushers let the words 'black widow spider' slip, and he damn near got trampled to death in the rush. They found it, though. But I guess you heard that already."

Rhianna shivered. She hadn't heard that, and she couldn't really say she'd wanted to. She'd been hoping that particular part of the night had been a figment of her overactive imagination.

"I think I'll get changed," she said, rising to her feet before Sam could launch into the gory details. "You never know, we may have to leave here in a big hurry."

When she emerged from her bedroom ten minutes later, Sam had her face buried in the account of the Roadside Diner's demolition.

"It says here that the doctor involved felt that the loss of the diner might have been a contributing factor in Marcie Noble's death," she commented without lifting her head. "Must have been some upstart quack from the city who came to that conclusion."

Rhianna tucked her shirt into her jeans. "Why do you say that, Sam?"

Her friend stabbed a finger at Marcie Noble's grainy newsprint picture. "Because there isn't any way that lady's blood vessels seized up over anything as ordinary as a foreclosure. She was one super strong woman. A real fury when it came to putting up a fight."

Rhianna plunked herself on the floor next to Sam. "There isn't any chance that she didn't die eleven years ago, is there? I mean, if Gage could be bought, isn't it possible that the doctor who signed the death certificate could be guilty of the same thing?"

Sam cast her an uneasy look. "That's the creepiest idea I've ever heard," she declared. "What would make you think something like that?"

"Oh, I don't know." Rhianna sighed. "I guess I'm just having a hard time envisioning Billie bashing Brodie on the head and dropping him behind a brick wall. The only other things I can figure are, one, that Marcia Noble's still alive, or two, that Billie's schizophrenic."

"Yeah?" Rising to her feet, Sam lifted the hem of her tattered shroud and started for her bedroom. "I definitely don't like the way your mind's working tonight, fancy britches. I'm going to change. Why don't you stick a tape in the VCR and make us a batch of popcorn. Maybe that'll keep your ghoulish thoughts at bay for a while."

Maybe. But even as she stuck *Star Wars* into the machine and headed for the kitchen, Rhianna's imagination was hard at work.

It sounded ludicrous, but what if Marcie Noble really hadn't died? And if she had, what if her hold over Billie was stronger than anyone in town suspected?

God, Sam was right, those were ghoulish thoughts. Ghoulish and frightening.

Shivering a little, Rhianna forced herself to concentrate on finding the popcorn. When the kernels were popped and ready she wandered back into the living room, plucked Sam's bracelet from the TV and once more turned her attention to the baffling series of numbers inscribed on the inside.

THE MURDERER SAT huddled in the cloying darkness, knowing that Mark would permit no action tonight. Knowing that time was running out.

A hazy mind saw the last grains of sand trickling through the hourglass, falling as Brodie Morgan had fallen when he'd been struck from behind that hot June night so long ago. The same mind saw anguish and pain and suffering—so much more satisfying than it might have been under different circumstances. It saw death, and it saw ten long years of torment. It saw Reed Morgan and it enjoyed the tortured sight. It reveled in it. And it relished the thought of seeing all those things again . . .

"YOU WORK TOO HARD, dear."

Marion's canny observation came as she trudged across the parking lot, her arms laden with Tupperware containers, contributions of food from the museum's employees.

"Where's your sister?" Mark retorted rather irritably.

Marion seemed disinclined to comment on his cranky mood. She motioned toward Blueberry Road. "Sleeping like a baby, thank the Lord. She was quite disoriented, babbling on about Mama for much of the night. I finally had to give her a strong sedative."

"You're sure she's asleep?"

Marion eyed him levelly. "Yes, I'm sure," she replied. "Now, for heaven's sake, Mark, why don't you follow her example? You look like walking death."

Which was about the way he felt after a night spent in cramped surveillance. He shot her a warning glance, however, forestalling any further comment she might have made.

"Dump that stuff upstairs, will you, Marion?" he said, running a weary hand through his hair. "I need you in the office today."

"Today! But what about the party?"

"Sam and Rhianna can sort out the last-minute details."

"But—"

"No buts, Marion," he cautioned her, and wisely, she snapped her mouth shut. "Among other things, I want to talk to you about Billie. And then there's the matter of the insurance settlement for the fire.''

"Yes, of course, the fire.'' Emitting a resigned sigh, Marion nodded. "Give me five minutes, Mark. I'll speak with the girls.''

"I'll speak with them,'' Mark countered firmly. "You check on Billie.''

"But—''

"Marion.''

Her lips thinned. "As you wish,'' she relented. "I'll meet you back here, shall I?''

"Five minutes,'' he told her. And he turned away to look up at Sam's apartment.

Abstinence, he reflected wryly. They said it was good for the soul, but he'd had enough to last a lifetime in the past twenty-four hours. He could still feel Rhianna's soft skin against his body, and the emotions she'd awakened in him during the past few weeks.

Wearily, he closed his eyes and shoved the haunting images away. Later, he promised himself. Later, when the murderer had been apprehended, and there was no one stalking her. He'd think about her, talk to her, make love to her...

The plan had failed last night, but, of course, he'd half expected that. True, the killer was unstable; unfortunately, there was a part of her that was also extremely smart, not quite crazy enough to go off half-cocked. She was playing a waiting game, and the best he could do was play it along with her.

Damn, Mark swore softly to himself, as he strode across the lot. He didn't like this one bit. His gut instincts warned him that something was going to break. Like the summer, this whole thing was poised to end.

Today, tomorrow, he couldn't be sure when. But it would be soon, very soon. And Rhianna was still dead center of it all, still the murderer's primary target. She was still in a great deal of danger.

With a shudder, he vaulted up the balcony stairs.

THE DAY WORE ON in hot, sultry waves. To Rhianna, it seemed as endless as the night before. "Stay with Sam," Mark had said, and although she would have preferred paying Billie another visit to finishing up with the party decorations for the fifties' dance, she'd agreed to remain on the third floor. She felt edgy, though, restless and tense, like a caged animal prowling behind steel bars.

It was after seven, and Sam was in the midst of adding a final bottle of cranberry juice to the enormous punch bowl. The streamers were up, the posters hung, the makeshift bandstand ready, the dance floor clear. The room resembled a high-school auditorium of thirty years ago. All that remained now was to shower and dress for the party.

Tired of waiting for her friend, Rhianna walked to the door and stepped out into the sunshine. The heat had abated a bit, but the humidity was still incredibly high. Far to the east, a black thundercloud was creeping over the horizon. The air was motionless. Not a hint of a breeze stirred the leaves on the trees.

Like the calm before a storm, Rhianna thought. Nothing was moving. The entire area seemed to have settled into a preautumn stupor.

She couldn't seem to do the same. All last night, she'd sat in the living room studying Sam's bracelet, running the numbers over and over again in her head, trying to figure out the code. Birthdates were out. So was numerology. There was only one thing left to try, and naturally, it was the most logical thing of all. Take all the names she did know, transpose each number to a letter and work backwards from there on the one series of digits she didn't understand.

Simple, right? So simple, in fact, that it hadn't occurred to her until just this moment.

She ran up the stairs and into the apartment, grabbing the first piece of paper she found. Two minutes later she was staring at double and triple combinations of letters for each number on the murderer's bracelet. This wasn't quite so simple after all, she realized. As far as she could see from what she had here, the letter B was represented by a 2, the second number on the murderer's bracelet. If Billie was indeed the guilty party, that B should come first, as it had on Brodie's bracelet.

Folding the scrap of paper thoughtfully, she tucked it into the pocket of the dress she planned to wear that evening. Then she stripped off her grimy clothes and filled the bathtub with hot water.

Time to relax, she told herself. Logan was down in the lot watching for prowlers, and the side entrance to the museum was triple bolted. For the next hour, she planned to do nothing except relive the memories of Thursday night. That would dispel any remaining traces of apprehension.

With a grateful sigh, Rhianna sank into the scented bubbles, rested her head on the back of the tub and closed her eyes.

THE MUSIC OF FATS DOMINO and Buddy Holly drifted across from the production shop's third-floor windows.

It was nine o'clock; the museum was closed, and Rhianna had just finished applying the last of her makeup.

Standing, she surveyed herself in the full-length mirror. The dress she'd chosen was ruby red, strapless and snug-fitting in the bodice, full and flouncy from the waist down. Chiffon over satin over layers of crinoline heightened that fullness and emphasized the narrowness of her waist. She slid her feet into a pair of red and silver high heels, brushed her hair until it fell in glossy waves around her bare shoulders and clasped a white-gold serpentine chain around her neck.

She was ready, and just in time, it seemed. Sam was thumping loudly on her bedroom door, snapping a wad of bubble gum and hopping from foot to foot in her worn saddle shoes.

The next thing Rhianna knew, she'd been transported back in time to the do-wop days of early rock and roll. A local band was tuning up onstage, and the room was brimming with ponytailed twisters, Sandra Dee prom queens and slick Brylcremed clones of James Dean. The overhead lights were up. Judging from the laughter of the first wave of arrivals, everyone appeared to be having a wonderful time.

"Here you go, ladies." Joe grinned, handing Rhianna and Sam a crystal glass. "A little punch to wet your whistles."

Rhianna thanked him, then glanced over his shoulder. Mark was nowhere to be found in the throng. If she hadn't known better, she would have sworn he was avoiding her again.

For a while, she chatted with a group of production-shop employees. They were raving about some new figure or other they'd completed late in the day, enthusiastically awaiting Mark's comments on the finished product.

"He said he'd be down to see it," Dag groused, "but he never showed. Oh, well, come on sweet thing." He grabbed Rhianna's hand. "Let's you and me show these punkers how to bop, fifties' style."

That was easier said than done on the crowded dance floor. Rhianna wound up with a flailing elbow in her ribs no less than five times in as many minutes. Nonetheless, she persevered.

For a solid hour, she danced with different partners, all the while keeping her eyes unobtrusively trained on the door. More people arrived, among them Renee in her walking cast and Marion, looking cool and collected in her *All About Eve* poster dress and Bette Davis bob.

Rhianna passed the office manager on the threshold. The air in the third-floor room had grown unbearably stuffy. She needed something fresh in her lungs. And while she was at it, she'd check the lot for Mark's car.

"I believe he's changing his clothes, dear," Marion informed her above the pounding music.

Rhianna grinned. "He, who?"

"He, Mark. Who else?" Marion remarked, smiling as she puffed away on one of her Virginia Slims. "You must tell him to slow down, Rhianna. Between the two of us, I'm not sure who's the more tired. He had me checking on Billie every hour on the hour today."

"Is she all right?"

"Heavens, yes." Marion waved a dismissing hand. "Well off in slumber land. I slipped a sleeping pill into her morning orange juice and another in her evening tea. She won't wake up until sometime tomorrow."

That was a relief. Rhianna offered up a silent prayer of thanks while Marion vanished into the mass of gyrating bodies.

Leaning over the rail, she breathed in the fresh night air. She could see Mark's car near Blueberry Road. She also noticed that there was a light on down in the pit. And then her eyes zeroed in on a hunched figure passing stealthily in front of that light.

Immediately, she straightened up. The figure belonged to Billie Noble. Although it had been swallowed up now by the looming shadows, Rhianna knew she hadn't been mistaken in what she'd seen.

So Billie was sleeping soundly, was she? Evidently, she'd ditched her evening tea behind Marion's back. She was prowling the grounds, and there was only one way to find out why.

Rhianna didn't stop to think rationally. She started down the steps, her courage bolstered by the music behind her and the light in front. When she reached the lot, she ducked past the door leading to the pit, eyes alert for any shift in the blackened shadows.

There was nothing. No movement. No sound of crunching gravel or scuffling penny loafers.

She considered running up to the apartment for her gun, but dismissed the idea quickly. She'd lose Billie for sure if she did that. Assuming, of course, that she hadn't lost her already.

What she needed was a pair of infrared glasses. Billie had to be hiding somewhere in the creeping darkness. But where? And what was she up to? Was she planning to torch the south wing this time? To destroy the heart of the wax museum once and for all?

Rhianna stood absolutely still beside the stone wall outside the pit. The minutes ticked by in a slow, arduous succession. Finally, she could take it no longer. There was a dim light burning in the office complex. Maybe Mark was in the back. If she could find him, they could hunt for Billie together.

As quietly as possible, Rhianna made her way to the glass doors. They swished open easily.

"Mark?" Tentatively, she called his name. "Mark, are you in here?"

No response. She risked a backward glance. The door had swung closed behind her. No one had followed her inside. And yet, she could feel... something. An evil something. A presence of some sort, or perhaps more correctly a premonition of impending danger.

Far, far in the distance, a low ripple of thunder rolled through the sky. A chill blast of air from one of the vents rushed over her, raising goose bumps on her bare arms. Chiding herself for her ridiculous overreaction, she ventured deeper into the building.

The door to Mark's office was wide open. The coffee machine was humming away on low, and the top drawer of his filing cabinet was drawn back slightly.

Instinctively, Rhianna walked over to it. As she'd half suspected, his nine mm automatic was missing. Now what on earth, she wondered frowning, could that mean?

With a sigh, she sank down on the padded chair behind the desk. This was all so frustrating. Mark, wherever he was, had apparently taken his gun with him. Billie was skulking around the museum grounds when she should have been home asleep. Everyone else was upstairs enjoying the party. And she was sitting here, still tossing numbers and letters around in her head, trying to make sense of even one part of this puzzle. Talk about a screwed-up mystery.

On impulse, Rhianna picked up the phone and dialed the number at Reed's place. She might have missed Mark. Maybe he'd been driving off while she'd been standing by the pit listening for Billie.

Ten rings later, she dropped the receiver back onto the cradle, glaring balefully at the round dial. The sight of it reminded her of the picture she'd found in Billie's parlor. Quelling a rising sense of futility, Rhianna forced herself to concentrate on the facts of the case. There were certainly few enough.

Billie... She turned the woman's name over in her mind. The coded bracelet she'd found had started with a six. As far as she could tell, that number translated to three letters, none of which was a B. Did that mean Billie was innocent? She remembered the numbers: 627466. Damn, what did they mean? What did they refer to? There weren't enough of them to make up a phone number.

She drew the folded piece of paper from the pocket of her dress. Double and triple letters for each digit. Her eyes locked on the first set of letters, M, N, O, then the second, A, B, and the third, S, R.

Thoughtfully, her gaze shifted to the phone. The telephone-dial picture...Billie's prize collection... The piece of cord wrapped around her neck...

Telephones! Oh, God, that was it! It had to be. The numbers on the phone dial—the corresponding letters!

Hastily, Rhianna matched letters to numbers. Brodie's name, Dag's, Sam's, they all worked. It was a telephone code. The murderer's identity was linked to Ma Bell, spelled out on the instrument's dial.

Rhianna's heart leaped into her throat. She looked again: 627466. From MNO she picked M, from ABC, A; from PRS, R. MAR...

That was as far as she got, as far as she could go. It was too far, too horrible to accept.

Mark's name swam before her eyes. Markus! Six numbers, six letters. No. Rhianna swore to herself. She couldn't believe what she had discovered. It couldn't be true. She wouldn't believe it. There had to be another explanation.

A tiny whisper of cloth penetrated her numbed reverie. Jerking her head up, she focused on the door to Mark's office, and the figure standing there. A shocked second later, she was scrambling out of the chair.

Billie Noble was hovering on the dimly lit threshold. And she was clutching a butcher's knife in her hand!

Chapter Fourteen

"It's wrong to kill ... Wrong."

Billie's whispered statement seemed oddly out of context with her menacing stance. Rhianna took one look at the scrawny woman, saw the bold flash of steel and plunged straight into the library adjoining Mark's office. Somehow, she was able to dash out into the corridor before Billie could move from the threshold.

She knew she couldn't get to the reception area. Her only chance was to head down into the basement. If she could make it to the pit, she might just be able to escape.

"No! No!" Billie shrieked from behind her. "Wait for me! Wait! Mama..."

Some snatch of Rhianna's memory sparked at Billie's final desperate pleas. That was it! Mama. Not Markus, but Marcie, Marcie Noble. Marcie and her dominated daughter. Marcie and Billie together—and wielding a deadly knife.

Even in heels, Rhianna made good time along the narrow passageway. Grasping for the cellar door, she yanked it open and launched herself into the confined stairwell. She could hear Billie trotting nimbly behind her, issuing strident pleas for her to wait.

"Not there! No, no! Not down there!"

Rhianna ignored the imploring wails and raced down the stairs. Gasping for breath, she skidded across the cement floor, slid sideways on one heel and had to claw at the stone wall for support. Hastily, she kicked off her shoes. If there was any justice at all in the world, Billie or Marcie or whoever the hell she was tonight would trip over them and fall flat on her face on top of the knife.

By applying her full weight to the warped wooden door, Rhianna managed to inch it open. She squeezed through the aperture and into the steamy pit.

Despite the fact that there was no one working tonight, the vats were still hot and hissing. That was wrong, and she knew it. The machinery should have been long since shut down.

In her blind flight, she collided full force with the newest figure. She winced as Medusa toppled backward to land with a dull broken thud on the floor.

"Wait! Wait!"

Billie's screams quickly got her moving again. In desperation, she ducked behind one of the huge, bubbling cauldrons. The smell of hot wax and cigarette smoke hit her. Now that was very strange. Mark never let Dag smoke down here. It was simply too dangerous, with so many combustible substances around.

Through a white haze, Rhianna spied the red exit sign. Her skin was slick with perspiration. It was almost too hot to breathe, let alone move—more like a bad dream than a slice of reality. She had to force her unsteady legs to carry her across the smooth stones.

Sheer strength of will kept her going. She had no idea where Billie had gotten to. The billowing white clouds of smoke and steam had pretty much obscured her vision.

The only plus was that they had probably blinded Billie as well.

For a split second, the heavy swirls parted, shaken aside, it seemed, by a sullen rumble of thunder outside. In that tiny, fleeting moment, Rhianna saw a shape rise up in front of her. To her relief, it wasn't clutching a knife.

Marion's concerned face appeared through the roiling whorls. "Rhianna," she exclaimed dropping her Virginia Slims and crushing it beneath the heel of her pump. "Good God, dear, what are you doing here?"

MARK SHOVED A FRESH CLIP in his nine mm automatic, flipped off the safety and jammed the gun into the waistband of his jeans. "How the hell could you lose her, Logan?" he bit out angrily.

"Man, I only went into the john for thirty seconds," Logan defended. "She couldn't have gotten across the dance floor that fast."

"Yeah, well, she did." Pausing by the stone wall, Mark glanced into the office complex. It was empty. From the pit, he detected a low grinding of machinery. A clever ruse or the real thing, he wondered, motioning for the Brylcremed men behind him to hold up. "Dave, you and Bryan check the museum. Joe, you and Lonny take the north-wing cellar. Logan, you phone the cops again. Make sure they're on their way."

Heaving himself away from the wall, Logan started across the lot, pausing only briefly to glance at Mark. "You could be wrong, you know," he grunted.

"I'm not wrong. She murdered Brodie, and now she's going after Rhianna."

"Maybe her sister can stop her, then. I saw her earlier. Maybe she'll stop her."

The muscles in Mark's jaw bunched. "I doubt it," he muttered. "She's never been able to stop her before." He reached for the brass handle, and something inside him twisted like the cold, steel blade of a dagger. The door was locked!

RHIANNA SCRAMBLED from behind the number-two cauldron, relief coursing through her at Marion's unexpected appearance. "Billie," she croaked, her voice seizing up from the heat. "She's got a knife."

"A knife! Oh, Lord, no... Billie!" Marion commanded brusquely. "Billie, you come out this instant." Her gaze strayed to a point just beyond Rhianna's left shoulder. "Put it down, dear," she intoned a trifle more gently. "Do as I say, and no one will harm you."

Rhianna chanced a surreptitious look to the rear. Billie was indeed advancing on her, the butcher's knife held aloft in one hand. Yet, strangely enough, she didn't seem to be aiming the blade at her back.

"Give me the knife, Billie," Marion ordered again.

"No. It's wrong!"

"Billie!" This time Marion's tone resembled that of a general. "Give me the knife. Now!"

Billie's sunken eyes blinked slightly. She had stopped not three feet from where Rhianna stood. And still she didn't bring the knife down.

"Mama..." she whispered dazedly. "No more... No more... To kill is wrong, even to protect."

Mama? Protect? Rhianna's head snapped up. This was all wrong.

Then, suddenly, a feeling of unbridled terror gripped her. Swiftly. Dreadfully. Not Billie. Not Marcie. She thought, 627—MAR. What was the 466? ION! Oh, God! It was Marion! Marion was the murderer! The bracelet belonged to her. Marion had killed Brodie!

In one agile lunge, Rhianna reached Billie's side. She twisted the knife free and spun around. Marion's sharp brown eyes watched her with deadly calm.

"Nicely done, dear," she congratulated almost indifferently. "I see that you've figured out the truth." A sardonic smile touched her lips. "I wondered how long it would take you to realize that I am in control here."

Marion or Mama Noble? Rhianna wondered, tightening her grip on the knife. She'd hoped she'd jumped to the wrong conclusion. Apparently, she hadn't. God help her, she hadn't. "You've been using Billie all these years, haven't you, Marion?" she ventured bitterly.

"Not at all," Marion replied, lighting a fresh cigarette. "In the beginning, I had only to play upon her grief. It was quite simple, really. I had no trouble whatsoever convincing her that she should find a way to avenge Mother's death and the loss of our diner. Bureaucratic dimwits. It was kind of me to simply steal from them." She blew a stream of smoke into the vaporous air. "Oh, do put that down, Rhianna," she scoffed. "You can't possibly hope to use it." To emphasize her point, she drew a gun from the pocket of her dress.

Rhianna lowered the blade but refused to drop it. "So that's the answer, is it, Marion? Kill me the way you killed Brodie?"

A throaty chuckle emanated from the woman's throat. "Heavens, no. That would be too merciful. Brodie was no problem. He deserved a quick, easy death. You see, he simply stumbled across the truth that night.''

Rhianna swallowed the bile in her throat. "The truth?" she asked shakily. "What is the truth, Marion? What exactly did he see?"

One languid brow arched. "See? Why, nothing, my dear. He saw nothing. Nothing except Billie and me having a—" her lips curled into a reminiscent smile "—well, let's just say we were having a discussion."

"A—discussion?"

Marion shrugged. "A strategy meeting, if you will. You see, stealing from those who had a hand in the diner's destruction was fine for the general masses. But somehow, it didn't seem like quite enough when it came to Reed. Even having Billie recruit his son to aid our cause wasn't quite enough. No, I felt that Reed deserved something more for having my diner torn down." Her eyes sharpened. "Understand, dear, I had big plans for that diner. Very big plans. Reed destroyed those plans when he purchased the land and had the place torn down. He had to be punished for that. He deserved the ultimate punishment."

"You mean, you were planning to...kill him? To kill Reed?"

The smile grew cruel. "But of course. What else would you have me do? Unfortunately for him, Brodie chose that particular night to renege on his agreement. He was going to tell Billie that he was leaving her little group of thieves. I'm afraid, however, that he never got the chance. He overheard our conversation. I knew he had when I saw him bolting across Blueberry Road. And so the plan changed."

Rhianna's palms were clammy, her mouth totally dry. "So you killed him instead."

"Naturally. And as for Reed..." She paused, her expression perhaps a trifle dreamy. "Well, there just didn't seem to be any real need to kill him once Brodie was dead. It was so much more fun just to watch him suffer over the loss of his only son. So much more gratifying."

"I'm sure it was," Rhianna muttered, inching cautiously back a pace. The woman was mad. How had they all missed that?

Marion noticed the move. "Now, stop that," she ordered imperiously. "I don't intend to shoot you, but I certainly will if I have to."

In her peripheral vision, Rhianna saw Billie swaying on her feet. She might still have a chance. As cold-blooded as Marion was, she might have a feeling or two left for her sister. If Rhianna could just keep the woman talking.

"I...ah—it was you who attacked me in the Pullman, wasn't it, Marion?" She wondered if she sounded as parched as she felt, as terrified. "How did you know I had your bracelet? It could have been Brodie's, or even Sam's."

"It could have been," Marion agreed. "But I knew it wasn't. I saw you, you see. Down in the north-wing cellar. I could have disposed of you right then, but, of course, you're very fast on your feet, and Mark has the worst possible timing."

"That depends on your point of view."

"True. You're still a very lucky girl, my dear." The gun shifted to Billie, who was cowering now behind Rhianna. "My darling sister here has this funny quirk about killing. That knife you're clutching was to have been used on you at the Pullman. But Billie came after me that night; we struggled and I lost it in the underbrush. She must have gone back for it this evening." Marion shrugged her shoulders nonchalantly. "Ah, well, such is life—or rather death."

Rhianna's skin crawled. She was almost too scared to feel it. Her heart pounded wildly against her ribs. Licking her lips, she ventured a raw question. "Did you lock Sam and me in the Chamber of Horrors?"

"Of course."

"Why?"

"I was going to put the black widow spider in your bed, just as I put the tarantula in your car. A lovely scare tactic, I felt. Mark, however, interrupted me. I'm tempted to kill him for that, but I think I'll settle for killing you right now. Perhaps I'll let my sister go on believing that Mark is Brodie's ghost. I'm sure she'd love nothing better than to make him go away again... And stop edging toward Billie," she commanded sharply. "She can't help you. If I have to, I'll go through her to get to you."

Grinding her back teeth together, Rhianna prayed for good aim. In a frantic gesture, she spun the knife around and launched it straight at Marion. It jostled her arm in passing; unfortunately, it did nothing more serious than that. But the slight contact did give Rhianna the opening she needed. She shoved Billie ahead of her and slipped out of sight behind the bubbling vat.

Marion's guileless chuckle drifted through the swirling fog. "It won't do you any good to run, dear," she shrilled. "The doors are all locked. I've seen to that. And

Mark, dear boy, will be sound asleep by now. A double dose of sleeping pills in his coffee has taken care of him.''

"Mama..." Billie whimpered helplessly.

"Not Mama," Rhianna hissed, pushing her forward. "Marion. She's your sister, Billie. She's been using you."

"No more," Billie moaned. "Please, no more."

God, if only that were true. If only Mark were here. If only...

Beside her, Billie stumbled against the workbench. A pot of uncapped blue dye crashed to the floor, splattering both women.

"I hear you," Marion called out, her voice a playful taunt. "Come to me, my little Joan of Arc. We'll take a page straight from the movie script. You'll be immortalized. Forever the martyr."

Like hell, Rhianna thought, more angry now than frightened. If anyone was going to be dipped in wax, it would be Marion, not her.

A blast of cooler air swirled around her ankles. Peering through the haze, Rhianna tried to discern its source. Marion could have lied about the doors. They might not be locked at all.

Dragging a resisting Billie, she made her way around the cooling tanks in the rear of the pit. The room was a veritable maze. There were only two exits: one at the front and one at the side. She had to get to the side exit before Marion blocked her path.

Amazingly, she felt Billie shrink away from her. Then, to her horror, she felt a barrel of cold, hard steel digging into the small of her back.

"You're all lucked out, Rhianna," Marion told her, her tone ice-filled and venomous. "Up the ladder. I've had enough of you to last a lifetime. My lifetime, that is. Now move!"

Rhianna's blood froze in her veins. She couldn't climb that ladder. She wasn't going to die. This couldn't be happening to her.

Her fingers wrapped themselves around the metal framework. Her heart was skipping every other beat, and her breathing was growing increasingly uneven.

"Move, now," Marion warned her. "My patience with you is wearing extremely thin."

Rhianna reached for the ladder. "This won't work, you know," she said with more defiance than she felt.

"Oh, I think it will. Now climb."

Joan of Arc... Images of a new wax figure appeared through the swirling steam to dance dizzily before Rhianna's eyes. This had to be a bad dream. She couldn't possibly be climbing into a cauldron of hot wax. She wasn't going to die. She wasn't!

Three rungs up the ladder, Rhianna tightened her grip on the slick metal bars, summoned every ounce of strength she possessed and spun around. Her heel impacted squarely in the middle of Marion's chin.

The gun clattered to the floor—but not quite out of sight. And Marion still had the advantage. She was already diving after the gun. Rhianna's only hope for escape was to knock her off balance before she could reach it.

She jumped from the ladder. Wispy tendrils of steam curled around her legs. Clenching her fists, she steeled herself to lash out once more.

The chance never came. Before she could so much as shift her weight, an arm snaked itself around her waist, hauling her roughly off the floor and practically tossing her behind the gurgling vat.

"Stay there," Mark told her, then he turned his attention, and his nine mm automatic, to Marion. "Forget it, lady," he snarled as her fingers closed around the barrel of her weapon. "Stand up and leave the gun."

The woman's head snapped around. She retained her grip on the gun. "Not this time, Mark," she growled. She raised her voice. "Make him go away, Billie," she shrieked. "Make Brodie go away for Mama."

Rhianna saw the spindly woman then. She emerged from the gray-white haze, her fingers wound tightly around the handle of the butcher's knife. She was behind Mark, moving up on him like a hobbling vapor.

"It's wrong to kill, Billie," Rhianna whispered desperately, knowing Mark couldn't possibly turn around.

"Make him go away, Billie," Marion entreated her.

"Killing is wrong, Billie."

"Listen to me, Billie," Marion commanded. "Make him go away!"

"I..." Billie faltered. Marion was on the floor. Mark was covering her. Rhianna was sprawled behind the vat. For the longest time no one moved.

"Put the knife down, Billie," Mark ordered the woman, "or I'll put a bullet between your mama's eyes."

"I..." Swaying on her feet, Billie appealed to Marion. Marion, who was inching her gun ever higher.

A shot rang out, and Rhianna seized the opportunity to tackle the indecisive woman. She had no idea who'd fired. She only prayed it had been Mark.

"No!" Billie's scream bounced off the churning cauldrons. "Mama! No!"

"Let her go, Rhianna," Mark said tiredly, crouching down beside her. "Let her go to her mama." His arms enveloped her as Billie scrambled off to where her sister was lying, holding her injured right shoulder. "It's over," he murmured. "Brodie's murderer's been caught."

Relief coursed like liquid honey through Rhianna's body. Relief and a spreading warmth like nothing she'd ever felt before.

Out of the corner of her eye, she saw Marion glaring at them. "The police chief won't . . . I have as much on Gage as you have on me. Bribery. Kickbacks. Payoffs. He'll get me out."

Mark shrugged. "I doubt that, Marion," he drawled. "Gage is gone. You'll have to take your chances with his replacement."

Rhianna barely heard him, so glad was she to be safe. Through the mist, she saw Logan and four uniformed officers swarm in to handcuff Marion and draw her sister away.

Mark turned his eyes downward. "It's over," he said, sliding his gun into his waistband. "Your Jawa's going to prison."

"But how . . ."

"I found a Virginia Slims cigarette butt in the lobby ashtray at the theater." His jaw hardened. "I knew Marion was the murderer. I just didn't know how to prove it."

"You what?" Relief turned to rage. Rhianna extricated herself from his arms. "You mean you set me up? How dare you?"

"You were never in any real danger," Mark revealed calmly. "Marion hasn't been out of my sight all day."

"Like hell she hasn't. She damn near killed me. You had no right to...oh, what the hell." Giving her head a shake, Rhianna let her outrage seep away. Marion was being taken out of the pit, as was a howling Billie. The murderer had been caught and that was all that really mattered. That, and the man beside her. The man who had set her up and then helped her nail Brodie's killer. Now, what did he deserve in payment for all of that? she wondered.

A tiny smile curved Rhianna's lips. She could think of only one fitting answer. And wrapping her arms around his neck, she lifted her head to find his warm, waiting mouth.

Chapter Fifteen

"Conversing with Nosfuratu, are you, fancy britches?"

Sam's voice floated out from the dim reaches of the wax museum's twisting maze of paths. Summoning a tired grin, Rhianna averted her head just as her friend's pink-poodle skirt came into sight.

"At least I know he's not a murderer," she replied. "Is Mark back from the hospital yet?" It was a hopeful question.

Mark had gone over to Bremerhaven General with Joe and the four uniformed officers who'd swarmed into the pit to take Marion and Billie away. He'd promised to return just as soon as he'd given his statement to the police and talked to the doctors who would be dealing temporarily with both women. Evidently he hadn't done that yet, for Sam gave her head a distracted shake.

"Uh-uh. But Joe just called from there. I gather Marion's ranting up a storm. Something about sticking to her original plan and how none of this would have happened if Reed had died instead of Brodie. Do you know what she's talking about?"

Rhianna nodded. Arms folded across her chest, the black jacket Mark had been wearing earlier now draped over her shoulders, she sank onto the raised dais in front of the pallid-skinned Nosfuratu. "Her original plan was to steal from those people who'd had any part in the loss of her family's diner, and then to kill Reed for buying the land and tearing the building down. What she ended up doing instead was killing Brodie."

Sam shuddered. "So then she could just sit back and watch Reed suffer. God, that's horrible. But it makes sense, I suppose, in a warped sort of way." She dropped down beside Rhianna. "Where exactly did Billie fit into all of it?" she queried. "I mean, Joe said something on the phone about her thinking Marion was Mama Noble, but how long has she been under that delusion? And how did Marion pull it off, anyway? I wouldn't say she particularly looked like her mother—except maybe a little around the eyes."

"She had her mother's strength of will," Rhianna reminded her. "With Billie already so deluded, I doubt it took much more than that to convince her that Mama's ghost had returned from the grave."

"So you're saying that Billie knew Marion was Marion when the whole thing with the east-end robberies got started. But by the time Brodie's body was discovered, she thought Marion was her mother come back from the dead."

"Something like that," Rhianna concurred. "Although I doubt if anyone will ever know for sure how Billie's mind works—or rather, how it's been working for the past few weeks."

Sam's brow puckered. "I don't get this. Did Billie know that Marion had killed Brodie, or not?"

"She knew." This from Mark, who'd just come in through the museum's side entrance with Joe. "She torched the north wing because she happened to catch a glimpse of Rhianna. It was her way of trying to cover up the crime."

"She torched the north wing!" Sam's eyes widened. "Would somebody please mind filling me in on a few of the details here?"

Joe chuckled. "I will, Sam," he agreed. "Come on, let's go over to the Raven's Wing. I'll tell you the whole story over a pitcher of Budweiser."

Rhianna waited until Sam and Joe were gone before arching a speculative brow in Mark's direction. "Your turn," she said as he came to sit, cross-legged, facing her. "What did I have to do with Billie setting the north wing on fire?"

A grin worked its way across his lips. "Among other things, she thought Brodie's ghost was going to tell you about Marion's plan to kill Reed. I think she also figured that as long as he was back, he'd try to extract a little revenge on his partners in crime."

"Brodie's ghost? You mean, you?" She paused for a second. Paused, then turned to face him. "So Billie did think you were Brodie, come back to haunt her."

"As far as the doctors can tell, she did. She's not especially coherent right now, and she's more worried about Marion—"

"Mama," Rhianna interjected. "She thinks Marion's her mama."

"Whatever." Mark shrugged. "The point is, Billie torched the shop to make Brodie's ghost go away. She felt it was all right to get rid of a ghost; unfortunately for Marion, she's never liked the idea of killing anyone or anything else. So... when Marion murdered Brodie ten years ago, Billie was forced to make a choice. She could either turn Marion in or keep the secret. She kept the secret, and the doctors feel that has a lot to do with why she's so screwed up today.''

''And what about Marion?'' Rhianna asked.

''What about her?'' Mark returned flatly. ''She's crazier than her sister. The way she was going on at the hospital, it sounds as though she really believes she's Marcie Noble. She just lays there barking at Billie to be still, to keep quiet and let Mama think of a way to get the incriminating bracelet back.''

''The bracelet,'' Rhianna murmured, glad when Mark reached over and drew her closer. His warm touch dispelled the icy shards of remembered fear that were shooting along her spine. Confused by a hazy recollection that had been plaguing her for the past few hours, she met his clear blue eyes. ''Why did Dag keep his bracelet with him, Mark? Sam said she really had to hunt to find hers.''

Grinning, Mark slid his arms around Rhianna's waist, tugging her gently onto his lap. ''You're forgetting why Dag agreed to take part in the robberies to begin with. It was all one big kick to him. Something he could get away with, to prove to himself, if no one else, that he was as tough as anyone in the west end. For some reason, he's always equated toughness with crime.'' Mark continued, ''His thinking's a little twisted in that way, but I imagine he'll come around now.''

Emitting a small sigh, Rhianna let her fingers trail across Mark's forearm, the one that was holding her so securely. ''How did you happen to stumble across one of Marion's cigarette butts at the theater?'' she queried, wanting to wrap this up once and for all. ''And why—''

she twisted her head around to send him one final accusing stare "—didn't you tell me what you'd found?"

He smiled at her, that slow, lazy smile of his. "Finding it was just a stroke of luck," he told her. "I remembered passing a werewolf usher when I went into the washroom that night. I also remember smelling smoke. When I found out you'd been attacked by a werewolf, I took a chance and sifted through the sand in the ashtray by the men's room door."

"You still could have told me about it," Rhianna reproached him.

"Yeah, I could have, but knowing you, you'd have decided to try and catch her all on your own."

"If you'd given me half a chance, I probably could have caught her—under much less dangerous circumstances than the one your plan called for."

"Uh-huh." Mark shifted her around in his arms, sliding his fingers around the nape of her neck. "You know, I think that's what I love most about you, Rhianna. You're as stubborn as hell."

"What did you say?" she demanded.

He grinned. "I think you heard me."

Tempted though she was to plunge her fist into his stomach to make him repeat himself, Rhianna settled for placing her palms flat against his chest and smiling up at him. "If my dreams weren't normally this vivid—" she laughed "—I'd swear I was upstairs in bed, conjuring this whole night up in my sleep."

Mark's lips twitched. "You're not, but it isn't a bad idea," he drawled. "Some of us haven't slept much since you arrived in town."

"According to Marion, you should have been sleeping soundly after drinking your doctored coffee."

"Yeah, well, I think she had other things on her mind when she slipped that mickey into my mug." A muscle twitched in his jaw. "I almost lost her then," he murmured, frowning.

"Aha, so you admit you're not a one-man army." Rhianna slid her arms around his neck. "I was in just a little bit of danger, wasn't I?"

"For a minute or two," Mark conceded, his expression both troubled and slightly humorous. "Somehow, though, I had a feeling you'd survive. You're a very strong lady, Rhianna. Just one more reason for me to love you, I guess."

"I guess." She brushed his mouth lightly with her lips. "So what's next, Mark? Are you going to start a new branch of your construction company here in Bremerhaven? Maybe find yourself a new manager for the wax museum?"

"Is that an offer, Vampira?"

"If you want it to be, it is."

He raised a questioning brow. "You sure you want to give up life in the big city to stay here?"

"I'm sure." She pressed herself closer to his warm, responsive body. "I never was a spoiled little rich girl. I love it here in Bremerhaven. I love the wax museum. And I love you, too."

Mark's lips curved into an amused smile. "In that order, Rhianna?"

"No." She paused, biting down hard on her lip. "I really didn't think you murdered Brodie, Mark. I want you to know that. I mean, the throat lozenges threw me a little, and the bracelet scared me for a second, but—"

"No buts." Mark cut her off, sliding his thumb over her chin. "Let's just put the past to bed and leave it there, huh? I think it can use the rest."

Rhianna couldn't argue with that. The past was the past. It was time to move forward. And as Mark lowered his head to cover her mouth with his, she felt the last of the ghosts slipping off into oblivion.

COMING SOON

Harlequin Historicals

**Exciting, adventurous, sensual stories
of love long ago.**

*Be sure to look for them this July wherever you buy
Harlequin Books—you won't want to miss out.*

Can you keep a secret?

You can keep this one plus 4 free novels

MAIL-IN-OFFER
OFFER CERTIFICATE

I have enclosed the required number of proofs of purchase from any specially marked "Gifts From The Heart" Harlequin romance book, plus cash register receipts and a check or money order payable to Harlequin Gifts From The Heart Offer, to cover postage and handling.

002

CHECK ONE	ITEM	# OF PROOFS OF PURCHASE	POSTAGE & HANDLING FEE
	01 Brass Picture Frame	2	$ 1.00
	02 Heart-Shaped Candle Holders with Candles	3	$ 1.00
	03 Heart-Shaped Keepsake Box	4	$ 1.00
	04 Gold-Plated Heart Pendant	5	$ 1.00
	05 Collectors' Doll Limited quantities available	12	$ 2.75

NAME _____

STREET ADDRESS _____ APT. # _____

CITY _____ STATE _____ ZIP _____

Mail this certificate, designated number of proofs of purchase (inside back page) and check or money order for postage and handling to:

Gifts From The Heart, P.O. Box 4814
Reidsville, N. Carolina 27322-4814

NOTE THIS IMPORTANT OFFER'S TERMS

Requests must be postmarked by May 31, 1988. Only proofs of purchase from specially marked "Gifts From The Heart" Harlequin books will be accepted. This certificate plus cash register receipts and a check or money order to cover postage and handling must accompany your request and may not be reproduced in any manner. Offer void where prohibited, taxed or restricted by law. LIMIT ONE REQUEST PER NAME, FAMILY, GROUP, ORGANIZATION OR ADDRESS. Please allow up to 8 weeks after receipt of order for shipment. Offer only good in the U.S.A. Hurry—Limited quantities of collectors' doll available. Collectors' dolls will be mailed to first 15,000 qualifying submitters. All other submitters will receive 12 free previously unpublished Harlequin books and a postage & handling refund.

OFFER-1RR

GIFTS FROM THE HEART

from *Harlequin*

FREE BY MAIL

With proofs of purchase
plus postage and handling

A. Hand-polished solid brass picture frame 1-5/8″ × 1-3/8″ with 2 proofs of purchase.

B. Individually handworked, pair of heart-shaped glass candle holders (2″ diameter), 6″ candles included, with 3 proofs of purchase.

C. Heart-shaped porcelain keepsake box (1″ high) with delicate flower motif with 4 proofs of purchase.

D. Radiant gold-plated heart pendant on 16″ chain with complimentary satin pouch with 5 proofs of purchase.

E. Beautiful collectors' doll with genuine porcelain face, hands and feet, and a charming heart appliqué on dress with 12 proofs of purchase. Limited quantities available. See offer terms.

HERE IS HOW TO GET YOUR FREE GIFTS

Send us the required number of proofs of purchase (below) of specially marked "Gifts From The Heart" Harlequin books and cash register receipts with the Offer Certificate (available in the back pages) properly completed, plus a check or money order (do not send cash) payable to Harlequin Gifts From The Heart Offer. We'll RUSH you your specified gift. Hurry—Limited quantities of collectors' doll available. See offer terms.

603R

GIFTS FROM THE HEART

ONE PROOF
OF PURCHASE

To collect your free gift by mail you must include the necessary number of proofs of purchase with order certificate.